Blind Man's Bargain

TRACY WINEGAR

OMNIFIC PUBLISHING
LOS ANGELES

Omnific Publishing
1901 Avenue of the Stars, 2nd floor
Los Angeles, CA 90067
www.omnificpublishing.com

First Omnific eBook edition, April 2014
First Omnific trade paperback edition, April 2014

Library of Congress Cataloguing-in-Publication Data

Winegar, Tracy.
Blind Man's Bargain / Tracy Winegar – 1st ed.
ISBN: 978-1-623421-07-6
1. Murder Mystery — Fiction. 2. New Adult — Romance.
3. Cold Case — Fiction. 4. Private Investigator — Fiction. I. Title

10 9 8 7 6 5 4 3 2 1

Cover Design by Micha Stone and Amy Brokaw
Interior Book Design by Coreen Montagna

Printed in the United States of America

For Brynlee.
My own little Cleo in the making.

CHAPTER 1

The old man's eyes were a frightening sight, with a thick film covering the unnaturally pale blue, almost white, shade of his irises. Nelson knew right away that although this stranger was staring directly at him, the man could not *see* him. He was blind.

Out of politeness, Nelson held his tongue and waited for the man to speak, glad that his curious expression could not be observed by his guest. He was sure that if the man knew or could sense what he was thinking, he would get up and leave. The stranger sat just opposite Nelson, his shoulders rounded and burdened by age, in a chair that was set up for his clientele.

Nelson's office was a minuscule room filled with mismatched office furniture. The space was bare bones minimum. There was only enough to conduct his business, but it lacked in quality, and certainly there was no flair for design to be found in the second-hand, industrial-looking desk and chairs. Perhaps if the blind man could see the shabby nature of the place, he would have thought twice about his purpose in being here. What's more, if he could have detected the tender age of the young man whom he was endeavoring to confide in, the session would have ended before it had begun.

Unable to be biased by such factors, however, the man leaned forward, putting his weight onto the cane that was propped between his legs. He appeared to be waiting, content to allow Nelson to initiate their conversation. This only made Nelson more uncomfortable. What should he say? What would a professional with years of experience under his belt say? He cleared his throat several times and then dove in. "So what is it that I can do for you, Mr. — "

"Fletcher. Harry Fletcher," he answered in a voice that was deep but intensely quiet.

"What is it that I can do for you, Mr. Fletcher?"

"I don't suppose that I have to tell you I am in need of a private investigator?" the old man said, the corner of his lip twisting up in the smallest ironic grin. Despite all that he had seen in his long life, he managed this jest easily. Nelson could see a great deal of character in his face, baring a slight resemblance to the actor Sir Anthony Hopkins, he thought. Perhaps that likeness was what made Nelson like him from the start.

"Most people who visit me say the same general thing," Nelson replied.

"I don't know if you recall our conversation over the telephone when I called on Wednesday of last week?" Harry inquired.

"I'm sorry, sir. I don't remember the specifics of it," Nelson admitted.

"I wanted to know what you charged, what your going rate was. When you told me, I was a bit surprised because it was just a fraction of what some of the others had quoted me. A bargain, you might say."

"And…" Nelson prodded.

"Do you stand by that quote?" Harry asked, pushing his head forward even further, cocked so that his ear was pointing directly at Nelson, his eyes unfocused and rolled to the corners of his sockets, waiting for the crucial reaction that would determine if he would continue on with this private investigator or if he would go home without having accomplished the thing he had come for.

"I absolutely stand by it, sir."

"I'd like to say that money is no object, that a price couldn't be put on peace of mind, but in my current circumstances that isn't quite true," he apologetically confessed.

"So, you're on a budget?" Nelson posed, hoping the amusement in his voice wasn't too obvious.

"Well, yes. I suppose that's a good way of phrasing it," he agreed with a vague grin.

"And what is it you need a private investigator for, sir?" Nelson wanted to know, unable to imagine what his visitor might say.

"I want you to clear my name of murder." The old man grew solemn, his dead eyes swiveling to gaze right through Nelson, who was motionless and transfixed by the stranger's admission. He couldn't help but wonder who exactly Harry Fletcher was, and if it were destiny or some cosmic foul up that had determined that their paths should have crossed.

CHAPTER 2

Harry knew that he was in hot water. He had called to tell Caroline that he was running late but on his way home. That was nearly an hour ago. *The Dinah Shore Show* would be on now. They usually watched that and *You Bet Your Life* together; it had become their Thursday night routine after he'd purchased their first color television a year ago. But he couldn't even get that right, that one simple thing. As much as Harry was berating himself, he knew that she would probably punish him further, make him sorry that he had let her down. He braced himself for it as he dropped his briefcase and keys on the credenza in the hallway and went straight for the kitchen. Caroline was bent over the trash can, pointedly scraping her roast and vegetables from the roasting pan into its graveyard depths. She looked up at him just as she finished her task with a sulky frown.

"Dinner ready?" he lamely joked. She did not dignify it with an answer, but went to the sink to wash the pan under running water and left it in the dish drain to dry.

"You're just a barrel full of laughs," she told him as she squeezed past him, intentionally not touching him as she fled to the bedroom. Harry sighed heavily, feeling too tired to go through this scene, but he turned to pursue her, as his role dictated.

"Caroline, I'm very sorry that I was late," he called after her. He got to the bedroom door in time to see her throw herself across the bed with her face turned toward the wall.

"Late? Late? Late would have been if you had come home the first time you called to say you were running behind. It is nine thirty, Harry. Dinner was ready to be served three hours ago," she fumed.

"I tried. I really tried to make it home on time," he defended.

"I don't believe that. Not for a minute."

"What exactly am I supposed to do here?" he asked, sitting down on the edge of the bed. "I'm trying my darndest to get my business on its feet. If I have someone come in asking me for help, even if I've already closed for the night, I'm not going to turn them away."

"Fine, Harry. Whatever you say." But her mind raced with a thousand angry things she would like to shout and didn't. Bitter, hateful things that scorched in her throat where they remained lodged. For a moment, she felt actual loathing toward this man she had promised to love, honor, and obey. She had agreed to marriage, thinking it would be the answer to all of her problems. But Harry was just a disappointment. He was shattering all of her illusions of what being a wife should be like.

"You know, I'm doing this for us, so that you can have nice things and we can get a bigger house. You want new clothes and your hair and nails done and a new washer and dryer. I'm doing this for you," he said, his voice agitated.

She sat up quickly, swinging her legs over the edge of the bed to face him. "Let's get this straight, Harry, you aren't doing this for me!" she said vehemently. "I never asked you to leave me alone, to make me feel like a single woman. You leave me to deal with everything. I'm just expected to be here when you come home and act like everything is wonderful. You aren't doing this for me; you're doing it for you, because I don't want it. I only want you, here, like it should be. Every other wife has her husband home by six."

His lip curled into a sneer. "That's easy to say. You don't worry about paying the bills. You don't worry about keeping up with the pressures of paying for the car, groceries, the roof over our heads. As long as it's there in the bank account to spend, you don't care where it comes from."

"I'm sorry that taking care of me is such a burden!" She was glaring at him, feeling the contempt building up inside, ready to burst.

Harry changed his approach. He could see that he had only made her more angry, and although he felt that he was justified in what he had said, he had never intended to make Caroline feel like a burden, only to make her feel a little guilty, make her come around and see reason. "That's not what I was saying, Caroline."

"So, what exactly were you trying to say, Harry?"

"I have to work. Things aren't free. I'm just doing my best to take care of you. It's not like I'm hitting the bars or out with my buddies or something. I'm just working."

"Do you think that because you aren't out drinking or out with your buddies that it's justifiable to spend all of your time at work and neglect me? You think that makes it right?"

Harry stretched his arms out, his palms up. "What do you want from me, Caroline? I have to work, don't I?"

She began to cry. "I know you have to work. But you're just there all the time. Don't you want to spend time with me? Don't you love me anymore? Or are you just trying to avoid me?"

Harry collected her tenderly into his arms. "Of course I love you, Caroline. You're my whole life. Do you really have to ask?"

"I'm so lonely," she sobbed. "You're gone all day and I'm alone. So completely alone. I wait all day for you to come home, and then you don't even come home. My roast was just a dry lump of burnt meat. I spent all day on it, too."

"I'm sorry. I'm really sorry about the roast," he soothed, stroking her hair. "I didn't know you were making a roast."

"I went and got it fresh from the market this morning, and now it's just ruined," she went on.

"Caroline, I'm sorry about the roast. I am," Harry offered.

"And the vegetables…" she continued.

"I'll get you another roast, Caroline. It will be all right."

"I don't want another roast. I wanted that one."

"I'm sorry, sweetheart. If I can just get this business on its feet, things will be better. Can you hold out for just a little longer? Can you be strong for just a little longer? Caroline?"

She grew silent, pulling away from him and looking into his eyes. Those darned blue eyes of his, so irresistible, so alluring. How could she stay angry at him with eyes like those? She sniffed and cleaned her face up by running her fingertips over the tear tracks that coursed down her cheeks. "Yeah, Harry. I can be strong," she squeaked reluctantly.

"That's my girl," Harry said, pulling her close again. "That's my brave girl."

She began to cry again, softly this time. "I love you, Harry."

"I love you too, sweetheart," he whispered into her ear. "I always have and I always will."

CHAPTER 3

"Hey, Nelson," Cleo called out as she saw the familiar figure of Nelson Rune coming down the hall. He looked up as if surprised, perhaps oblivious to the fact that she was there. He often appeared to be in his own world, consumed by his thoughts, working over perplexing concepts that hurt the mind if one lingered over them too long.

"Hey," he shot back, digging in his pocket for his keys.

"Aren't you going to offer to help?" she asked.

He saw, then, the garbage bags in her hand and nervously sprang forward to grab them from her, feeling stupid that he hadn't noticed them before she had pointed them out.

"Oh, yeah, sorry," he said. He stood with a bag in each hand, looking unsure of himself as she watched him. Cleo found his awkwardness endearing. There was something so sweet about his boyish demeanor. He was a good-looking guy, but didn't know it. He had no inflated ego, no cocky self-confidence, although he had good reason to, and that was what she found so appealing about him. The boys her age were consumed with trivial things that meant nothing in the grander scheme. They were content so long as they were not the lowest man on the totem pole. But Nelson, he lived in the real world. He had serious and sober things to think about.

A moment passed in silence. Nelson shifted his weight from one leg to the other as if he were waiting for something. Cleo smiled. "The Dumpster's downstairs."

"Right." He spun around and headed for the stairway with Cleo following close behind. They made their way to the first floor's lobby area and then outside to the parking lot, where Nelson disposed of the trash in the Dumpster. The lid shut with a bang.

"Thanks," Cleo told him.

"Yeah, no problem," he said with a shrug. She was pretty, with her big blue eyes, the darkest, deepest blue he'd ever seen. She had strawberry blond hair and a pale, clear complexion, with a ruddy glow to her cheeks. It seemed as if she was always surrounded by friends or admirers. The girl never lacked the ability to speak, to laugh, to draw people to her. It left him feeling sheepish, like a total loser when he was around her.

"How about I share some of my fresh baked cookies with you to say thanks?" Cleo offered, trailing him back into the small apartment building.

Nelson nodded, keeping his eyes down. "Sounds good." He waited outside the door of Cleo's apartment as she swung it wide open.

"You don't have to stand out there. You can come in, you know," she said, giving his arm a little tug.

Nelson came in reluctantly, taking in the decidedly feminine décor. It was just Cleo and her mom. No man to insist on a La-Z-Boy, to toss a baseball cap on the table, to protest floral patterns or the feminine color palette. He felt out of place, like a fish out of water. It was too nice, too easily messed up, too cluttered with ceramic figurines, potted plants, and framed photos.

Cleo watched him slouched next to the bar, and a sly smile played at her lips. "Sit down," she ordered.

He obeyed her a little too quickly, pulling the chair out in a clumsy jerk and swiftly planting himself there. He resembled a school boy, in trouble for some sort of mischief, waiting for his scolding with his hands tucked between his knees and his head bowed slightly. Cleo took the cookies from the Tupperware container and set them on a saucer, then poured a tall glass of milk and set it in front of him. She took the chair opposite him, resting her chin on her hand as she watched him eat.

"Thanks, these are good," he said.

She thought it looked like a commercial, the way he took the bite and then held it up for her to see as he praised it.

"No problem," Cleo responded. "How long's it been since you've had homemade cookies?" she asked.

"Probably the last time you gave me some," Nelson answered as he took another bite, remembering her impromptu visit at Christmas time to deliver a tin of sugar cookies to his apartment. He suspected that she felt sorry for him. He had experienced a lot of that in his relatively young life. So much pity begins to make one self-conscience, like a man with a blemish on his nose. No one can help but look at it, and you know why they're looking, but there is no way to hide it.

"So, awhile," she joked.

"Yeah."

"It's my mom's birthday," she informed him.

"Oh."

"Well, she doesn't like cake," Cleo explained. "Kinda weird, huh?"

Nelson bobbed his head in agreement.

"So anyway, I made her cookies instead."

"She at work?"

"Yeah, but she'll be home soon. I think she said we were going out for dinner to celebrate."

"The cookies are really good." Nelson was unsure of what else to say. He realized, with chagrin, that he had already given this endorsement. Cleo didn't seem to mind.

"Thanks." She waited a minute or two. "Why don't you come with us?"

"Oh, no. I'd just be in the way. It's your mom's birthday. She probably doesn't want anyone else tagging along."

"She wouldn't mind, Nelson. She's really cool that way."

Instead of trying to argue the point, he fell silent, drinking a loud gulp from his milk. Then he said, "You're lucky, you've got a really nice mom."

"Where's your mother?" Cleo asked.

Nelson looked at her, a little bewildered, and then looked away hastily, brushing some crumbs into a pile on the table top to keep himself carefully busy. "I don't know where she is right now. Last time she called she was in New York." He sniffed. "She doesn't stay put in one place for very long."

"My mom says she visits every now and then."

"It's rare."

"But why?" Cleo genuinely wanted to know.

"She's always been a free spirit type. Guess she just never got it out of her system."

"So, she's always been like that?"

"Yeah. When I was a kid, I remember just riding on the bus a lot. She shuttled me back and forth all across the States and sometimes into Canada even."

"So, how'd you end up here if she's off somewhere else?"

"Ended up with my grandpa."

"And she was okay with that?"

"I don't know. My grandpa said she was different before, but it must have been before I came 'cause that's always how I remembered her."

Something about the matter-of-fact, non-emotional way he answered puzzled her. She was all about emotions. She was more than tuned in to how she felt, how other people felt around her. But he was incredibly hard to read, which made her want to read him all the more. "I know you a little, Nelson, but you've never really told me anything about yourself. It's hard to really get to know you. Don't you get lonely living on your own like that, never talking to anybody?"

"Not really." He didn't care for her scrutinizing gaze. "I can take care of myself."

"I know," she said, seeing that she had made him uncomfortable. And then out of nowhere she dropped the bomb. "Nelson, would you go to a dance with me?"

Nelson stared hard at her. "What dance?"

"Sadie Hawkins dance. Girls are supposed to ask guys."

"Isn't there somebody else you'd rather ask?"

"No."

Nelson finished his milk and got up. "I should go," he said, balancing the saucer and empty cup in his hands. He didn't want to be rude and tell her no, but he also didn't want to be cornered in to going to some dance that would serve as a venue for highlighting his every social defect. The thought made him skittish. He pictured himself in the crowd of people, the music booming loud and staccato. He felt the safest route at this juncture was retreat.

"Are you turning me down?" She had raised her eyebrow as if she was mildly amused. She generally was not the type of girl to get turned down. Cleo was a go-getter. If she wanted something, she asked. If she was told no, she asked again. Life was there for the taking, and she took. She had not been given a reason yet to let go of her youthful optimism.

Put so bluntly, Nelson couldn't bring himself to say no. He didn't have the *nerve* to say no. But he wasn't ready to agree to it either. "When is it?" he asked, still noncommittal.

"At the end of next month," she responded. "On November twenty-ninth, so it's really almost two months if you need time to think about it." Her tone and manner were meant to be persuasive. An act she had perfected since her toddler years, when her father would cave almost immediately to her eyelash batting.

"I don't know if I can. Let me check on some stuff, and I'll get back with you."

"Okay," she responded a little too eagerly. Nelson noted this and was confused by it. Why should she care so very much? It did not make sense to him.

"Your mom's probably going to be home soon," he said, taking the glass and saucer and putting them in the sink. He backtracked through the apartment with Cleo following. She opened the door and let him out.

"Thanks for taking my trash out," she called after him as he went to the door, two doors down and on the opposite side of the hall. He absent-mindedly picked through his pockets for his keys and let himself in, shutting the door behind him with a quick second glance at the girl who had just shared her cookies.

Cleo was his same age, eighteen. Amazingly enough, their birthdays were only weeks apart in the month of September. He had never really related to anyone his own age, but she seemed to talk to him effortlessly. She did not treat him as if he were different or as if she was uncomfortable in his company. Maybe she was more mature than other people their age. Maybe that's why she appreciated him, why he appreciated her. Regardless of her reasoning, she looked for opportunities to speak to him any chance she could. And yet Nelson hesitated to let her in. He had never really needed human companionship. His grandfather was the only real attachment he had ever formed with a person. But his grandfather had a familial obligation to love him unconditionally.

Nelson always wondered in the back of his mind if she pitied him, felt sympathy for his situation, alone in the world, on his own, and a complete oddball. He didn't like the notion of being someone's pet project, some reject charity case. He was "special," something he had been aware of from a very young age. He didn't go to high school like the other kids his age. He worked for his living. Nelson had gotten his high school diploma when he was only twelve years old. At sixteen, he had graduated from college easily with a double major in criminal psychology and forensic science. While many of his peers were fretting over learning to drive cars, anticipating their sixteenth birthdays so they might get their driver's license, Nelson was mulling over what to do with his college diploma and charting a course of action.

Ever since he could remember, he had wanted to be a detective. He'd had visions of attending the police academy, gradually working his way up, achieving his life's goal through diligent persistence and hard work, until someday he would finally hold the title of Detective. It was something he had single-mindedly and doggedly pursued. There was never any question in his mind as to what he would do with his life.

Nelson remembered when he was only six, his grandfather had bought him a pair of toy handcuffs with a plastic, silver badge and a cap gun. He played with them endlessly, growing proficient in cuffing his perps with just one hand, smilingly broadly as the rounded, swinging, jagged arm clicked and locked into place.

He watched *Law and Order* religiously and was nearly angry with himself for being able to guess the ending long before the show was over. He would like to have been surprised every now and again. He memorized episodes and repeated back lines from the show. The other children thought he was strange when he spouted off some quote that had popped into his head. But he was too oblivious then to see their scorn for him. Those days had been the most carefree, the most stable time of his life.

His life's goal had been frustrated when he discovered the police academy did not accept applicants under the age of eighteen.

Furthermore, even if you were accepted into the academy, there was no point in attending until you were twenty-one, because no one was going to hire a kid fresh out of the academy that wasn't old enough to carry a weapon. The irony of the situation had not escaped Nelson. With his extensive college experience, he knew more in theory than all of the rookies, and he would have known as much with on-the-job experience as seasoned veterans with their legitimate badges, yet his dream was just beyond his reach. He still had another three years before he could think of applying.

What would he do while he bided his time? He took what little money his grandfather had left him when he'd died, and he started his own business as a private investigator. What was he thinking? Nelson had asked himself that question many times over the past two years. It barely paid the bills, but Nelson tried to look at what he did as a stepping stone to bigger and better things. So, at sixteen he found himself the owner of his own weak and failing business. For the last two years, he had struggled to make his living doing something he had a passion for. And yet, lacking any real opportunity for substantial cases, he felt as if he were headed straight for a brick wall. His life was headed for a dead end that made him feel almost claustrophobic.

At first it had been difficult getting anyone to hire him as a private investigator. He was young, inexperienced, and his college diploma didn't do much to impress, despite his genius status. To remain competitive, Nelson lowered his fee — drastically. He got plenty of work now, not always from the most savory of characters, but at least he had something to keep him busy. Generally he dealt in cheating spouses, locating lost relatives, checking out bogus worker's comp claims, background checks, and the like.

But as Nelson threw himself across his futon that evening, it was the blind man's freakish eyes that dominated his thoughts and floated through his mind. Harry Fletcher. Who was he really? It seemed incredible to Nelson that after two years of nothing but the mundane, he had landed something extraordinary, something mysterious and fascinating. What was coming he could not guess, but he thrilled at the prospects, delighted at the break in routine.

CHAPTER 4

Harry was a man who had everything he had ever dreamed of. His business was thriving. He enjoyed driving his '54 Ford Crestline Sunliner Convertible. True it was a few years old, not brand new, but he always felt like a man to be envied when he drove it to work with the top down. He loved to wave at the passersby as he parked the car in the lot next to his office. His new home — a three bedroom, two bath with an attached garage — was all that he had hoped for. His wife, young and beautiful, the love of his life, met him at the door each night when he came home from work. He had known since he was sixteen that she was the one for him. Everything was as it should be in Harry Fletcher's world. Things were looking up for him. He noticed with pleasure that people looked at him with respect and envy as he passed them on the sidewalk. Harry Fletcher had a spring in his step and a smile on his face these days.

When the telephone rang, he was delighted to hear Caroline on the other end of the line, her slightly husky voice low and pleasant. He leaned back in his chair, crossing his legs and extending his free arm above his head in a deep stretch. "What a nice surprise," he said into the receiver.

"Yes, well, you won't be so happy when you find out why I'm calling."

"What's the matter?"

"I know we had planned on having lunch today, but I won't be able to make it," she told him, sounding immensely disappointed.

"Why not?"

"I'm afraid I forgot that I was meeting with Marnie today."

"Tell her you can't come," he persuaded. "I want to see you."

"I normally would, Harry, but she's been a little blue lately, and I think she needs some cheering up, you know?" Caroline replied.

"What's the matter with her?"

"I don't know for certain. Well…I'm sure she'll be fine. But really, what kind of a friend would I be if I wasn't there for her?" she asked. "She's always been there for me, and now she needs someone to be there for her."

"You really think it's that serious?"

"I don't know, Harry. You should have heard her. She just sounded so down when I spoke to her."

"I see," he said, genuinely concerned. "I suppose I'll have to make do without you, then."

"You and I can just have lunch tomorrow," she consoled. "Would you be able to arrange that?"

"All right, tomorrow," he agreed. "Tell Marnie hello for me."

"What will you do for lunch?"

"Nothing, I suppose. I'll probably just finish some things up here. I don't really have a reason to go out now."

"Oh, I feel so badly," she said.

"Don't worry about it. I'm a big boy, aren't I? Just take care, then, sweetheart."

"I will. I'll see you tonight when you get home," she promised.

"Yeah, tonight," he said and then hung up the telephone.

He labored for the better part of the afternoon over a particularly complicated account but finally gave in to his growling stomach. Securing the "Be Back in Half an Hour" sign in the window, he went down the street to get a sandwich. Harry sat at the bar of the local diner by himself and ordered a burger. He ate it in a few bites, savoring it very little, before rushing back to the office, unwilling to waste too much time on a lunch break.

As he passed the drugstore, who should he bump into but Marnie Donner. She was coming out of the swinging doors just as he approached from the sidewalk. She smiled up at Harry. "Fancy meeting you," she said.

"Well, hello, Marnie," he said. His eyebrows came together in concern as he asked, "How are you feeling?"

"I'm just fine," she replied. "Just fine. No need to worry. I'm not here for me," she explained. "Only grabbing Chuck's blood pressure medicine." And she held up her sack, waving it back and forth to show him.

"How was lunch today?" Harry asked with a broad grin.

"Lunch?" she asked, confused. "I guess it was all right. Just a liverwurst sandwich I threw together at home. Nothing special."

"Huh. Didn't Caroline drop in to see you today?" He was bewildered by the turn of events.

"No. No, just me and my liverwurst," she told him with a laugh. "Was she supposed to drop by today?"

"You know I probably just got the days mixed up," he said quietly. His gut churned within, and he felt a strange mixture of nervous jitters and sickening dread. Acidic bile began to rise, and he felt its scorching effects in his throat as immediate heartburn ensued. Trying to hide his panic, he swallowed hard a few times and straightened his tie. Marnie noticed the change in his demeanor and grew worried.

"Are you all right, Harry? You look sick," she told him.

"I'm fine, Marnie. You know, you and Chuck haven't been over in a couple of weeks. We'll have to remedy that," Harry offered.

"That sounds good. You just let us know when, and we'll be there."

She took her small paper bag and headed on down the street. Harry spent the rest of the day trying to push thoughts of Caroline out of his mind. There could be a million reasons why she hadn't had lunch with Marnie. After all, plans change. Things come up. It was simply a misunderstanding. That was all.

When he got home that evening, Caroline was her usual charming self. She took Harry by his hand and pulled him to the table, pushing him into his chair. She removed his hat and ran her fingers through his dark brown hair and then went to put the hat on the coat rack by the front door. "I made your favorite," she cooed when she returned.

"It smells great," he said, all the while his stomach lurching within. The thought ran through his mind over and over again that he should confront her. But she seemed oblivious to his preoccupied mood. After all, he would feel very bad indeed if he were to accuse her of something she was not guilty of when there might be a completely reasonable explanation for her not having lunch with Marnie.

"How was work?"

"Oh, I don't know. Same old," he said, faltering. "How about you? How was your day?" And it was the moment of truth. He nearly held his breath in anticipation of what she might say.

"It was all right," she told him, dishing a healthy portion of meatloaf and mashed potatoes onto his plate. "Marnie was a bit of a sour puss, but I think she was glad that I came," Caroline went on. She helped herself to a smaller portion and turned to set the dish on the counter.

"Did you find out why she's so down?" Harry asked.

"You know how women are, Harry. Sometimes we just get moody," she teased, sitting across from him at the table. "I think she'll snap out of it soon. As a matter of fact, she seemed on the mend when I left her."

"You don't think it's anything serious? Maybe I should give Chuck a call," Harry suggested, carefully keeping his eyes averted. Why? Because he couldn't stand to look at her while she was lying to him. He didn't want to know if she could look him in the eyes while she so convincingly told her fabricated bull.

Caroline cocked her head to the side with an eyebrow lifted as she spread her napkin across her lap. "Now, Harry, I don't think it warrants a call to Chuck. I'm sure that she'll be fine. And, really, it's none of our business. I think it's best if we just stay out of it. Maybe they're quarrelling or something. That could be awkward if we got in the middle of it. We should just leave it alone."

"You're probably right," he responded slowly.

"Of course I am. Aren't I always?" She watched him toy with his fork, his eyes glued on his plate. "Aren't you going to eat?"

"Sure, sure," he said, picking up the fork, loading it with food, and forcibly putting it in his mouth. He swallowed with difficulty. Harry doubted if he would ever be able to eat this meal again without remembering these events and playing it out in his head. The meatloaf was like a brick in his stomach—the tomato sauce too tart and the meat greasy on his tongue—but he soldiered on. If he could swallow her story, he reasoned, he could certainly swallow this bite of food.

CHAPTER 5

Nelson began his research at the library, looking over old newspaper articles on microfilm — some difficult to read because of the quality and age of the paper that had been photographed. He skimmed through dozens of articles that were specifically about Harry Fletcher's case, reading each gruesome detail with a sick sort of enthusiasm, with a fiendish appetite for the particulars of what had happened the night Caroline Fletcher had met her maker. He learned that Harry had spent thirty years in prison, always maintaining his innocence, but strangely enough, never filing for an appeal or seeking parole. This made no sense to Nelson. If he were an innocent man, wouldn't he do everything in his power to prove he had not committed the crime? Furthermore, Nelson felt that the story Fletcher had told seemed incredible, a lame account that didn't hold up under scrutiny, easily poked full of holes.

The papers had splashed photos of the couple across the front page. The young Harry seemed an apparently mild man, his eyes soft, a strange disparity to his muscular build. Next to him was a beautiful woman, her oval face carefully done up in makeup, her lips in a bright smile, her black hair reminiscent of Jacqueline Kennedy. Nelson thought she was quite stunning, the sort of woman, he mused, that would draw attention from any man. It was not difficult to see why the murder and ensuing trial had drawn so much attention.

He read over the trial coverage, which was very blatantly biased against Harry Fletcher. The press felt he had to be responsible for his wife's murder. His flimsy story simply did not hold up under scrutiny. He claimed to be at work up to the wee hours of the morning, although there was no way of knowing if that had been the case, despite his ex-mistress's claim that she had seen him there. No one had believed the former lover's assertion, supposing she had backed the story to protect Harry and hide the truth.

Yes, the public sentiment had definitely not been in his favor. Nelson assumed this must have hurt Harry's case considerably. This was years ago, when a bias because of an affair may have played a big part in getting Harry put behind bars. Nowadays, even with substantial DNA and forensic evidence, someone could still get off with reasonable doubt. In Nelson's mind, it was obvious that Harry Fletcher hadn't gotten a fair trial. And yet Nelson wondered how he was going to solve a murder from 1964, nearly thirty years before he had even been born. Surely, Harry Fletcher was doomed to remain guilty.

The last and most recent article that had featured Harry Fletcher's name was dated only two weeks earlier and had nothing to do with the actual murder itself, although references were made to it. Nelson skimmed through the paragraphs detailing the murder and ending with the specifics of Christy Fletcher's death. Christy Fletcher, the only person in the house when her mother was murdered. Christy Fletcher, only child of Harry and Caroline Fletcher, had died at the age of fifty-one after suffering for over a decade from Huntington's disease.

The only material witness was gone, just two weeks before the mysterious Harry Fletcher had secured him as a private detective. Nelson jotted details in his notebook as he went over and over the information in the newspapers. After several hours of reading, he leaned back in his chair and stretched, rubbing his blurred eyes. He felt he had gleaned all that he could from this source and decided to pay a visit to the courthouse. Nelson collected his things, climbed into his grandpa's old pickup truck, and headed downtown.

With a little finagling, he was able to secure a copy of the court transcripts, which he loaded into his backpack and took home. Sitting on his futon with the pages fanned out before him, he began reviewing and taking notes on the testimony of each witness, picturing the trial in his head as if he were watching a movie. A knock at the door startled him. Nelson had been totally immersed in what he was doing, and the unexpected interruption made him jump slightly, the papers in his hand giving a little quiver. His eyes fell to the clock, and he realized with some surprise that it was nearly eight.

Cleo was smiling brightly at him when he opened the door. This made his heart beat a little faster, and perspiration wet his armpits in an instant. She didn't wait to be asked in, just breezed past him with a "Hello" as she entered. Nelson shut the door and tagged along after her into the living room area. She surveyed the mass of papers and turned to him. "What's all this?"

Nelson scrambled to try to collect the grisly black and white photos of Caroline Fletcher laid out on the kitchen floor of her home, her vacant eyes peering up at the camera. "Work," he replied.

Cleo caught a glimpse of the photos and grimaced. "*What* are you working on?"

"Just stuff," he answered, running his fingers through his hair.

"You don't want to tell me?" she said accusingly.

"A case. I'm working on a case."

She could see she was making him nervous and switched modes. "You had dinner yet?"

He hesitated. "No."

Cleo walked over to the refrigerator, opened it, and surveyed its contents. "You can't exactly eat dinner with no food in your apartment."

"I think I have some macaroni and cheese," Nelson told her as he joined her in the kitchenette and began rummaging through sparsely stocked cabinets.

"But you don't have any milk to make it with."

"It works with water too."

"That sounds really good," she joked. She had no doubt why his frame was so tall and lean. The guy didn't eat, or at least not enough. "I wouldn't mind a cheeseburger myself." Cleo waited for a moment, but when Nelson did not respond, she bluntly blurted, "That was a hint. A pretty obvious one, too."

"Oh," Nelson replied, setting the box of macaroni and cheese on the countertop.

After an awkward moment's silence, Cleo persisted. "So, are you going to take me to get a burger or not?"

"Yeah, I can do that," Nelson said reluctantly. He wondered why she had shown up, why she was hanging around, why she wanted him to go with her to get something to eat.

"Good," she said as he went to get his keys.

He drove her to the closest place, a Wendy's a few blocks away. They sat at a small two-seater table with their meals before them, quietly regarding one another—Cleo with her double cheeseburger, Nelson with his grilled chicken salad. Cleo stuck a few fries into her mouth with relish.

"Why don't you want to go to the dance with me, Nelson?" she asked with a hint of a whine, not bothering to look up at him. She knew she was throwing him off guard, and in fact that was her intention.

Nelson was surprised by her straightforward question. He was hoping that his lack of commitment and his attempt at dodging the subject would effectively shut her down. He cleared his throat nervously.

"I never said I didn't want to go," Nelson said.

"Yes you did," Cleo argued.

"I don't remember saying that," Nelson stammered, trying to mentally recall using that verbiage.

"Well, you didn't say yes, and then you tried to avoid having to answer at all. That was pretty much you saying you didn't want to go," Cleo pointed out, watching him closely for his reaction.

"All right, I don't want to go."

"But why? Is it me?"

"No, Cleo." He took a moment to word it right. "I just don't like stuff like that. I don't like being around people and crowds, you know? Besides, I don't know how to dance, and you'd probably have a rotten time with me anyway." How could he make her understand that going to that dance would make him feel uncomfortable, out of place? He was painfully aware of how different he was, and he was also aware that everyone else knew it too. They treated him with the same sort of disdain that they treated women who grew beards, or men who could swallow strange things like nails and glass, or conjoined twins, or people born with terrible birth defects like extra limbs. He was an aberration to them. He had been called a freak often enough to know what everyone thought of him.

"Have you ever been to a dance before?" she asked.

"No."

"Then how do you know you wouldn't like it?" she asked.

"I just know," he insisted.

"So, you *are* turning me down?"

He didn't respond. Nor did he move. His eyes were still trained in her direction, but they were unfocused, as though he were avoiding her direct gaze.

"Okay, Nelson, you don't have to go with me. I guess I'll just ask somebody else."

Again, Nelson said nothing.

"Jeez, Nelson, could you just try and pick up on the tactfully subtle manipulation? It would make this a whole lot easier on me."

"What do you mean?" he asked, his eyebrows drawn together and one side of his mouth drooping as though he were confused by what she was saying. She could see he really did not understand.

"I mean, you're supposed to say, 'No, Cleo, I'm not turning you down,' or 'No, Cleo, don't ask anybody else, I'll go with you. I want to. It would be my pleasure.' It's called reverse psychology. When a girl works it, especially as strongly as I'm working it, you should be polite and do whatever it is she's trying to get you to do, so she doesn't have to come right out and *tell* you what she's trying to get you to do."

"So, you wanted me to go with you, even though I said I'd be uncomfortable? Even though I said I didn't know how to dance?" Nelson asked, confused.

"Exactly," Cleo affirmed.

"Well, all right, I guess."

"Really?"

"You won't take no for an answer, will you?" he asked.

"No, I won't," she said. "I'll probably just keep bugging you until you say yes."

"I guess I'll have to go then," he replied with a shrug. Nelson did not like feeling so put on the spot. He figured that if his honest opinion didn't deter her, nothing would, and he didn't want to make a scene.

"Good, I'm really glad you decided to."

"Okay," he said simply.

"Nelson, you don't know a lot about girls do you?"

"Absolutely nothing," he admitted. "I mean that literally, too. Like, nothing."

"Then let me tell you just a little, ya know, for future reference. With boys, they usually just tell you flat out what they expect or want or what they think or whatever. Girls are different. We're a lot more devious and mostly use mental warfare to get our way. You have to try and read into whatever we're saying, because we rarely say what we really mean. It's all between the lines. See?" Cleo told him, growing winded near the end of her discourse. She took a long sip from her straw until it made a noise to indicate that she was out of soda.

"I guess." Nelson had never particularly related to the female gender, and now that Cleo had finished with her long-winded explanation, he had some understanding as to why. He always said what he meant and expected that everyone else did the same. For the first time, he had a small glimpse into the inner workings of a woman's mind. While it was fascinating, it was also terrifying. He had never been very good at double meanings, innuendoes, or passive-aggressive behaviors. They were like a foreign language to him. This new knowledge made him feel incredibly insecure and guarded.

"So, now that that's settled, why don't you tell me what you're working on," she suggested.

"I have a confidentiality thing with my clients. I don't know if I really should," Nelson told Cleo reluctantly.

"Oh." She thought for a moment. "But I don't know who your client is. If you didn't mention any names and I promised not to tell anyone, don't you think it couldn't hurt?"

"You have kind of a big mouth, Cleo."

She laughed. "Thanks a lot."

"I didn't mean it that way, I j-just…" he stammered, feeling immediate remorse for his blunder.

Cleo noted his red face and sought to ease his discomfort. "Don't worry. I don't get offended easily. Lucky for you. You're probably right anyways. I do have a big mouth."

"That doesn't mean that I don't like you. I mean—well, that didn't come out like I wanted it to. You probably think I'm a blubbering idiot." Nelson was picking frantically at his salad with his plastic fork while his foot drummed a hyper and steady beat on the tiled floors. It was as though he couldn't force his body to be still.

"Do I make you uncomfortable?" Cleo asked suspiciously. She had noticed before that he fidgeted a lot, but she wasn't sure if it was because of her, or if it was just a particular habit of his.

"No. I think I'm more comfortable around you than I am most people." He said it as though he had just only realized it for himself, as though it were somewhat of a surprise.

"Really?"

"Yeah."

"Well, that's a great compliment, Nelson. Thanks."

"It's a murder case," he blurted, diverting the conversation to something he felt safe with. It was easier to talk about something he knew than to remain in this uncertain territory he currently found himself in.

"What is?"

"I'm working on a forty-five-year-old murder case right now."

"Really?" Cleo seemed excited by the prospect.

"Really."

"Well, what kind of murder case?"

"This guy, Harry Fletcher, he was accused of his pregnant wife's murder, served thirty years in prison, then out of nowhere he comes to me yesterday and asks me to prove he's innocent," Nelson went on.

"Bizarre!" she said, her eyes wide and disbelieving as she took a mammoth bite from her burger.

"No kidding."

"But, why now? Why not before?" she asked and took another bite.

"That's the thing that's bugging me. Why now?"

"Why do they say he killed his wife in the first place?" Cleo probed.

"Hard telling. He lied in court under oath about a relationship he had with another woman. They tried to say that he killed his wife because she found out about his infidelity."

"I think it would be the other way around. It would be the wife that killed the husband, if she caught him cheating. Don't you think? I mean, I would anyway, if it was me. I'd kill the snake. I'd cut his—"

"I get the picture," Nelson interrupted as he pushed his salad around with his fork.

"I'm just saying…" She trailed off.

"I can't really imagine being angry enough to kill anybody. It seems a little extreme, doesn't it?" Nelson asked.

Cleo smiled to herself; she couldn't imagine Nelson being that angry either. He just wasn't the type. But Nelson was not the norm. She imagined that there were plenty of people out there with healthy, hot-blooded tempers that were very capable of murder. Given the right circumstances, anything was possible.

"I don't know. There are a few times I've daydreamed about killing Miss Clayborn," Cleo admitted with a mischievous smile.

"Who's Miss Clayborn?"

"The gym teacher."

"Sometimes I forget that you're still in school," he commented.

"Yep, we can't all be a genius like you, Nelson, but I finish this year, and I'm out of there. And believe me, I'm counting it down."

"You don't like school?"

"I have a lot of friends and stuff, but I'm just kind of sick of the whole scene. It's like nobody knows that there's life after high school, that this is just a blip on the radar. It's not forever. You know what I mean?"

"No. Not really."

"Well, I guess you wouldn't," Cleo realized out loud. "It's just that most of the people I know now, I won't ever see again after this year. Why should I care what they think?"

"Maybe. You never know, though. Harry Fletcher married his high school sweetheart," Nelson said dryly.

"Harry who?"

"Fletcher. The guy that was convicted of killing his wife."

"That was a long time ago. It was pretty common then, I guess, to marry your high school sweetheart. Not so much now. Usually people that get married out of high school don't end up staying together. It ends up in splitsville."

"All of their friends and acquaintances swore up and down that he was head over heels for her, had been since they were kids, that she could do no wrong. They all said that the two of them were the ideal couple."

"Maybe that's how they made it look. Doesn't mean that's how it was. Why'd he have an affair if he was such a doting husband? That's just sick and wrong, by the way. And perfect relationships don't tend to end in death!" she said contemptuously.

"I don't know. In my estimation things never are as they seem. Appearances are shallow."

"Well, maybe you should ask him about it," Cleo recommended.

"I plan on it. Something else that's off, his daughter died two weeks ago. I'm not sure if it's a coincidence that he came to me now or not."

"What's his daughter got to do with it?"

"She was the only one there that night when the wife was killed."

"So, you think he waited until the only witness was gone to try and say he didn't do it because she knew something?"

"It's possible."

"Very possible. The creep. Did she see anything? Do you know?" Cleo asked eagerly, sitting a little taller in her chair.

"No. She was sleeping. Slept through the whole thing," Nelson said as he shook his head.

"How'd this poor woman die?"

"She was stabbed nineteen times, which is a little misleading, actually. Some of the wounds were defense wounds." He indicated his forearms with his hands. "Some hit and misses, and then some were right on the mark, most of those inflicted once she was down for the count. Someone was pretty angry with her."

"It seems like she would have cried out or something. You don't go quietly if someone is stabbing you repeatedly."

"I wouldn't think so either," he agreed. "But the little girl was sleeping soundly in her bed when the aunt arrived."

"That's gotta damage a kid." She took another drink from her straw. "You gonna eat that?" she asked, eyeing his baked potato.

"No. You can have it." He pushed it toward her.

"Thanks," Cleo told him. "Here's the thing, if this Harry guy knew his daughter was in the house, would he really kill the wife right under the little girl's nose? It seems like he would wait, figure out another way to do it, sometime when they were alone."

"That's why he only got thirty years. They found him guilty of second degree murder, meaning he didn't plan on killing her; it was just heat of the moment, a crime of passion. It certainly seems like a crime of passion, stabbed nineteen times. A little bit of overkill, wouldn't you say?"

"I guess so. Sounds like a very angry person."

"They never found the murder weapon, although they were pretty sure that it was a knife from the Fletcher home. There was a knife missing from the set in the kitchen. The house was very neatly burglarized. Drawers open, a few things turned over, some jewelry items missing from the wife's collection. Most likely staged. It was all a little too neat. Even more disturbing to me is that they didn't test to see if she had been sexually assaulted, they didn't process blood and dirt found at the crime scene, they didn't test a partially-smeared shoe print and a perfect print on the walkway outside to see if it matched any of Harry Fletcher's shoes, they didn't examine the contents of Caroline Fletcher's stomach, and they didn't take into account that Caroline's front teeth were nearly ripped out, indicating she bit the person who attacked her."

"So? What does that mean?"

"You have to bite someone pretty hard to pull teeth like that. You see, she sinks her teeth in, the person she bites pulls away from her so forcefully that the teeth get yanked too."

"Gross. I'm trying to eat here," she teased.

"Sorry."

"I'm just giving you a hard time," she said with a smile. "So, did Harry have bite marks?"

"No, he didn't. Not a mark on him, besides an injury to the back of his head," Nelson replied. "Then they found a cigarette butt next to a shoe print just outside the back door that leads into the kitchen, which conveniently disappeared from evidence. But neither Harry or Caroline smoked."

"What do you mean 'conveniently' disappeared?"

"I mean they thought Harry did it and they didn't want any evidence that might refute that claim. It would have been easy to accidently misplace it. Things were a lot different in nineteen sixty-four. That wasn't the only thing that disappeared, either. The shoe print was destroyed too."

"So, what exactly is Harry's story?"

"All I know is what I've read in the newspapers and court transcripts. He claims he was working late, came home and the bedroom light was on, which he thought was weird because it was so late. He walks into the house and is hit over the head with something, and it knocks him out. When he comes to, he goes to check on his six-year-old daughter, who was sleeping, and then his wife. She's not in bed. He runs through the house looking for her and finds her in the kitchen.

"There she is lying on the floor, dead from the stab wounds. Here's where it gets hard to believe. He doesn't call the police right away.

He calls his sister, Dinah, to come over. When she drives over in a hurry, Harry tells her what happened and has her take the little girl back to her house before he decides to call the police."

"He pretty much stamped a guilty sign across his forehead. He didn't call the police right away?"

"Nope. He said he was only trying to protect his daughter. His poor sister got all wrapped up in it. She swears up and down that Harry couldn't have done it. She said that he was always looking out for the daughter and that he was just trying to keep her from seeing or hearing anything that would have messed her up."

"Little too late for that, wouldn't you say?"

"Guess so."

"So, it's just his word that she was asleep. There's no way of really knowing for sure if he's telling the truth," she pointed out.

"When they interviewed her later, she said that she didn't hear anything, that she was sleeping. That was her testimony too."

"That still doesn't mean that was the truth. Sweet Aunt Dinah could have been coaching her before the police had a chance to question her, you know."

"I guess that's something we'll never really know, since we can't ask the daughter ourselves," Nelson granted.

"I'm finished," Cleo announced. She collected her trash and put it all on the red tray lined with paper that their meal had arrived on. "Aren't you going to eat the rest of your salad?"

"No, I'm not really hungry."

"Guys don't eat salad, Nelson."

"What do they eat, double cheeseburgers with fries, a soft drink, and a baked potato with a frosty?"

Cleo scowled. "When you put it that way, it's very unflattering."

"Here, let me get that for you." Nelson grabbed the tray and took it over to the trash can. He watched the contents slide into the dark hole with a thud and went back for Cleo. She was still a little sulky.

"Don't worry about it," he soothed. "You need your protein, right?" Before she could give him any sort of a biting rebuttal, his cell phone began to ring. He pulled the small black device out of his back pocket and checked the caller ID window.

"Shoot. Miss Bombeck," he muttered.

"Who's Miss Bombeck?"

"Just a client. Look, do you mind if I run an errand before I drop you back off at home?" he asked, sincerely sorry for the inconvenience. "Ah, never mind. I'll drop you off first."

"I don't mind running an errand. What is it?" Cleo's curiosity was piqued. She had nothing better to do than tag along with Nelson. It was infinitely more interesting than sitting at home doing nothing.

"I gotta go pick up a cat," he said in irritation.

"A cat?"

"Yeah, a stupid cat."

Cleo's puzzled expression did not abate, but she shrugged her shoulders in a resigned agreement. "Okay."

"Hello, Miss Bombeck," he said as he answered his phone. He listened for a moment and then replied, "No worries. I'll try and find him for you. Okay. Okay. All right, I'm leaving right now. Okay, Miss Bombeck. Okay. Yeah, goodbye."

Once they stepped outside, she shuddered a little from October's evening air. "It wasn't this cold when we left," she noted. "I probably shouldn't have worn shorts. I'm freezing."

Nelson was wearing a T-shirt with a long-sleeved flannel buttoned over the top of it. He took off his shirt and handed it to her. "Maybe this will help," he offered.

"You'll be cold now," she protested.

"I'm fine," he insisted. "I'm not cold at all." He opened the door for her, and she climbed in, draping the flannel shirt over her legs as if it were a blanket. Nelson turned the heater on so she'd be more comfortable.

He drove down Main Street, confident in the route he was taking, behaving as if he were slightly preoccupied. Cleo examined him with a curious amusement. It was interesting to watch him at work, his one-track mind tuning everything else out as he focused on the business at hand, a propensity for centering his attention on the immediate task. "So, why are we picking up a cat?" she finally interjected, breaking into his thoughts.

"Miss Bombeck calls me when her cat goes missing, and I go find him. I mean, she pays me for it and all," he explained.

"But how do you know where to find it?"

"The cat?"

"Yeah."

"He's in the same place every time," he said.

"I see." She waited a moment before she asked, "So, why does she pay you to get the cat if he's in the same place every time?"

"Well, she genuinely didn't know where the cat was the first time he went missing. I did have to figure out how to find Mr. Darcy then, but—"

"I'm sorry, but did you just say 'Mr. Darcy'?" she interrupted.

"Yeah, Mr. Darcy. That's the cat's name."

"Like *Pride and Prejudice* Mr. Darcy?"

"Uh, yeah. Anyway, since that first time, I guess she just thinks it's easier to call me than to have to go get him herself. Only, she makes this big deal out of it, like she's afraid he's gone for good this time. Not likely."

"Why not?"

"Oh, for several reasons," he said as he pulled the truck up to the entrance of Bonsai Sushi Bar. "For one, he has unlimited fresh fish in this Dumpster, and for another, he's a tom cat who hasn't been fixed and the owners have a very attractive Siamese. I'd be too lucky if the stupid thing were to get hit by car." He got out of the truck and headed down the dimly lit passageway between the back walls of two restaurants. She could hear him calling, "Here, Mr. Darcy, here, kitty."

She could hardly suppress her laughter as she watched from her vantage point. Nelson came back shortly cat—black with white socks and a tuft of white fur just below his studded leather collar. Nelson opened her door, holding the cat in the crook of his arms. "You mind if I put him in here? You allergic or anything?"

"No, I'm not allergic," she said, fighting a smile. "So, this is the infamous Mr. Darcy? He's so cute. It's like he's wearing a little tuxedo."

"He knows how to live the good life, that's for sure," Nelson grumbled as he dumped the cat in the cab.

"Sounds like you're mad at the poor thing," she mused as Nelson climbed in next to her.

"This cat is the bane of my existence."

"Why's that?"

"I have to go pick him up at least once a week. No sooner do I bring him back, and he's run off again."

"Why don't you just tell her you can't pick him up anymore?"

"I don't know. I don't feel like I *can* say no to her. She's a nice lady."

Cleo smiled at him, impressed by his soft hearted nature. He seemed embarrassed when he caught her glance.

"And I get paid, anyway. Just a few more blocks now."

"Nelson, what's wrong with the cat?" she asked, watching Mr. Darcy suspiciously.

"I don't know," Nelson told her. "What do you mean, what's wrong with the cat?"

Mr. Darcy's eyes seemed wide and dilated as he paced between the two of them frantically. He made a low growling sound in the back of his throat, jumping down onto the floor of the cab and then back up onto the seat again.

"What's it doing?" Cleo gasped, holding her hands out with her head cranked back, ready to defend herself from attack.

"Mr. Darcy, stop it!" Nelson yelled. The cat paid him no notice, continuing his odd behavior. It was as if the thing were in a panic, urgently looking for an escape route. "He's never acted this way before," Nelson assured her.

"You don't think he has rabies or something?" she speculated, a disturbed look on her face.

"I doubt that. Knowing Miss Bombeck, that cat has definitely had all of its shots," he said.

Mr. Darcy was like a cat on crack. It was as if he were in some sort of frenzy, a fur ball from Hell. He jumped up on Cleo, putting his front paws on the dashboard, his back paws still on her lap, and then let loose with a huge pile of poop right onto Cleo's legs. Cleo reacted with a stifled shriek. "Nelson! Nelson!" she cried, flailing her hand to get his attention.

He pulled his eyes from the road, looked over at her, looked back for a split second, until it dawned on him what Mr. Darcy had just done. "Holy crap!" he yelled, swerving wildly while pulling the truck to the side of the road with an urgent squeal of the brakes.

"That seems pretty appropriate," Cleo said dryly, "considering the circumstances." She realized there was not a whole lot that could be done about the situation at this point, and she didn't want to make Nelson feel any worse than he already did. She shrugged it off as if to say, *What are you going to do about it?* Meanwhile, Mr. Darcy jumped off of her lap and sat politely between the two of them like a perfect guest now that his business was done.

"I am so sorry," Nelson apologized.

"Uh, I'm pretty sure your shirt is ruined," she said with a grimace. "Lucky for me you let me borrow it."

"Stupid cat!" Nelson fumed, unbuckling the seatbelt and jogging around to Cleo's side of the truck. He gathered the flannel gingerly into a bundle, turning away from her and searching in either direction for a place to dispose of it. Spying a garbage can at the side of a brick home, Nelson made a beeline for it. He wrenched the lid off, tossed the shirt in, and slammed the lid back on.

By the time he had gotten back into the truck, he was noticeably flustered, his face red with embarrassment or anger. Cleo wasn't sure which.

"Are you all right?" she asked.

"Jeez, I'm really sorry. That couldn't have gone any worse," he mumbled. "You shouldn't be worried about me. I'm not the one that got dumped on. I can't believe he did that! What a lousy thing to happen…"

"It's okay." Cleo saw Nelson shoot her a doubtful glance. "Really it's not that big of a deal," she assured him.

By the time he pulled into Miss Bombeck's driveway, he'd calmed down a little. He picked up Mr. Darcy, restraining his desire to launch the cat at the door and drive away. Instead, he carried Mr. Darcy up the sidewalk to deliver him personally. Two curt knocks, and Miss Bombeck answered. She was a middle-aged woman wearing a floral polyester blouse that stretched over a vast expanse of bosom, reminiscent of twin torpedoes bundled side by side.

"Oh, thank you!" she gushed as Nelson handed her the cat. "You've brought him back to me safe and sound. Mr. Darcy, you bad thing," she scolded as if talking to a child. "Hold on for just one minute while I get my check book." She put the cat down and went back into the house, leaving Nelson to wait for her. Mr. Darcy ran the length of his body against Nelson, arching his back and purring, while Nelson shook his leg to try to get the cat to leave him alone. Cleo was watching from the truck and worked to suppress a laugh, afraid that she might get caught in the act of finding the awkward situation amusing.

When Miss Bombeck came back, she was in the process of writing the check. She ripped the check from the book and handed it to him with a wide smile. "Twenty dollars, as usual. You're a life saver, Nelson. Thank you so much for your help. I don't know what I would do if anything happened to my Mr. Darcy."

"No problem, Miss Bombeck."

"Who's that in your truck?" she asked, craning to get a peek at Cleo waiting in the driveway.

"Just a friend. Take care, Miss Bombeck," he said, watching Mr. Darcy make his way to the window on the far wall just behind his owner. The window was open, and Mr. Darcy jumped onto the sill, stretching himself out before he agilely leaped from his perch on the sill and outside to freedom again.

Nelson returned Cleo back home in mostly silence, saying good night at her door before he headed back to his futon and his piles of papers that needed to be reviewed. He always felt soothingly secure in his tiny apartment. The close space gave him a sense of safety, of comfort. After a night like this one, it was a refuge. Trying to distract himself from the burning memory of the cat dropping a load on Cleo's lap, Nelson immersed himself in work.

He pulled his cell phone from his jeans pocket and dialed a number that he had carefully written on a scrap of paper. He waited for someone to pick up on the other end. "Yeah, could I please speak with Dinah Gert, please?"

CHAPTER 6

Nineteen fifty-eight was the year that brought a slow downward slope to complete estrangement for Harry and Caroline. When Caroline had told Harry that she was going to have a baby, there was no joy in his reaction. If anything, he seemed indifferent. Some expectant fathers doted over their wives, taking care of their every need, providing for their every comfort. They would affectionately chide their wives for doing too much, for not taking care of themselves as they should, telling them not to reach too high, not to work too hard, not to physically exert themselves. They would insist that, in such a fragile condition, their wives should sit with their feet propped up under a plump pillow or take a nap in the middle of the day.

Not Harry. No, he felt no empathy, no compassion for the woman who carried his child. Caroline was terribly ill with morning sickness for the first four months. She was lucky if she could keep down an occasional slice of toast and a glass of water in the beginning. Odors and the sight of food left her running for the bathroom, and she looked pale and weak, not her usual naturally beautiful self. He didn't express concern, didn't do anything to change his routine so that he might help her out. On the contrary, he lived his life as he always had, keeping to his same routine as if nothing were out of the ordinary. He ate his meals in the morning and evening without regard for how the smells or the sight of it might affect her. He left his dishes by the sink for her to wash. In general, he was quite thoughtless, as if nothing had changed in their lives.

Caroline resented it. He knew it but didn't care. As her pregnancy progressed and the sickness abated, the rage she felt toward him abated a bit as well. She tried to include him in the blessed joy of anticipating a baby. She informed him as to how her trips to the doctor's office went, including the details of first hearing the heartbeat through the doctor's stethoscope, and that their baby was due in late September. Harry listened politely, but never showed the sort of relish she wished he would. He was a completely different man from the doting lover she had married.

One evening, she attempted to cuddle up next to him. Gingerly taking his hand, she pressed it against her tummy so that he could feel the baby moving. "Do you feel that, Harry?" For a moment, he held still, with the hint of a smile on his lips, because he could indeed feel the ripples of movement below her skin. "That's our baby moving in there."

Harry promptly drew his hand away as if he had come in contact with a hot iron. He pulled free from her and left the room, abandoning a bewildered Caroline, leaving her to cry alone. Their frosty silence and cold demeanor only grew worse as the months languished on. Her middle grew and so did her fears, but there was no one to share them with.

Marnie had just had her own baby, a boy named Steven. But Caroline was embarrassed to go to her with any questions or complaints. It seemed as though, whenever they spoke about pregnancy, Marnie would gush about how happy she was, how miraculously her experience had unfolded. She would brag about Chuck and how tender he was, how kind he had been to her, how generous he was during her delicate condition. He rubbed her feet. He massaged her back. He let her sleep in in the mornings. He was the saint of all expectant fathers. It made Caroline not only feel forlorn and neglected, but it also made her terribly jealous of Marnie. She began to think maybe she should have married Chuck. Simple as he was, at least he would have treated her better than Harry did. Maybe then she would be excited too.

The unknown was the thing that plagued her the most. She couldn't imagine attending to a child's every need. Would she be a good mother? She simply couldn't fathom what childbirth would be like or how she would get through it. The prospect of actually delivering filled her nightmares, made her panic in her waking hours, permeated every thought she chanced to think. She was frightened beyond her ability to control it. Whenever Caroline dwelt on her impending doom, she would dissolve into tears, with a sick feeling in the pit of her stomach. The closer she came to her due date, the farther away she wanted to run. One evening, she weakly confided in Harry.

"I don't think I can do this," she told him, her voice growing thin and emotional.

"Do what?" he asked, oblivious. Perhaps, deep down, he knew what she was thinking, maybe even understood, but then, if he admitted it to himself or to her, he would have to be responsible. He would have to do something about it.

"I don't think I can have this baby," she said. "I'm terrified. What if I can't handle the pain? What if I die?"

"Well, it's too late for that now, Caroline. Probably should have thought of that before you got pregnant. At this point, there's not much we can do about it, now, is there?"

She looked at him in shocked horror. "You are so cruel to me," she moaned. "How can you be so cruel to me?"

He shrugged indifferently. "I'm only telling the truth. It's too late for regrets. It's done." He watched the tears spill down her cheeks, and his conscience pricked him a little, but in the back of his mind, he was telling himself he was justified; he was only pointing out the reality of it, wasn't he? Caroline could use a good reality check. She was so spoiled and pampered. Someone needed to force her to grow up and face the consequences of her actions. Still, perhaps he shouldn't be so hard on her…It was so difficult to see her cry and not give her some solace.

"How can you treat me so thoughtlessly? Don't you care? Don't you care about me anymore?" she raged.

"It has nothing to do with that. You simply must have the baby, and there is nothing to be done about it. You're getting yourself all worked up over something that can't be changed."

"I hope I *do* die!" she wailed. "I hope I die, and then you'll be sorry for the way you've treated me! You'll be sorry when I'm gone."

"You're being hysterical, Caroline," he scolded.

"At least I feel something, anything, you cold-blooded fool." And she ran from the room sobbing. Though they had been bad before, things between Harry and Caroline were never the same after that. She didn't even try to share her feelings or her ideas, her hopes or her dreams with him. Their relationship was over, to the extent that they were as two strangers living under the same roof. Dinner was eaten in silence. Evenings were filled with empty hours to be endured until bedtime. The truth was that Caroline had felt detached from him for some time, but it was only now that she had grown to despise him, had discovered just how angry and disdainful her feelings toward him were, how deep they ran. There was nothing she really cared to contribute to their marriage any longer. As her baby grew within her womb, so did her longing to run away, to be rid of this place and this man. But she was trapped and she knew it. She was trapped by her own circumstances. No respectable woman divorced without a very good reason for it. What could she say? He didn't give her the attention she wanted? And then there was the baby to think about. She had no means of providing for a baby on her own. The thought of living her life as a single woman was something she couldn't even fathom. To have people looking at her, talking about her, scorning her — that was too much to even consider.

When Harry got the call he had so dreaded, that the baby was on its way, he was at work. In attempts at prolonging the inevitable, Harry finished the paperwork that was before him prior to going home to collect his wife. She was in a state when he finally pulled up in the drive. It all seemed surreal when Caroline rushed out of the front door, lugging her suitcase, her hair disheveled, her coat buttoned crooked. Harry got out of the car and opened the trunk so that he might put the suitcase in. When he tried to take it from her, she refused, snatching it furiously from his grasp, and instead lifted it herself with a loud grunt and dropped it into the trunk with a thud. She didn't wait for him to open the door for her either.

Once he had situated himself in his seat and jammed the keys in the ignition, he turned and got a good look at her. Her face was pinched and pale. He recalled their argument just a month or so ago and how she had said that she wished she would die. What if she did die? His heart began to pound, and he was reluctant to go. There were so many things he wanted to tell her, so many tender words that swelled up inside of him. Harry wanted to reach out to her, to hold his wife lovingly in his arms. Things should have been different; he should be on cloud nine, full of euphoria, of joy. Caroline was his only love, his whole life. And he contemplated how it had come to this.

A memory floated before him, as clearly as if he were observing it as a third party. Caroline was sitting upon the front porch of a white house with a black door, the place she grew up in on McKinley Street. She was lazily rocking back and forth on the wooden swing with the push of her toes. He sat next to her, glad to feel her there so close to him. At that moment, Harry was completely content not to speak, just pleased to soak in the time that he had with her.

"You're awfully quiet tonight," she had chided.

"Just enjoying the view," he'd replied, turning toward her and slipping his arm around her.

"The view, huh?"

"That's right. Now come a little closer here and give me a kiss."

"Why would I do that?" she teased.

"'Cause you like it," he said, matter of fact.

"Maybe so, but you have to earn my kisses."

"How do I do that?" he asked, still in a playful mood.

"Well, Jim Garr brought me a box of candies yesterday, and he didn't even get a kiss," she informed him.

Harry withdrew his arm and sat up straight, pouting slightly. "So, maybe you ought to be sitting on the front porch with Jim Garr," he told her.

"Oh, stop your sulking, Harry. I don't want to sit on the front porch with Jim Garr. I sent him packing right off."

"Why's that, if he brought you a box of candy?" Harry asked, continuing to hold a grudge.

"Because I love you, silly. You and no one else, though I can't say why."

Harry looked at her with a stupid grin spread across his face. He slid closer to her and took her in his arms. "And I'll never give you a reason to regret it," he whispered, brushing his lips against hers. She wanted more. Caroline pressed her body closer to his, her embrace more insistent, more passionate.

She had always been so zealous, so full of life, which may have been a part of what drew him to her in the first place. His mind was so far away that he had forgotten where he was presently and that Caroline was sitting next to him in pain.

"What are you waiting for?" she asked with a gasp. "Would you have me deliver in the car?"

Immediately he snapped out of it, put the car in reverse, and pulled out of the driveway.

The baby did not come as soon as Caroline had hoped. She spent twelve long hours in labor, suffering alone, praying that it would end, begging for relief. Twelve hours was nothing short of eternity to her. She questioned in her mind why any woman would willingly agree to such torture. In terror, she fought against each pain that ripped through her. She was frightened and alone. No one seemed to care that she was suffering so. The nurses advised her to relax to let the labor do its job. They threatened to restrain her, to give her medication if she couldn't calm herself. After a while, she told them to shut up…to leave her alone. Finally, they grew tired of her belligerence and forced her wrists and ankles into the fur-lined leather straps at the head and foot of the bed. They administered a dose of medicine through a hypodermic needle, telling her it was for her own good, although she cried out and begged them not to.

Caroline felt her body grow languid and refused to respond to her mental commands. It was as though she were trying to move through water, the resistance impeding her ability to move her limbs. Now too exhausted to battle against the labor, she lay limp, feeling the flow of pain spread upward over her belly, groaning but still. Near the end, with the doctor and nurses telling her they could see dark hair, encouraging her to push harder, with her feet in the stirrups, she wailed loudly, not even ashamed at the fuss she was making. She was beyond the point of caring what anyone else might think of her or how she must look.

When Harry was finally allowed to see her, Caroline was tucked in to her bed, with the sheets fitted closely to her body. Her hair fanned out across her pillow, her skin drained of color and unnaturally ashen, she didn't seem herself at all. The room was sterile, all shades of grays and whites, with a bedside table next to the metal hospital bed and one hard chair against the wall. He felt ill at ease in this place, in his white medical smock and cap and gloves. They had given him a white cloth mask to wear. To protect Caroline and the baby from his germs, they said. But he had pulled it down around his neck, feeling that he might suffocate if he had to cover his mouth and nose with it.

The nurse that followed him in to the room whispered, "Don't wake her; she needs her rest. Poor thing had a very difficult delivery." Then she indicated the chair. "Just have a seat, and I'll bring the baby in."

Harry sat heavily on the chair and watched Caroline as she slept, her breathing even and rhythmic. It was the only thing that, to him, indicated that she was not dead after all. The nurse returned shortly, wheeling a small, clear plastic bed labeled *Fletcher, Baby Girl* in front of her. She picked up the bundle, wrapped in pink, with a little bow nestled in the dark mass of fine hair, and carefully handed it to Harry. He accepted it awkwardly, worried that he might inadvertently crush the delicate little creature.

"I'll be back in a little while to check in on her. Just press the button if you need anything." And Harry was left alone with the baby.

She stretched and yawned, wrinkling her tiny nose, and then stuck her fist into her mouth and sucked until she soothed herself back to a full sleep and lay quietly in the circle of his arms. In the hush of the room, holding the little infant, Harry was suddenly a changed man. No words could express it; no feeling could adequately convey it. He looked upon that baby girl, and he fell in love. She was perfection in a pink flannel blanket, and he stroked the silk of her hair. He pulled back a corner of her blanket and inspected her feet, as they were curled up next to her body, her knees drawn up to her abdomen, like a little ball. He extended her fingers out from her fist, marveling at the sliver of fingernails and the minuscule joints and knuckles.

In that hushed space and time, Harry adored his new daughter. At one point, she lazily opened her eyes, regarding him with what Harry thought was recognition, and he felt the tears burning his eyes. He blinked hard to keep from crying. He was a man, and men didn't cry.

"I wish you could see the silly grin you've got on your face right now," Caroline murmured from the bed.

Harry immediately straightened up in his chair, the grin gone. "How are you feeling?" he inquired.

"As if I'd gotten hit by a train," she said flatly.

"I'm sorry," he replied, his tone dead.

"I bet you are."

"Do you need anything?"

"No."

"They brought the baby in," he informed her, holding the baby up just slightly.

"Yes, I can see that," she acknowledged.

"Do you want to hold her?"

"No, I don't. I'm tired."

Harry drew the baby in closer to his chest. "You were a real trooper," he told her.

"How would you know, Harry? You weren't there."

"They wouldn't let me be there," he said as an apology.

"It was awful," she complained. "I never want to do that again."

"It's probably a bad time to decide something like that right now. You've been through a lot."

"I mean it. If you want another, you can just get that out of your mind, Harry." Her words were filled with a ferocity that made him shudder. He didn't want to exchange angry words in front of the baby, so he took it and remained silent.

"What are you going to name her?" he asked after a moment.

"I like the name Christy," she murmured as she began to doze once more. When Harry was certain that Caroline was fully asleep again, he turned his full attention back to the baby he held in his arms.

"Little Christy. Do you hear me? Do you know who I am? I'm going to be your father," he whispered against her soft round cheek.

Life had no sense of normality for many months after. Harry would return home from work, hearing Christy's wails before even reaching the door. Caroline bounced from angry to sobbing and back to angry again as she described how the infant had cried all day long. Harry would pick the baby up, and she would immediately grow calm.

In her mind, Caroline unreasonably thought it was some sort of a conspiracy. The baby she had gone through such agony to bring to this world did not like her and was openly working against her with the man that couldn't have cared less when she had cared so much. Harry would make the bottles, bathe, diaper, and dress the baby while Caroline would shut herself up in the bedroom and cry. She felt inadequate, disillusioned, abandoned. And then she felt nothing.

CHAPTER 7

A middle-aged woman, dressed in a long flowing skirt, a T-shirt, and jean vest, opened the door to Nelson. She looked him over, thoughtfully comparing him to the age of her own children. Not one to be impolite, even in the most difficult situations, she stepped back and allowed Nelson to come in. The entryway was well lit from the sun spilling in through the cathedral style window that loomed on the wall above them, the spacious feel courtesy of the vaulted ceilings. As grand a scale as the home offered, it seemed quaint, welcoming, warm, with the tan paint on the walls and the overstuffed furnishings that he eyed in the living room just beyond.

"I'm Cheryl, Dinah's daughter," the woman informed him as they drew further into the entryway.

"Thank you for having me, Cheryl," he replied.

"Why don't you go ahead and sit down," she offered. "I'll go get my mother."

Nelson obligingly did so, waiting expectantly on the down-filled sofa for Cheryl to return. She wasn't gone for very long, pushing Dinah in a wheelchair in front of her. Nelson jumped from his seat when they entered, allowing the other two to get settled before he reclaimed his place. Cheryl parked the wheelchair beside the coffee table and sat down next to it. Nelson could see that she wasn't about to leave her mother alone. However, she still remained politely pleasant toward Nelson, despite her obvious mistrust. It did much to put him at ease.

"This is my mother, Dinah," she said.

"Harry said you were young, but I expected someone a little older," she admitted.

"I'm older than I look," Nelson lied.

"Well, anyhow, I don't usually entertain visitors, especially one of your profession, but Harry asked it of me, so…" She let the words trail away.

"I certainly appreciate you being willing to visit with me," he said. "I'm Nelson Rune." He held his hand out, and she accepted, giving him a feeble hand shake. At this point, he drew the digital recorder from his pocket and set it on the coffee table. "Do you mind if I record our conversation, you know, so I don't miss anything? Helps me keep the details in order."

"I guess not," Dinah replied, but Nelson could see that Cheryl seemed nervous by the prospect. He leaned forward and pushed record.

"Obviously I'm here to try and find out what happened to Caroline. Any information you have would be helpful," Nelson said, addressing Dinah.

"I suppose that woman got what was coming to her," Dinah told him in a matter-of-fact tone. "She caused a good deal of trouble, you know."

"In what way?"

"In every way," Dinah said with a snort. "She thrived on it. I think she liked to feel like she was in control, and her way of doing that was to put everyone else on their ears."

"What did she do to cause trouble?" Nelson asked.

"Well, for one, she tried to make everyone angry at everyone else, kind of a pot stirrer. For another, she said things to try and make you angry, try and irritate you. She was very good at figuring out how to get under somebody's skin. And then she flirted a lot with the men folk. That drove all the wives crazy. She was carrying on with half the county, from what I knew of it."

"And you know this first hand?"

"Certainly I do," Dinah said adamantly. "I saw her once driving with a man in her car."

"When was this?"

"Just shortly before she was murdered."

"Did you report this to Harry?"

"He knew all about her running around. He didn't need to be told," she informed him with a disapproving shake of her head.

"And he put up with it?"

"Different times back then. Divorce was a dirty word."

"Can you tell me what Caroline and Harry's relationship was like?"

"Poor Harry. He was my kid brother. I sure didn't like to see him in such a sad situation. But what do you do? He was always such a sweet boy, very thoughtful and very decent, you know." Nelson noticed the tremors in her hands, her weak and fragile condition, the frail quality of her shaking voice, her transparent skin laced with blue veins. He wondered if he should have come, if he should be here now, dredging it all up again. Still, he had a job to do. Dinah grew reminiscent. "When he was only thirteen, he got the mumps, real bad case of 'em. Most kids that get them don't get them that bad, but Harry lost the hearing in his left ear, and we weren't sure if he would make it. We thought he would die. I wonder now if that wouldn't have been better for him." Her voice didn't falter, although she grew a little teary eyed.

"Mother, are you all right?" Cheryl inquired, a concerned look on her face.

"Yes," she said, nodding slowly.

"Could you tell me, Mrs. Gert, what you remember about June third of nineteen sixty-four? Anything at all."

"It's hard to forget," Dinah stated. "It didn't just change Harry's life; it changed everyone's."

"What happened?" Nelson prodded.

"They had been arguing for months. She was doing a real good job of making his life completely miserable. He called me just before it all happened and said he was afraid she would leave, that she would take Christy away. He was crying when he told me. It hurt me to see him like that. He loved that girl, would have done anything for her."

"You mean Christy?"

"Yes, Christy. She was everything to him. They were like two peas in a pod, he and Christy. What's sad is Caroline didn't so much as look her way, didn't care a thing for her, but to hurt Harry, she would have taken the girl. Well, he had me in knots, worrying over him. I didn't know what to do. I couldn't bear to see him that way. I tried to tell him he'd be better off without her. The thing is, he didn't see it that way. Caroline was all he really knew. He had dated her in high school, and they had been married for nearly twelve years at that point. I suppose he thought it was the end of the world."

"But she didn't leave?"

"No. I think it was just a cry for attention. I don't know. How could you know with her? It was like the boy who cried wolf. You hear it enough, you start to ignore it. Then, close to two weeks later, we got a call in the early morning. My husband, Rich, woke me up and told me that it was Harry on the phone and would I come speak to him."

"How did Harry sound?"

"Like he was scared. I mean really scared. He said to me, 'I think they've killed Caroline.' Well, my blood just ran cold."

"What do you think he meant by 'they' when he said 'they'd' killed Caroline?" Nelson asked.

"Got me. At the time, it didn't seem real. None of it. He wanted me to come get Christy. He was worried that she would wake up and find out what had happened. I tell ya I didn't even bother getting dressed properly. I put my overcoat over my nightdress, threw on some shoes, and jumped in the car."

"How did you find things when you got there?"

"Harry was so pale. He'd been hit over the head, and he seemed confused and just spooked. He told me to wait by the front door while he went and got Christy. She was asleep in his arms, wrapped in her blanket, and he carried her out to the car and put her across the back seat. She stirred at that point, and he tried to comfort her. Once she went back to sleep, he told me to get out of there. I was shaken. I did what he told me to. I took Christy back to my home. I know everyone says that he killed her, but it's not true."

Nelson gently asked, "How can you be so sure?"

Dinah grew slightly defensive. "His injury alone proves he was telling the truth. He couldn't have clobbered himself in the head. They said so. They said someone else had to have done it."

"Who said so?"

"The doctors. They said there was no way he could have done that to himself. No way. They testified to it in court, under oath!"

"There were other witnesses for the prosecution that say it could have happened when Caroline was fighting for her life. You don't think that's possible?"

"You don't know a lot, do you?" she scoffed. "Harry was six feet tall. Caroline was five-three. You think she somehow got behind him during the struggle and hit him on the head with enough force to crack his skull?"

"You testified on the stand, under oath, that when you arrived Harry was dazed, appeared to possibly have a concussion? Is that right?"

"That's right. And the doctors said so too. They said he had a concussion. I was the one to pay for it, though. They crucified me and my family for trying to stick up for him. No one else was. Nobody was standing up for him. Not even his friends. Just abandoned him."

"I was only five, and I remember it," Cheryl muttered. "As children, no one wanted us to know what had happened, but they couldn't keep it from us for long. Pretty soon everyone was talking about it."

"Not that I minded helping Harry out, he was my kid brother, but I hated what it did to my own children, to my own family," Dinah confessed.

"What about Christy? Did she ever let on that she had seen or heard anything?" Nelson asked.

"She swore she didn't hear anything, that she had been sleeping. I asked her myself. She was a different girl after that, but who wouldn't be? She lost her father and her mother, and, well, there was no hiding it from her that her mother had been murdered, and all the details that came out with it. It was splashed across every paper and on the evening news. Then they put Harry in jail for it. They made a saint out of Caroline and a monster out of poor Harry. But I tell you right now, he never could have done what they say he did. I know he couldn't have." She grew adamant in her declaration.

Nelson wondered how often a loving relative would have sworn on a stack of Bibles that their husband, son, father, brother were innocent, even in the face of some very stiff evidence. His skepticism seeped into his next question, which didn't escape the two women's attention. "Can you tell me, Mrs. Gert, why he waited until Christy passed away to hire a private investigator to clear his name?"

She looked thoughtful. "He probably just wanted to spare her. She went through a lot. He didn't want her to have to go through any more, I suppose."

"You don't think that's slightly convenient?" he pressed.

Cheryl broke in at this point. "Uncle Harry loved Christy very much. It seems insensitive of you to infer that he didn't, Mr. Rune."

"I'm sorry if I offended you. I was only saying it is quite a coincidence."

"I don't think it was any coincidence," Dinah admitted. "I think Harry has always tried to protect her. I think that was his only reason for doing many of the things he did," she scoffed.

Nelson could see he had crossed the line, had insulted her.

"He certainly had nothing to do with her death, if that's what you're getting at," she added.

"Does Huntington's disease run in your side of the family, Mrs. Gert?"

Dinah grew upset. "Never even heard of it till Christy was diagnosed. She was only thirty-nine when she found out she had it. She suffered horribly in the end. It was a blessing when she went."

"My mother has been through quite a lot. I feel very sorry for my uncle, but I really don't feel that she should be made to suffer over this any longer. Perhaps you should finish up so that she can rest," Cheryl suggested, speaking to Nelson much like she would one of her own children.

Nelson's confidence weakened a bit in the face of her authoritative voice. He leaned forward and turned off the recorder. "I regret very much causing you any sort of discomfort, Mrs. Gert. That really wasn't my intention. I'm simply trying to get to the bottom of all of this, as I was asked to do."

"No one else has been able to get to the bottom of it. Pretty presumptuous to believe that you could, don't you think?" Dinah Gert scoffed. Either she was angry with Nelson or she was annoyed with being asked the same questions that she had been asked for all of those years. She looked for a moment as if she might cry, although there was something a bit defiant in her face as well. "The only person who really knows what happened that night was Caroline, and ghosts don't talk."

Nelson stood and pocketed his recorder. "Thank you for your time. I appreciate you allowing me to come in to your home," he told the two women sitting across from him. Cheryl got up from her chair as well, leading Nelson back to the front door.

She waited until he was on his way out before she whispered, "She really is very fragile. She shouldn't be put through this kind of mental strain. It's just too much for her."

"I'm sorry that I bothered you," he said.

"If you need any more information, please just call Uncle Harry," she said, polite but pointedly firm.

He managed a nod. "I'll do that."

CHAPTER 8

The family spent Memorial Day weekend, 1962, at the beach. The sand was warm against Harry's skin as he dug with his fingers. Catching what he might in his hands, he worked to quickly transport the sand to a pail before it slipped from his grasp. He watched as Christy, decked out in a miniature bathing suit and white sandals with her legs stretched out before her, used a red plastic shovel to scrape up a small mound and then toss it hastily into the same pale. She was losing most of it in the transaction. Once the wet sand was filled to the rim of the bucket, Harry pressed his hands heavy against the top.

"See, Christy, you have to press it hard so that it gets all smashed down in there so that it stays the same shape," Harry told his little daughter.

Her round face turned up to him with a broad grin splashed across her rosebud lips, a single dimple appearing along with it. Her head bobbed as if she were agreeing with him, blond ponytail nodding with it. The little girl watched as Harry flipped the pail over, lodging it into the sand and pounding the bottom. She would be four soon. Another year was slipping by. It amazed Harry how quickly it all went once he had a child to measure the time.

"Are you ready?" he asked.

"Yes, Daddy," she confirmed eagerly.

Harry pulled the pail straight up, revealing a bundle of sand the exact shape and size of the cylindrical pail. Christy clapped her hands, immensely impressed by his feat.

"It's a sand castle," he informed her.

"Good job, Daddy."

He traced a few windows and a door into the side of his castle with the pointed end of a stick and then moved back so that Christy could get a closer look at it. Christy stood up on her round stocky legs, her pot belly pushed out, knees locked, observing it for a short while. Then she pulled her leg back, landing her sandal into the structure, toppling it into a jagged lump.

Harry gave a mock gasp of horror. "Christy, you broke my sand castle!" She giggled with glee. Positioning himself onto all fours, he faced her with an overdone scowl on his face. "You broke my castle," he growled.

"No, Daddy," she squealed, turning to run along the beach. Harry was in hot pursuit. He could hardly keep from laughing at her as she trotted away from him, looking over her shoulder at regular intervals to see if he was still after her. She ran to Caroline, who was sun bathing on a striped beach towel, and wedged herself against her mother's side. "Mommy, Mommy, Daddy's tryin' to get me," she said breathlessly. By this time, Harry had caught up and was roaring ferociously, baring his teeth, lurching toward Christy, who was laughing in delight.

Caroline frowned, trying to push the little girl away. "Harry, do you mind? I'm trying to relax."

"Sorry," he said, attempting to smooth things over. "Come here, Christy, let your poor mother alone." He grabbed her below her armpit and swung her high up, catching her leg and pulling it around his shoulder. She sat perched there, laughter still spilling from her. "Do you want to play in the water?"

"Yes, Daddy," she said, holding his hair with her fists to steady herself.

"Don't go too far. It's nearly lunchtime," Caroline yelled after them. She rolled over onto her stomach and faced Marnie, who appeared to be asleep as she soaked up the rays of sun. "I'm thirsty," she complained.

"There's a soda pop in the cooler," Marnie informed her, eyes still closed.

"I don't want to walk all the way back to the car," she moaned.

"You said yourself it's close to lunchtime. Just wait and the boys will bring it down for you soon," Marnie said.

"Chuck!" Caroline shouted out, watching as Chuck and Steven approached with their fishing poles, Steven proudly carrying his catch held high in front of him.

"What?" he hollered back.

"Go get me a soda from the cooler," she commanded.

"Go get it yourself," he shot back.

Caroline laughed mischievously, amused by her own antics. Four-year-old Steven, a year older than Christy, brought his fish to Marnie who sat up to view it.

"Steven, what a beautiful fish you have there," she bragged.

"Pop helped me catch it," Steven told her with a smile and a shrug. He was playing modest.

"We have an excellent fisherman on our hands here," Chuck said, patting Steven's shoulder. Chuck was a tall man with jet black hair, brown eyes behind his thick, black-framed glasses, a broad chest, and massive forearms. He wore only his pants, and they were rolled up at the hems.

"We must put this fish in the cooler so that we can cook it when we get home," Marnie recommended.

"Guess who we spotted while we were fishing?" Chuck asked.

"I wouldn't even know who to guess, Chuck," Marnie said. Caroline leaned in eagerly to get in on the conversation.

"I love to guess. Let me. Is it someone I know too?"

"No," Chuck said.

"Oh, well then, never mind," she replied, rolling her eyes slightly as she collapsed back onto the towel.

"Well, who was it?" Marnie pressed.

"Lonnie and Theresa Sheraton."

"You should invite them to join us," Marnie suggested.

"Who are Lonnie and Theresa Sheraton?" Caroline broke in.

"Chuck works with Lonnie down at the tow yard," Marnie told her.

"I already invited them over," Chuck replied. "Steven and I are going to clean this fish and put it in the cooler in the car."

"Stay away from the cooler that has our lunch in it," Caroline ordered as Chuck took Steven by the hand and led him toward the parking lot. Chuck chose to pay no attention to her. "And bring me a soda!"

"Leave him alone, Caroline."

"He's just a big hunk of meat, isn't he?" she mused.

"Chuck's a lot more than that."

"Really? Pray tell, what more is there to him, besides that massive body of his?"

"He's very smart and very kind. Well, he is to everyone but you," she said as a smile spread across her face.

"Smart for working in a tow yard anyhow," Caroline retorted.

"Stop poking fun at my husband, Caroline," Marnie peevishly replied. "I don't make fun of Harry."

"You can all you want. Anything you could poke fun at Harry about would probably be justly deserved," Caroline said with a look of boredom.

"The way you talk, poor Harry."

"Yes, poor Harry."

Chuck and Steven returned from their hike to the car, Chuck lugging a large cooler and Steven struggling to carry the picnic basket. Marnie got up and went to help them, snatching up one of the handles of the basket so that Steven would still feel as if he were helping. They plopped it in the sand next to Caroline, who didn't seem to notice they were there. She was watching a set of figures in the distance as they approached.

"Are those your friends?" Caroline asked, shielding her eyes with her hand.

Chuck glanced in the direction she was looking. "Yep, that's Lonnie and his wife."

"Are you going to sit there doing nothing, or are you going to help me?" Marnie said, trying to come across as if she were joking, although she wasn't. "Here, spread the blanket out."

"Yes, ma'am," Caroline huffed, grabbing it from Marnie's hand. She unfurled the blanket, shaking it out on the breeze, and then allowed it to drift slowly to the ground, straightening it out at the corners. As she finished, Lonnie and Theresa Sheraton arrived, carrying a long rectangular basket between the two of them.

"Hello, you two," Marnie addressed them. "It's been a while. How have you been?" And she went over to give Theresa a little hug.

"We're good. It's funny we should meet like this. Lonnie and I were just talking about you the other night," Theresa said to Marnie.

"You remember Steven," Marnie said, taking Steven by the shoulder and drawing him near.

"Of course we remember Steven," Lonnie threw in. "How are you, son?"

"Good, sir." Steven held his hand out to Lonnie for a shake. The adults all chuckled at his grown-up gesture. Lonnie took his hand and shook it.

"Aren't you going to introduce me?" Caroline put in, her eyes meeting Lonnie's with a doe-eyed grin. "Chuck and Marnie seem to have forgotten their manners."

"This is our good friend Caroline Fletcher," Marnie said. "Her husband is around here somewhere…and her little girl."

The next few hours were spent in discomfited agony. Harry returned with Christy, after they had played for a time in the water. He carried her all wrapped up in a towel, the two hungry and ready to eat lunch. He warmly welcomed the new additions in the beginning but was displeased and brooding for the remainder of their visit when he witnessed how shamefully Caroline was throwing herself at Lonnie Sheraton. She commented on how strong he was, going as far as squeezing his biceps. She gushed about how interesting he was, how refined his sense of humor was, laughing at even the hint of a joke.

A bewildered Theresa Sheraton sat quietly, her large eyes the only indicator that she found any of it out of the ordinary. Lonnie didn't seem to know how to react to all of the attention. He was somewhat nervous but managed to remain polite, although he was pointedly aloof toward Caroline. He was more than aware of his wife and how she must be feeling by a strange woman's advances, and he didn't wish to make it any worse than it already was.

At one point, Chuck followed Caroline off to the side as she bent over the cooler to get a bottle of Coke. "Cut it out, Caroline. You're making an idiot out of yourself," he whispered in a low, menacing tone.

"Why, Chuck, I have no idea what you mean," she said with an innocence that was far from genuine.

They had only made it through lunch when Theresa gave a flimsy pretext for excusing Lonnie and herself from any further interaction with the group. They picked up their basket and left, heading speedily for the parking lot and their automobile. Caroline didn't seem to notice the others' sudden un-festive manner upon Lonnie and Theresa's departure. She went off by herself, leaving the rest of them to clean up what remained of lunch.

"I think I'm in the mood for a swim," she declared, and she headed off toward the beach at a trot.

CHAPTER 9

Cleo rapped soundly on the door and waited. When Nelson didn't come right away, she rang the bell. Nelson looked through the peep hole and saw Cleo practically dancing in the hallway. He unlocked the door to let her in. She brushed past him in a flurry of excitement, toting a book under her arm.

"Guess what I found at the library?" she burst out.

"I don't know, Cleo. What'd you find at the library?"

"*The Darkest Night*." Cleo beamed.

"What's *The Darkest Night*?" Nelson humored her.

"A tale of lust, lies, and murder most foul," Cleo replied, holding the book up to his face for him to see. Nelson took it from her, turned the book over, and read the synopsis.

"The murder of Caroline Fletcher, huh?"

"Yep. Why, Nelson, you landed yourself *the* murder mystery of this century! I've been skimming through it. There's no end of twists to this thing. Did you know that Caroline's best friend Marnie Donner claimed that Caroline was miserable and had confided in her that she wanted a divorce from Harry? Then there's the newspaper boy who claims he saw a man that was not Harry Fletcher kissing Caroline goodbye at the door one morning when he was delivering papers just a few short days before she was murdered. Looks like old Harry wasn't the only one with someone on the side."

"Caroline was cheating too," Nelson confirmed unenthusiastically. Cleo's eyebrows drew together, as if to say that she felt hurt over the fact that he hadn't told her about this sooner. "I know, I know. It just gets more and more warped, doesn't it?" He flipped through the pages of the book. "Harry never said anything about her running around," Nelson confided, "but his sister did."

Cleo shrugged. "Maybe he didn't know."

"Oh, I think he must have."

"Well, the twists didn't end with all of that. There's the house painter that showed up with Caroline's brooch fifteen years after the murder. He somehow talked his way out of getting into trouble for having it and then got busted five years after that for attempted robbery and assault."

"Sounds like you know more about it than I do," he complained.

"So, maybe Harry really isn't guilty. There's an endless number of suspects that could have done it besides him."

"Maybe," Nelson admitted, sitting on the futon and inspecting the table of contents. "But I gotta tell you, Cleo, there's something not right with this guy's story. I mean, if you walked in on your dead wife laying there on the kitchen floor, what would your first reaction be?"

"I already told you, I'd call the police."

"Exactly. But Harry's sister Dinah says that his first thought was Christy. His first thought was to call his sister and have her come get his daughter."

"So, you interviewed her?"

"Yeah, yesterday."

"Why didn't you tell me?" she asked accusingly.

"Sorry," Nelson said simply. Why would he run over and tell her? After all, it wasn't like he and Cleo were an item. They were barely friends, if that. He was observing her closely as she plopped herself down on the bean bag, thinking she was adorable in a very quirky sort of way.

"What'd she say?" she prodded.

"You know what she said; you read the book. Chapter two."

"So, nothing that would help you answer the big question of who done it?"

"Nope."

"What's your next step?"

"My next step is to go check out Jason Stuart," Nelson replied.

"Who is Jason Stuart?"

"Some guy that's claiming worker's comp," Nelson informed her.

"What does he have to do with Caroline Fletcher's murder?"

"Absolutely nothing," he answered.

"I thought you were working on the Caroline Fletcher murder."

"I am. But I still have to pay the bills. I gotta go." Nelson got up and went over to the bar in his kitchenette, grabbing his camera from the Formica countertop. "Smile," he commanded as he clicked a candid picture of her. She ignored the camera.

"You're leaving?" Cleo challenged. "I just got here."

"Sorry, but I've been staking this guy out for the past week, and he's going to be home from his physical therapy session in like—" he looked at his wrist watch "—a half an hour."

"No cats involved this time around?" she asked with a chuckle.

"No, no cats," he replied. He was a bit embarrassed that she brought up the last disastrous job. He would like to have been able to forget it completely.

"Can I come with you?"

Nelson wondered why she would want to. It was just work, after all, certainly not a good time to be had. One more thing to add to the list of things that gave him pause and made him question how Cleo's mind worked. She was a constant curiosity.

"Seriously, Cleo, this is about as boring as it gets. I just sit there and watch and hope he screws up and does something that will prove he's not disabled."

"I can keep you company," she offered. "I'd really like to see you in action. Might be fun."

"Well, it's probably not what you think it'll be. Pretty sure you'll end up being bored out of your mind. Besides, I'm trying to keep a low profile," he told her.

"And you can't if I'm with you?"

He realized that if he answered that question he might say too much, so he held his tongue and pursed his lips, recognizing that he had lost this battle. "Fine, Cleo, but you gotta do what I say."

"All right," she conceded with a triumphant smile.

"When I say it," he went on.

"All right!" she agreed.

They each locked up their apartments and then headed to Nelson's car together.

"You know, there's probably an easier way to do this," she told Nelson on their way over to Jason Stuart's home fifteen minutes later.

"How's that?" Nelson asked as he came to a stop at a stop sign. He waited for a Toyota to go ahead of him and then began driving again.

"Where does this guy live?"

"Like, three and a half blocks from here," Nelson informed her.

"Is this the way he would come on his way home?"

"I guess," Nelson conceded. "This way or Main Street, but Main Street is usually pretty congested with all that construction going on."

"Stop the truck," Cleo commanded.

"Why?"

"Would you just do what I say?" she grumbled.

"Fine," Nelson snapped back. He pulled the pickup over to the curb and stopped. Cleo got out, slamming the door shut behind her as she went to the back of the truck, taking a peek in the bed. Nelson watched her came around to the driver's side, bending over and inspecting the rear tire. She tapped on his window and motioned for him to roll it down.

"Pass me my purse," she said. Nelson reached over, grabbed it, and passed it to her. She rummaged through it for a moment, extracted a fingernail file that tapered to a point, and went back to the tire. She promptly pressed the tip of the filer against the needle, letting the air out in a hissing rush.

Nelson jumped from his truck in agitation. "What are you doing?"

"You've got a spare," Cleo pointed out, finishing off the job.

"Yeah, I've got a spare, a spare that has a nail through it!" Nelson yelled.

"Sorry," Cleo said guiltily. "I didn't know."

"Great. Just great!" he fumed, hitting the side of the truck with his open palm. "You said you would do what I told you to. This isn't exactly keeping a low profile, Cleo."

"I said I was sorry," she defended. She quickly changed the subject. "What's this guy driving?"

"Why?" He was clearly still put out.

"*What's he driving?*"

"Dark green Tahoe," Nelson told her as he ran his fingers through his hair in agitation. "You wanna tell me what your plan is?"

"Just get your camera and go hide by that Dumpster," she told him, pointing across the street to a Dumpster outside of a small business in a strip mall.

"What?"

"We don't have a lot of time. Would you just get the camera and go?" she ordered.

Nelson reluctantly reached through the rolled down window, grabbing his camera from the seat. He jogged across the street and crouched next to the Dumpster, watching Cleo with a sour expression on his face. She stood next to the flat tire with her thumbs in her belt loops, looking in either direction to see if anyone was coming. A car slowed and a middle aged man popped his head out. Cleo looked over at Nelson who shook his head in the negative. This was not Jason Stuart.

"Hey, thanks for stopping but my dad's on his way," she explained. "I called him on my cell." And the Good Samaritan drove on. A few cars drove by without giving her a second glance, but Cleo remained vigilant. When she saw the Tahoe approach, she took a few steps forward, making it difficult for him to pass. He slowed and came to a stop just behind the old pickup.

"What seems to be the trouble?" the man asked as he approached, his posture that of a confident rescuer, his chest puffed out as he strutted toward her.

"I have a flat," she said, indicating the tire with an outstretched hand, like one of the game show beauties displaying a fabulous and expensive prize that could be won. He came closer, bending his knees to get a better look at the tire.

"Yep, you got a flat all right," he agreed.

"Do you happen to have one of those things you prop the truck up with? You know, those things that you crank to get them off the ground so you can change the tire? Oh, what's it called?"

Jason Stuart laughed, amused by her lack of knowledge and vocabulary. She was a pretty girl, a damsel in distress, and he figured it was his good fortune to have happened upon her. "Yeah, I got a jack." He went back to his Tahoe and opened the hatch, rummaging through his junk until he found the jack and brought it back.

"Oh, great," she thrilled. "Do you know how to change it?"

He eyed her somewhat suspiciously.

"I don't know how. I've never had a flat before," she explained. "I guess I'm pretty useless that way."

"Yeah, I know how," he said with a grin that promised mischief, dropping the jack on the ground and adjusting it under the frame of the truck. "You got a spare?"

"In the back." Cleo nodded her head toward the truck bed. She shot a quick glance over toward Nelson's direction, nervous and excited, knowing that he must be getting the evidence of fraud he had been looking for. She smiled nervously, as if she were proud of herself, but Nelson knew she was probably getting quite an adrenaline rush from the whole thing.

Jason Stuart brought the jack from the back of the truck and began to crank the lever, forcing the truck to slowly rise off of the ground. From where Nelson sat in the shadow of the Dumpster, he began clicking pictures as the man who claimed he had lost the use of his left arm went to work on changing Cleo's flat. At one point, he lugged his tool box to the truck and had to use all his strength to get the rusting nuts off of the bolts. Nelson documented it all.

Everything went smoothly until the stranger went to put the new tire on. "This one's flat too." He chuckled, showing Cleo the nail that had pierced the exterior of the tire.

"Oh, no. I guess I should have checked before I put you to all that trouble," she lied.

"No worries. Jump in my car, and I'll take you over to the repair shop on Granite," he offered.

"Maybe I should just call my dad," she said nervously.

"It's just a few blocks from here. Maybe they can patch it. You can't go anywhere with your truck like that," he coaxed, ignoring her reluctance.

"You know, I really appreciate all your help, but I just don't think I should do that."

"Why not?"

"I don't know you. I'm not going to climb into a car with some guy I don't know," she said with a little laugh, trying to play it off as amusing.

"Come on, if I was such a bad guy, would I have stopped to help you?" he coerced.

"Probably not, but I still think I should just call my dad. He would be pretty upset with me if I got into a car with a strange man instead of having him come help, ya know? He's really over protective."

Jason Stuart took hold of her arm and started to walk her back to his Tahoe somewhat forcibly, but still with a smile on his face, as if he would compel her to go with him just to prove his point. He would show her he was a guy who could be trusted.

Nelson tensed as he watched, the uneasy feeling that had plagued him since the start of her charade growing stronger, until it went beyond uneasy. It was now full-fledged panic. What was this guy pulling?

Cleo drew her arm away and seemed to be protesting. The two were in what appeared to be an argument, with her objecting and him insisting. She wrenched her arm free of Jason's grip and tried to walk back toward the truck but was thwarted by him as he stepped in front of her, effectively blocking her path. Nelson jumped out from behind the Dumpster and jogged across the street, the camera knocking against his chest, a horn honking as he cut in front of a car headed in the opposite direction, forced to stop to avoid hitting him.

Cleo looked at him with a warning in her eyes. Perhaps she thought he shouldn't have blown his cover to come to her aid, maybe thinking he was just making the situation worse, possibly feeling that she could have handled it on her own. At any rate, Nelson didn't care. His temper was reaching its boiling point. Without any plan of action, he grabbed Jason Stuart's shoulder and spun him around.

"What the...? Who are you?" Jason asked with bewilderment and a hint of an accusation.

"You keep your hands off her," Nelson said, pointing his finger into the man's chest, his face screwed up in rage.

"This is none of your business," Jason roared, pushing Nelson hard.

"Cleo, get in the truck," Nelson ordered, putting himself between her and Jason.

"Nelson..." Cleo began.

"Get in the truck," he barked. His tone warned her to do what she was told. She climbed into the truck, locking the doors and frantically rolling up the window.

It was then that Jason Stuart noted the camera that was dangling from Nelson's neck, and it dawned on him that these two strangers knew one another's names. Registration settled on his face when he realized that he was in a shake down. He backed away defensively with his hand in the air, as though he were motioning for Nelson to stop.

"Wait a minute. What's going on here?" he growled.

"You need to leave," Nelson replied.

"Just what are you trying to pull?" the angry man yelled, making a lunge for the camera. Nelson tried to side-step him but was hit squarely in the shoulder and knocked into the side of the truck. The pickup squealed and shook, still balanced precariously on the jack. Cleo shrieked in fear as she was jostled about. She began to fumble desperately for her phone while she watched helplessly from the inside of the truck as the two men fought with one another.

Nelson recovered quickly, just in time to block the other man's fist from slamming into his gut. He pointed the camera at Jason Stuart's face and clicked, the flash deterring him for only an instant. He let the camera flash again, again a moment's pause.

Jason Stuart finally landed a blow to his nose, and it began to spurt blood. Nelson was stunned but grew angry enough to fight back. He lunged forward with an uppercut to the man's jaw, knocking him off balance, making him stumble backward. Jason caught himself before he went down, renewing his efforts in earnest. He grabbed Nelson by the shirt, spinning him into the road and the oncoming traffic. A car honked in protest, swerving abruptly just in time to miss Nelson and his attacker. Nelson pushed him hard, away from the traffic, and the two of them tumbled together onto the road next to the truck.

Cleo was suppressing a scream, still observing their exchange from the front seat as fists flew and grappling ensued, at times not really sure who had the upper hand in the fight. Her heart raced; she wanted nothing more than to come to Nelson's aid. A few times, the image of her jumping on the other man's back and pounding his head with the tire iron that lay on the ground just outside of her reach passed through her thoughts. She wasn't sure what to do at this point. Would Nelson be angry if she called the police? Her hands shook as she dialed 9-1-1, but she hesitated to actually follow through with it. Finally, in desperation, she rolled down the window and shrieked, "I'm calling the cops!" and held up the cell phone for the two of them to see.

The knot of fists and legs suddenly broke apart, and Jason Stuart jumped up, backed away reluctantly, eyeing first Cleo and then Nelson. He turned toward his truck and trotted to it, climbing in and speeding away. Nelson had gotten up to pursue him and had to dive out of the way to miss the fury of the man's enraged driving. The Tahoe careened around the corner and was gone before Nelson registered how close he had come to being flattened by it.

Cleo jumped out of the pickup and rushed to his side, kneeling next to him with fear and concern in her blue eyes. She gasped. "Are you all right?"

"Fine," he snapped, pulling the hem of his dirty T-shirt up and pressing it against his bleeding nose. The white knit fabric spread crimson upon contact. Cleo got a peek of his six-pack and looked away with a guilty flush.

"Your arms are all scraped up," she said softly. He ignored her comment, picked himself up from the asphalt, and went over to duck into the cab. He opened the glove compartment with his free hand, the other still pinched to his nose, and took out a small first aid kit. Nelson pulled a few small square packages of alcohol-soaked wipes and a packet of ointment from it, dumping them onto the front seat.

Cleo intercepted, pushing him back gently with her fingertips so she could access his stash. "Let me," she said, tearing open one of the wipes and swabbing his arms, her concentrated gaze fixed upon his wounds. He appeared angry, but he let her. She then applied the ointment as gingerly as possible as he winced from the sting.

But it wasn't just the sting he felt. There was something else too. His heart was pounding loud and fast in his chest, and he struggled to swallow. This only made him angrier, with himself, with her.

On the drive home, Cleo could see that Nelson was fuming and didn't want to make things worse for herself. After Jason Stuart had sped away and Cleo had tended to his road burn, Nelson had rolled the flat to a gas station not far away, filling it with air so he could put it back on the truck. She came with him because he didn't feel it prudent to leave her alone at that point, but Nelson hardly acknowledged her at all, keeping his eyes safely on the task before him and carefully away from her.

Once they were in the safe confines of the pickup truck, he concentrated a little too closely on his driving, which made her grow more and more uncomfortable. Cleo needed words; they were her anchor. She was a girl that concerned herself little with what others thought, unless the others were people that she cared for, in which case she would do anything in her power to get back into their good graces. Whether she wanted to admit it or not, Nelson was one of the few that she sought approval from.

"I don't know why you're so mad at me," she said, breaking the quiet as she kept her eyes on the passenger side window. "I was only trying to help." She gave him a sideways glance to try to gauge his reaction. She noted that his grip on the steering wheel tightened, his knuckles whitening.

"Hey, thanks a lot for letting the air out of my tire and getting me involved in an altercation! I really appreciate it!"

"I didn't know your spare had a nail in it," she argued.

"It doesn't matter. Just drop it," Nelson replied vehemently.

"I said I was sorry. Are you going to accept my apology?"

"I don't think you are sorry," Nelson charged.

"Well, how was I supposed to know he'd flip out like that?"

"Oh, I don't know, maybe the fact that he's been receiving compensation for an injured arm that works just fine could have been some clue that he is an unsavory character, a whacko! That might have been a good indicator that he would flip out when pushed into a corner," he told her with his voice raised heatedly.

"You got your pictures, didn't you?" she asked defensively.

"Yeah, I got the pictures all right. I especially loved the one where he was trying to *pound* me," Nelson retorted. "Lucky my camera's not broken."

"So, you got the pictures. What's the problem?"

"The problem…the problem is he could have killed you!"

"But he didn't."

"Look, I know my job is a joke, but this isn't some sort of a game. That guy was dangerous. Do you think I want you getting hurt? You think I could have lived with myself if something had happened to you, Cleo?"

Cleo grew still, biting on her bottom lip nervously. "I never thought your job was a joke. I messed up. I really am sorry. Please don't be mad at me," she appealed.

Nelson was quiet, watching out the windshield with silent fervor. She was studying his profile, trying to glean what she could from his facial expression, but he had none. He was stoic to the point of aggravation. She sighed. "Fine, stay mad. I tried to apologize." When they pulled into the parking lot, she waited only long enough for him to come to a semi-complete stop and bailed out the passenger side door.

Nelson watched her storm in, amusement mingled with frustration. Life without people was so less complicated than this. It had him seriously contemplating taking up residence in a cave, or perhaps getting lost deep in the jungle, living with the tribes that had not kept up with time and civilization in their ignorant bliss. Something that he didn't want to admit and would never fully be able to express was that Cleo had grown on him, to the point that he actually craved her company. Or at least when she wasn't doing something sensationally stupid he craved her company.

He put the truck in park, turned the engine off, and pocketed his keys. When he got back to his apartment, he closed all of the blinds and grabbed a Coke from the fridge, slouching in the kitchen chair at the café-sized table where his computer sat. Nelson plugged his camera into the tower and pulled up the photos that he had taken of Jason Stuart, some of him helping Cleo with the jack, some of him taking swings and trying to pummel Nelson. And there was Cleo's bright face looking back at him in the picture he had snapped before they had left his apartment. He printed the photos and then deliberately covered her face with a file folder as he went into the bathroom to clean up. Once he had changed into a clean T-shirt, he headed back to the front room to watch TV in an attempt to relax into temporary, self-induced amnesia.

CHAPTER 10

Just as a diluted light began to seep through the blind at the window, Harry stirred. He did not know what had woken him, only that once he was awake, he was awake. A hush permeated the house in the predawn tranquility, and he savored it. He knew Christy was safe, sleeping in the room across the hall. He could hear Caroline's soft breathing in the bed next to him, and he felt a sudden sense of peace that was rare and fleeting for him.

He turned onto his side and could make out his wife's form in the dimness. With quiet stealth, he rolled out of his own twin bed and knelt next to her as she slept in hers. Harry had never tired of seeing her. She was a beautiful woman, with a smooth oval face and ebony hair that complimented her slightly olive complexion. Even now, nearly thirty years old, she looked much the same as she had when she was eighteen and they had married. She was a timeless thing, he marveled, the picture of youth. In many ways she was nothing more than a child. Perhaps, he reflected, that's why he couldn't stay angry with her for very long, why he always managed to forget how selfish and spoiled she could behave, why he couldn't hold her accountable for her often bad behavior. After all, she was emotionally more like a child than a woman. What was the point in being mad at a child? Really, he blamed himself for what had transpired between them. Harry knew she must have been through a distressing experience, and he thought of the moment in the car when he had been afraid he might lose her, and his heart softened toward her. He studied her with great care, tentatively taking a loose curl and wrapping it around his finger and fiddling with it.

In a sudden rush of regret and longing, he touched her cheek, stroking it with the tenderness of a man who felt something beyond affection, his emotions churning in his stomach. He wondered wistfully where he had gone wrong, where the deciding factor had been drawn, what he could have and should have done differently. His soul was cankered, and he wondered with a growing panic if it would always be this way, if he would always feel this sort of hurt, if this is what the rest of his life was doomed to be. Caroline's eyes fluttered open, as delicate as butterfly wings, and she took Harry in with a confused, concentrated gaze.

"Harry?" she whispered. She started to sit up. "Harry, what's wrong?"

"Sh. Nothing's wrong, Caroline. I'm sorry I woke you," he mumbled. "Go back to sleep."

"What are you up for?"

"I don't know. I couldn't sleep, I guess." But he was looking at her as if he might burst in to tears. She noticed he was swallowing hard, trying to maintain control over his emotions, and speculated at his odd behavior.

"Harry, something is wrong," she insisted.

"I never saw a more beautiful woman than you. No one has ever come close," he admitted. He bent down and kissed her lips in a soft, almost reverent caress. Harry realized he had overstepped his bounds and remorsefully pulled away. It had been so long since he had kissed her that he couldn't recall when. Maybe a year or more? Although she was his wife, it hardly seemed right. "I'm sorry," he said.

"If you're going to kiss me," she tempted in a hushed voice, husky from sleep, "kiss me like a man."

His eyebrows drew together as if he were baffled by her response. He had been afraid that she would rebuff his kiss, turn him away and tell him he had no right. He felt a jolt of electricity course through his body, his heartbeat accelerating. As he was not one to argue, he did as he was told. He collected her in his arms and kissed her with all of the feeling he had suppressed deep inside for so long. The anger, the sadness, the frustration and desire exploded like a geyser bursting violently from the earth. What amazed him the most was that Caroline was returning his affections, matching his passion in earnest.

He drew back for a moment, catching his breath. "I don't understand…" he began.

"Shut up, Harry," she moaned, pulling him to her again by the lapel of his pajama shirt. Somewhere along the way, they had drifted apart until a huge chasm had formed between them, and they faced one another across the gulf as strangers, as foes. In one brief moment, it all melted away. The gulf disappeared, and they were standing on the same ground once again, and she was welcoming him with open arms. While Harry had a difficult time understanding any of it, he did not question it too rigorously for fear of what the answer might be. He would take from it what he could and hope that it would last.

For several weeks, Harry was as close to bliss as he could recall being for a long time. He remembered how young he still was, and it seemed only an instant ago, a blink of an eye, that he and Caroline had been teenagers, enraptured with one another. Not so long ago, he thought. Now they had come full circle. In the back of his mind, though, there was a nagging that he simply could not dispel, throbbing with each rush of his pulse. He knew that he should pull it out into the open, bring it finally to the surface so that he could appease his sense of right and wrong for good. But then Caroline was looking at him again, touching him again, loving him again. He just could not find the words or the strength to speak them when there was a moment to do so, because he did not want to break the spell that they were under.

It was as if they were young lovers, eager to be with one another, counting down the time until they might spend a moment together, arranging chance meetings during Harry's work hours. She had a light in her eyes that she had lost somewhere along the way, and she seemed almost content, at peace with her lot in life. And still the guilt and shame persisted in tormenting and harassing him, until he simply couldn't live with it any longer.

He waited to raise the subject until one evening, after Christy had gone to bed for the night. Caroline caught him glancing cautiously at her several times as he feigned watching the news, looking away when she turned her attention to him. It was easy to see that he wanted to say something but couldn't. After attempting to ignore his obvious need to converse, she could stand it no longer and set her novel down with a sigh.

"Well, what is it, Harry?"

He looked startled. "What do you mean?"

"What's on your mind? I can see you want to say something."

He paused, as if he were proceeding with something delicate that required kid gloves. "I love you, Caroline," he said. "And I don't want to do anything that would mess up what we…I mean…I don't want to rock the boat. That's all I'm trying to say."

"Is there something that you feel would rock the boat? Is that what you're getting at?"

"I suppose so," he replied in a slow, drawn out way.

She regarded him with a serious and anxious expression. "I don't want to hear it," she admitted. There was a pleading in her eyes that should have stopped him there, but Harry couldn't carry the burden of it any longer.

"I don't want to say it," he countered, his focus still on the evening news, although he was no longer watching it. "These things seem to have a way of coming up. I'm afraid you would find out some other way, and I'd rather it be from me."

Caroline bowed her head, scrutinizing her hands as they rested on her lap.

When Harry turned to her, she would not look at him. "I've made a serious mistake," he told her, his voice shaking slightly, whether from nerves or emotion was unclear.

"Please…" she begged. But he went on.

"I've been unfaithful to you, Caroline. I was seeing another woman," he divulged.

There was a long moment of silence, Caroline studying the cuticles of her nails, Harry studying her. He could see her mouth growing hard, her eyes narrowing. "Is that it?" she asked, her voice almost mocking.

"I was seeing someone for several months, but I want you to know that it's over. I ended it."

"Well, good for you, Harry," she muttered. Her eyes slowly wandered up to meet his. "Who was she?"

"It doesn't matter," he said. "What matters is that it's over and I am sorry, so sorry."

"Who was she?" Caroline demanded, more forcefully this time. "I want to know who she was."

"Really I don't see —"

"Tell me!"

"It was Opal Armstrong," Harry admitted.

"Opal Armstrong? That little mouse that works as a seamstress at the dry cleaners?" Caroline spat. It was Harry's turn to remain still. Caroline grew disdainful. "I would have expected better, Harry. She's not the least bit beautiful. Dull as a dish pan, if you ask me."

"I want to apologize…"

"Apologize? For what? What exactly are you apologizing for?"

Harry grew defensive. "Look, Caroline, I'm not the only one who's made mistakes. I'm not the only one that's looked elsewhere. I know. I've known from the beginning. I'm not as stupid as you would like to think I am."

"You're right, Harry. You're absolutely right." She smiled maliciously. "Is that what you wanted? You wanted me to confess my sins before you as well?"

"No. I had something I needed to get off my chest and I did. I was wrong, it was wrong. I'm asking for forgiveness."

"Do you want to know what I think? I think every problem we've ever had was because of you. Everything you've gotten you've deserved," she said, staring him down.

"What have I done that was so wrong, Caroline? What have I done to make you behave so hateful toward me?"

"You didn't fight for me! You didn't care enough to keep me! If this is all about confessions, here's mine. I wanted to love you. I wanted you to love me back. When I didn't get what I needed from you, I looked for it with someone else. You drove me away. You pushed me aside and drove me away." She was nearly crying as she said these words to him. "I was never good enough, was I? Just not good enough for your time. And then you humiliate me by going behind my back with someone like Opal? She's not even pretty or smart. I could understand if it was someone better than me, but Opal?"

"I've done my best, Caroline. What I did I did out of love for you."

"You were with Opal Armstrong out of love for me?" she mocked.

"That's not what I meant…"

"What did you mean, then, Harry?"

"Huh, why bother?" was his caustic rebuttal.

"Explain how anything you've done has been out of love for me. Explain why you left me alone for years, when I begged you for attention, when I would have done anything to have your eyes on me. I want to know why you turned the other way when you knew that I needed love, needed affection. Why you buried yourself in work to avoid me. Tell me what it was that made you so cold and uncaring when I craved a kind word and some support when I was pregnant with Christy. I would just love to hear what you have to say about that!" Caroline ranted.

"I suppose it's easy to blame all of your problems on someone else, Caroline, take no responsibility for yourself, but you chose what path you took," Harry said in a quiet, self-righteous tone.

Caroline laughed scornfully. "If it makes you feel any better, Harry." Her eyes fixed back to her hands. "We're like poison, the two of us, and I think it's about time we end this before we self-destruct."

"What exactly are you saying?"

"That I want out...I want a divorce," she stated.

"Caroline...Caroline, you don't mean that," Harry said, crestfallen.

"We are hurting each other. We are ruining each other's lives," she whispered in horror. "I am appalled at what we've become. It's disgusting."

"What about Christy?" he asked, fear in his voice. "What will happen to our family?"

"Christy?" she asked, a deep disappointment flooding her face. "That's all you can say?" She stood and walked out of the room, leaving him to himself.

CHAPTER II

The nurse's white tennis shoes squeaked on the linoleum as she showed him down the hall to the faux-wood door with a gold name plate, *Marnie Donner,* posted next to it. She gave a short tap with her knuckles before she opened the door and peeked her head in. When she had seen Nelson, she seemed a little amused, perhaps expecting a grizzled, middle-aged man in a cheap suit, smoking cheap smokes, like something reminiscent of a mystery novel. From her candid surprise, Nelson could see she was not expecting an eighteen-year-old, smooth-shaven, innocent-looking kid—dressed in jeans and a button-up oxford—who could spout off the folly of cigarette smoking with great conviction.

"Marnie? You up, honey? Your guest is here to see you," she chirped cheerfully.

Marnie was seated in a small sitting area beyond her hospital-style bed, next to the window, in a chair that could electrically lift her to a near standing position. She had been gazing out onto the courtyard, watching a group of senior citizens make a slow pilgrimage with their walkers along the paved walk, like a gaggle of geese. When she saw Nelson, she didn't try to hide her surprise as the nurse had. "This is the private investigator?" she said with rude shock. "You're not even old enough to shave yet, are you?"

The nurse chuckled. "You need anything, you just buzz me," she told Marnie as she backed out of the room and retreated to the nurses' station.

Nelson cleared his throat. "I actually do shave, ma'am, but that's only just a recent development. I can understand the confusion." He held out his hand. "I'm Nelson Rune, Mrs. Donner."

Marnie grasped his hand in a firm shake, proving that she was not as delicate as she appeared, very much unlike Dinah Gert's unsteady hand. "I haven't got anything better to do. You may as well sit down and visit for a while," she said, thinking over the months of empty days that had transpired between her last visit from anyone. He quickly sat in the seat across from her before she could change her mind. "How'd you find me? The residents here are under private listings," she said as she cupped her hand next to her mouth as if she were telling him something confidential, "so some shyster doesn't come around and con us out of our retirement." Then she laughed at her own joke.

"Your grandson told me how to reach you," Nelson informed her.

"That boy surely doesn't use the brains God gave him. Sold his old grandma out just like that, huh?" She became bitter in her tone. "He moved off, you know. Doesn't live in state anymore. *I* never see or hear from him." Her cracking voice reflected her loneliness. "Still, he's all I've got left now. My husband went over twenty years ago; it was the emphysema. And my son, he was taken from me when he was only twenty-four. A drunk driver hit him when he was getting the mail. Just left him there in the road to die…"

"I'm sorry to hear that," Nelson consoled, thinking that loneliness made one's tongue loose. "Hard to imagine someone doing something like that. Leaving a person to die. That's a shame."

She looked at him astutely, trying to gauge his intent with this comment, then dismissed it as polite condolences. "Now I'm alone," she said with a half-smile.

"This seems like a decent place," Nelson replied.

"You really a private investigator?" she asked suspiciously.

"Yes, I really am."

"How old are you, anyhow?"

Nelson contemplated whether he should lie or not. He decided that she was not the type to gullibly believe anything that was fed to her. Her eyes were shrewd and suspicious. He felt that the truth would serve him better. "Eighteen, ma'am."

"They don't usually come that young, do they?" she asked. She could see that he was taking in every wrinkle, every white hair, the sagging skin about her jowls, the fine whiskers above her upper lip. He was young, naïvely unaware that his time was coming and coming fast. With the same fervor he had been inspecting her, she was watching him, remembering when she too had been fresh, had believed that the world was hers and that time would never catch up to her. She wondered if he relished the prospects, the endless opportunities he had before him now, or if he too would ungratefully squander those years, those months, those weeks, those hours of beauty, of strength, and newness. Could he sense what was to be his fate as he sat in this place of the half-dead? Could he sense it was just around the corner, waiting as surely as it had come for her?

"As I had mentioned on the phone, I wanted to speak to you about the Fletchers," Nelson said, politely attentive.

"When you get to be my age, it's difficult not to think on the past, fret over it. You got nothing better to do with your time. You just mull over it and over it." She paused and grew thoughtful. "I just dreamed about her the other night."

"Who?"

"Caroline," Marnie said wistfully.

"Does it bother you to talk about the Fletchers?"

"That seems to be the hot topic since nineteen sixty-four. Can't get away from it, even after all these years. Keeps coming back up, like the indigestion that keeps coming back up after Mexican Fiesta Night we have here once a week," she mused. "I never learn my lesson, either. I stubbornly get the beef burrito despite the burn."

Nelson was perplexed by her candor. He shifted uneasily in his chair. "I'm sorry to hear that, Mrs. Donner."

"I'll bet you are," she retorted.

"Do you mind if I record our conversation?" he asked, pulling the digital recorder out of his pocket and putting it on his leg where she could see it.

"I suppose not. I've already said it all before, and I don't see how it'll make a difference now, but if you want to, I won't stop you."

Nelson pushed record. "So, Mrs. Donner, you knew Caroline and Harry Fletcher well?"

"Caroline was my best friend."

"How long had you known her?"

"Oh, ever since grade school, when my family moved here from Colorado," Marnie Donner told him. "That's when I met her. I knew her probably better than anyone could know Caroline."

Nelson thought that was an odd thing to say. "What do you mean by that, Mrs. Donner?"

"She was an enigma. Even to me."

"How's that?" Nelson pressed.

"She just didn't fit in here, never did. She was too big for this place. Very beautiful, you know. She probably could have been a movie star or something. Probably would have had a very different life if she had been born twenty years later. That's why she had a hard time with folks around here."

"Did she not get along with other people?"

"Got along with the men just fine." Marnie smiled sardonically. "She was always getting *their* attention. She was a sensational flirt, you know, and it turned some of the women off, made them jealous and angry. Hell, she even flirted with my Chuck, and I was her best friend. I knew she was prettier than I was, but Chuck only had eyes for me, and I never really worried about it. She didn't intimidate me like she did the others. I understood that it was daddy trouble. You know her father left when she was around seven or so. Just took off one day, left her and her mother and Janie, her sister."

"So, you were her only friend?"

"I wouldn't go so far as to say that. They didn't like her, but they still gravitated around her. Everyone did. She was exciting and fun. One time, she threw this theme party. It was a Hawaiian luau, complete with a roasted pig, grass skirts for the ladies, and she had set up a little bamboo hut in the back yard where they served drinks in coconut shells. Well, the women didn't say no to that, I can tell you. Certainly they came, because everybody who was anybody wouldn't have missed it," Marnie confided. "That was just classic Caroline, a social butterfly, if you will."

"Did this strain her relationship with Harry?"

"Yes, well, Harry and she were like night and day," she said, her gaze shifting to the stiff curtains that were moved by the breeze. "He adored her, would have done anything for her. But one man wasn't enough to hold Caroline Fletcher. He knew it, too," she insisted. "He liked the small town, the quiet life, a real homebody, and it just wasn't for her. He *knew* it wasn't enough for her."

"You said in a previous interview that Caroline had admitted to you that she wanted a divorce, that she was unhappy with her marriage," Nelson pointed out.

"I said it, but no one listened to what I was really saying. They heard what they wanted to," she told him disdainfully.

"What did you really mean then, Mrs. Donner?"

Marnie shrugged. "She talked about leaving all the time. I don't know if she ever would have done it. The fact is Caroline was not meant to be happy. She was just an unhappy sort of woman. If she had gotten what she had wanted, she probably still would have been unhappy. She was born in the wrong time. If she had been a young woman now, well, it would have suited her. You can do just about anything these days and it's just fine, no penalties, no strings attached, all in the name of making yourself happy, right? As long as it feels good, it's justifiable."

Nelson did not really understand her response. He tried to change his approach. "Did she want to leave because Harry was unfaithful to her?"

"You're too young to understand half of what went on between those two," Marnie scolded. "It's something you'll never understand until you've loved somebody that doesn't love you back. Harry loved Caroline, was married to Caroline, wanted only Caroline, but she didn't exactly want him." The woman chuckled. "She did but she didn't. And he got lonely, I suppose, became weak, and I'm not saying he had a right to, mind you, but he strayed. He hid it pretty well. I guess he wasn't very proud of it, and the whole thing didn't come out until after…I only knew about it because Caroline knew about it, and she only knew about it because Harry's conscience got the best of him one night and he admitted it to her." She raised her eyebrows as if amused. "Big mistake."

"Did she express how she felt about it?"

Marnie frowned thoughtfully. "She thought it was laughable, I suppose. Opal Armstrong couldn't hold a candle to Caroline's beauty. Opal was a nice girl, though, a real nice girl." She stopped suddenly and looked at Nelson accusingly. "That wouldn't have been what put

Harry over the edge, if that's what you're getting at. Caroline already knew about it before…Well before…Harry had broken it off. He and Opal weren't even seeing one another anymore."

"Did you see her or speak to her the day she was murdered?"

"Not the day of. I saw her two nights before. She and Harry had Chuck and Steven and me over for dinner."

"Could you tell me about that night? The last night you had dinner together?" Nelson probed.

"It was a Wednesday. We got together often, Caroline, Harry, Chuck, and I. Caroline loved to entertain. Chuck wasn't crazy about Caroline, but he liked Harry a good deal. They were friends, just like Caroline and I were. My Steven was almost the same age as their Christy, so we all got along well. Anyway, that night we sent the children out to play in the backyard, and the men were in the front room while we finished up in the kitchen."

"Go on," Nelson encouraged.

"She wanted me to come on Saturday to help her with some pies for the Sunday social. We were always doing things together, the two of us. She helped me put together a quilt once, and there were always baking days and parties to plan. Back in the day, there weren't too many women who worked out of the home, so we kept one another company and helped each other through our days. Not that we didn't have our share of things to keep up with, but it wasn't as frantic as it is now. Our children had mothers that were there for them, and the house was our duty, and I like to think I took good care of what I was responsible for."

"So, you and Caroline were talking about the pie social…" Nelson said, trying to redirect her to the events of that evening.

"Yes, the pie social. She asked me if I would help, and I told her of course I would. Then she asks me if I had thought about it, if I could go to California with her."

"Why did she want to go to California, Mrs. Donner? Do you know?"

"Caroline had to have something to carry on about I suppose. Gave her a reason to blow off all that hot air she was full of."

"So, you don't think she really intended to go to California?" Nelson speculated.

"Beats me. She said a lot of garbage she never meant." She saw his surprise and quickly added, "We all do. Anyway, I told her I couldn't run off to California. I had my family to take care of, so she got upset at that, but said she'd go by herself anyway. Yeah, right. She wasn't capable of doing anything by herself."

"Co-dependent type, huh?"

"That's the nice way of putting it. She never could have gotten to California alone. She knew it, too, but she was good at lying, especially to herself. I don't know what she was thinking. It would have been good to have gotten a peek into the way she reasoned, understand how that brain of hers worked. Well, I wasn't about to go to California, and she knew she couldn't talk me into it, so she tried to make me feel bad about it. I asked her what she wanted to go to California for anyway. She said she wanted to get away from Harry."

Marnie removed her spectacles and cleaned them on her blouse. Nelson waited respectfully, glancing around at the somewhat impersonal room. There were no photos of loved ones to grace the sparse furnishings or the stark white walls. Marnie's bed was covered in a floral bedspread, and a knit throw was draped across the footboard. Some crocheted doilies lay atop the chest of drawers and bedside tables. She had a vase with artificial roses resting on the small table between them. That was it. He drummed his leg with his fingers, growing impatient with the silence.

"Can you think of anything else about that night, Mrs. Donner?"

"Stop butting in," she snapped, jamming her glasses back on her face with a scowl. "Like I was saying, she was mad at Harry, *again.* She told me that she had asked him for a divorce, *again,* but she probably wouldn't after all 'cause she found out she was pregnant."

"She told you she was pregnant?"

"Yup, but nobody else knew, and she wanted to keep it that way. She told me to keep it a secret."

"What did you say?"

"Not much. What was I supposed to say? She'd always told me she didn't want any more children. And to tell the truth, she probably shouldn't have had anymore," Marnie said with a no-nonsense attitude.

"Why not?"

"That woman was a terrible mother. She wasn't a good wife either. That just wasn't Caroline. She was the baby. She thought she was the center of the universe. How does someone like that take care of a baby that really *is* the center of the universe, that needs everything done for them and requires all the time and all the attention? Caroline never would have won Mother of the Year, that's for sure," Marnie said with a sarcastic huff.

"Not to be rude, Mrs. Donner, but did you even like her?" Nelson asked. "Because you seem very, I don't know, antagonistic toward her."

"I told you, I was her best friend, her only friend."

Marnie's profile was to Nelson, but she turned and looked at him with a look of torture and sadness all mingled together in her green eyes. "That was the very last time I talked to her," she whispered in a voice that was permeated with melancholy haunting. "How was I to know that would be the very *last* time? What would I have said differently? What would I have done differently, if I had it all to do over again?"

"Do you miss her?" Nelson asked, feeling sympathy for the woman who was now all alone.

She shifted emotions quickly and with a wry smile said, "No use crying over spilt milk."

CHAPTER 12

Nelson's mind refused to shut down. He had finished the last few pages of *The Darkest Night*, and now he could not stop replaying it over and over. What had really happened that night in 1964? Was Harry the innocent man or was he playing Nelson for a chump? Nelson could imagine what a guilty man might be thinking. Pay some cut-rate private investigator to prove his innocence, and then the doubt and blame would be deflected away from him and onto some other loser. Perhaps Harry thought that just the fact he paid a private investigator to probe his wife's death would make him look innocent, with or without the proof. Nelson was not sure what to make of any of it. Such a strange and entangled mess had played out that he couldn't yet make heads or tails of it. In his mind, he had targeted three prime suspects. Three people that could have done it, that had motive and opportunity.

First and foremost in his mind was the painter Dennis Harvey. Harvey was a teenager who got by on odd jobs. He would have known the Fletcher home intimately from his frequent visits to repair and repaint the entire interior. His mug shot picture was a frighteningly candid one, with a young Harvey glaring contemptuously at the camera, his collar pulled up, his hair disheveled. How many years had he flown under the radar?

The police first picked him up for petty theft. That was when the big discovery of Caroline Fletcher's brooch had been made, fifteen years from the time she had been murdered. When they questioned him, the police had asked him how he had come to possess it. Harvey had made up some ludicrous story about Caroline paying for his painting services with it. A flimsy excuse at best. The Fletchers were quite well off, owning a home in the premiere part of town, a two-car household during a time when most could only afford one, and a well-stocked savings account to boot.

The brooch had originally belonged to Caroline's grandmother, then her mother, and lastly to Caroline herself. She would not likely have given some riffraff handyman a family heirloom that was worth a considerable amount of money. The police hadn't bought it. They asked him, knowing full well that their question was not based on factual evidence, why his blood had been found in the Fletcher home after Caroline's murder.

Harvey concocted a wild tale of accidently cutting himself on a piece of broken glass and cleaning himself up in the kitchen sink. He insisted that he must have inadvertently left traces of his blood in the very room that Caroline Fletcher had been murdered. It was just too incredible to be true. But the police had nothing to hold him on. He served a short sentence for the theft and was let out. Just five years later he was brought in again, this time for the theft and attempted murder of an older woman he had been working for. Harvey had used the key given to him for the repairs that needed to be made to access the house late in the night when the owner was supposed to be away for the weekend. He had been surprised by her unanticipated presence, and in desperation, he had attacked her, landing her in the hospital in very serious condition.

Again the finger of suspicion was pointed at him. By this time, Harry Fletcher had served two-thirds of his prison term, without any substantial evidence against him in his wife's murder. Dennis Harvey had never been charged in connection to Caroline Fletcher. Why would anyone pursue that avenue, if there was already someone doing the time for the crime? Several years into his prison term for attempted murder, Harvey killed a man, a fellow inmate, and now served a life sentence. Nelson believed he was a strong candidate for the killing of Caroline based upon what he had read and what he knew of the man's past. But he very much wanted to interview Harvey for himself.

Next on the list was a bizarre but possible contender as well. The Fletchers did not know him. Indeed, he did not even live in their town. Gary Turner, a member in good standing with the Outlaws, a violent bunch in a motorcycle gang, had been serving a life sentence for his infamous crime spree in the summer of 1964, dying in prison in 1989. In a strange twist of fate, he was in the area around the time of Caroline's murder. He had spent several days before June third at his father's home just twenty miles from where the Fletchers lived.

Did Gary Turner happen upon the Fletcher home in the dead of the night? Did he see the lights on and stop in to find Caroline Fletcher alone? Did he then murder Caroline only to move on to the next town? He was a man that had proven he could be violent. He was a man that had been in the vicinity of the Fletcher home during that time. It very well could have been Gary Turner.

Still, although Harry Fletcher had hired Nelson to prove his innocence, Nelson could not rule him out. His story was just too incredible. And why hadn't Harry fought more grievously to clear his name all those years ago, instead of waiting until now? Surely he was hiding something. Surely he had kept quiet because he didn't want to divulge what that something was.

Nelson finally gave up and got himself out of bed. He showered and dressed, combing his hair with his fingers as he looked in the mirror. He sat waiting and staring at the clock until it was nearly eight, and then he went down two doors and to the opposite side of the hall and knocked softly. Sandi Franklin answered the door, her hair in curlers. It was a strange inconsistency in comparison to her tailored business suit and perfectly applied makeup. Sandi was a legal secretary downtown. When she saw Nelson, she gave him an all-knowing smile.

"Good morning, Mrs. Franklin."

"Morning, Nelson," she said, waiting expectantly. She was going to make him squirm a little.

"Has Cleo left for school yet?"

"No, she's just getting ready."

"Could I speak to her?" Nelson asked, shame-faced.

Sandi turned her head slightly, yelling toward the bedrooms. "Cleo, you have a guest!" Then she turned back to Nelson and smiled politely. "I hate to be rude, Nelson, but I need to finish getting ready for work. If you'd like to have a seat on the sofa, you're welcome to."

"Thank you, Mrs. Franklin. I appreciate that." Nelson slouched into the living room and sat quietly while he waited for Cleo. She came out looking warily at him, as if she suspected him of some sinister reason for being there.

"What do you want?" she asked, pulling no punches.

"I thought you might need a ride to school," Nelson offered.

"My mom usually just drops me off," Cleo said, unwilling to cave right off the bat.

"Oh, I see." Nelson got up from the sofa, looking about awkwardly. "Well, if you ever need a ride, I mean, if she can't take you for whatever reason, I wouldn't mind taking you."

"Sit down, Nelson. You're giving up too easily."

He immediately sat down again. "Look, about the other day...I shouldn't have been so mad," Nelson apologized.

"I know it wasn't entirely your fault. I shouldn't have let the air out of your tire," she admitted.

"Yes, well, that was a stupid thing to do — "

"Shut up, Nelson, before I kick you out."

"Okay." He fell silent.

"I realize that I was partly to blame, but I don't like being treated that way. You know? So, if you're mad at me, then talk to me about it and don't act like I'm not there, or worse, yell at me. I don't like being yelled at."

"I'm sorry, Cleo," he said simply.

She looked at him closely, weighing in her mind if she should accept his apology or make him suffer a little longer. There was just something very innocent and endearing about Nelson Rune. She couldn't quite put her finger on it, but to punish him any more than that seemed a bit cruel.

"Hey, Mom?" Cleo called toward the bathroom. "Nelson offered to drive me to school."

Sandi came in, running the brush through her hair as she talked. "That's fine, Cleo. Just call me when you get home this afternoon so I don't worry." Nelson noticed that Sandi's hair was a much darker shade of Cleo's reddish-blond. Cleo had her square chin, too, but that was where the resemblance ended. Even Cleo's build was different, Cleo being tall and thin, and Sandi being very petite. Sandi looked at Nelson. "You be careful with my daughter," she directed in what was meant to be an intimidating tone. "Take good care of her."

"Yes, ma'am," Nelson responded obediently.

"Mother, stop it. You'll scare him."

"Did I scare you, Nelson?" Sandi asked with a level stare.

"Maybe a little…" he confessed.

"Good. That's what I was aiming for," Sandi affirmed. "I'm her mother, and that's my job."

"Mom!" Cleo scolded.

"Don't forget to call," Sandi said, pointing the brush at her daughter as she headed back to the bathroom to finish getting ready.

"She can be so embarrassing sometimes," Cleo complained.

"I like her," Nelson said.

"Anyway, just let me grab my bag," she told him. "Then we can go."

When they got to his truck, Nelson opened the door for her. She thanked him and climbed in. "She's not usually like that, you know, that 'keep my daughter safe' crap, but I told her what happened the other day, and she was kind of miffed with me."

"You told her about my worker's comp case?" Nelson felt his face turn red. No wonder Sandi was so harsh with him. She was probably speculating what would happen next if she let Cleo go with Nelson.

"Yeah," Cleo replied wryly. "I tell my mom everything. She's all I've got, you know."

"What happened to your dad?"

"He died when I was younger. I don't remember a lot about him, just that I loved being around him, and he told jokes to make me laugh. He's the one who chose my name, you know. It's kind of a funny story," she said. "He was a history professor, and he wanted to name me Cleopatra. Well, my mom wouldn't hear of it, so she finally caved to Cleo. I guess after being given the option of Cleopatra, Cleo didn't seem so bad to her. But it means 'Father's glory,' which I think is kind of cool. Don't you?"

"I guess."

"Nelson is a little different too. What does it mean?"

"I don't know," Nelson confessed. It had never occurred to him to even care what his name meant. "Nelson's my middle name, though. I hate my first name, so I never use it."

Cleo's curiosity was aroused. "What's your real name?" she asked.

Nelson cleared his throat and then muttered under his breath, "Conroy."

"What was that?" she asked, trying to suppress the grin that was involuntarily spreading across her face.

"Conroy."

"That is way worse than Nelson," she concurred. "It sounds like a character from *Brokeback Mountain* or something." Cleo couldn't help it. Her own analogy made her laugh out loud.

"That's my crazy mom for you. Nothing she's ever done makes sense. Thanks, by the way. Nothing like being compared to a gay cowboy. Didn't care for it before, but now I *really* hate it."

Cleo shrugged, and the smile faded from her lips. She paused for a moment before asking him, "Why'd it take you so long to come around, Nelson?"

"What do you mean?"

"I mean it's been two days," Cleo pointed out.

"I've been really busy," Nelson explained.

"Too busy to make up?"

"I know I was a jerk, Cleo."

"I would agree with you there," she said with a broad smile.

"I wasn't even really mad at you. I was just...I don't know. The thought of that guy..." He couldn't seem to find the words to express himself. "I got you something," he told her.

"You did?" She seemed surprised.

"Yeah."

"What is it?" she prodded.

"It's there in the glove box."

Cleo was quite obviously excited about the prospect of a gift. She opened the glove compartment and spotted a small box wrapped in newspaper. "Is this it?" she asked, holding it up for him to see.

"Yeah."

Cleo ripped away the paper and opened the rectangular box. She pulled out a cylinder-shaped leather pouch attached to a key chain. "What is it?" She turned it over in her hands, inspecting it curiously.

"Careful. You don't want to get that in your eyes. It's pepper spray," he explained.

"Pepper spray?" She was a little befuddled. In truth, she was expecting something more along the lines of sentimental. Something like an 'I'm Sorry, Cleo' gift. While it wasn't exactly what she had anticipated when he had told her he had gotten her something, it was touching nonetheless. It had shown a great deal of thoughtfulness, she reasoned.

"Yeah. Keep it on your key chain, and then you'll have it if you need it."

"You're not really a flowers and candy sort of guy, are you?" she laughed.

"Well, if you don't like it—"

She cut him off. "No, I like it. It was very thoughtful of you," she insisted. "It's the gift that keeps on giving."

"I just thought if you ever got in a situation like the other day again, you'd have protection."

"I appreciate it, Nelson."

"It wouldn't hurt to think about taking a self-defense course or something, either. I took one a couple of years ago, but I could always brush up on it. We could go together maybe."

"Maybe," she said, noncommittal. "So, how's your case going?"

"I don't know." He shrugged.

"What's going on with it?"

"I read the book you brought over," he told her.

"Was it helpful?" she asked eagerly, apparently pleased that she may have been of some assistance to him.

"Somewhat. I still have a lot of interviews to conduct. I've been looking over the scene photos, and I agree with the scene investigator from the original analysis of the murder. The burglary looks staged, too neat. There were only a few things missing: the broach that showed up fifteen years later, a few pieces of costume jewelry that weren't worth anything, and the knife that was used on Caroline that belonged to a set in the kitchen."

"Generally, a professional thief is going to know the difference between costume jewelry and the real thing. Wouldn't you think?" Cleo reasoned.

"I know. He passed up a pearl necklace and two rings that were worth a little something for a few other pieces that had no value whatsoever."

"So, robbery was not likely the motivation behind the killing. If it wasn't Caroline walking in on the thief and getting killed in the process, then what was the reason for her being murdered?"

"Plain and simple: someone wanted Caroline dead. They most likely didn't plan it ahead of time, there was a confrontation, and whoever it was lost control. Like I said before, it was a crime of passion. You take everything else away and look at the bare bones of it, and that's all it boils down to. Someone she knew brutally attacked her, face to face, stabbing her until the knife broke. They must have been really angry with her."

"So, who on your list of suspects would have killed her out of passion or rage?"

"Harry."

"Who else?"

"It wouldn't have been a stranger, so that eliminates Gary Turner, the drifter. As far as we know, he'd had no previous connections with the Fletchers, no reason to hate her or want her dead. Dennis Harvey, the house painter, he knew them, but what would his motive be?"

"Is he still alive?" Cleo asked.

"Yeah. Still alive and serving a life sentence. I'm going to see him today."

"So, he could have done it. I mean besides Harry there's really no one else left. No one else that hated Caroline and would like to have seen her dead, as you put it, right?"

"I kind of think there were a lot of people that didn't exactly care for her." He suddenly grew silent, working over the beginnings of something in his mind. Cleo noted his mood change and grew alert.

"What, Nelson?"

He jerked his head toward her, as if he'd been caught doing something he shouldn't be doing. His eyes were wide and alert. "It's just that I thought of something that maybe I shouldn't even be thinking."

"What's that?"

"I probably shouldn't say it. Once I say it, I can't take it back, and murder is a serious accusation," he reasoned.

"Nelson! You have to tell me! You can't just leave me hanging! How am I supposed to concentrate on anything else for the rest of the day? It's cruel! Besides it's not like I'm going to talk to anyone else but you about all of this. No one else would even care. Come on," she complained vehemently.

"It's just that I went and talked to Harry's sister, Dinah…"

"The one who came and took Christy away in the night—"

"Yes, and…well, she didn't like Caroline at all. She told me that Harry would have been better off dead than saddled with her. She said that she thought Caroline had probably got what she deserved," Nelson finished.

"What if Harry never called Dinah to pick up Christy? What if Dinah was already there?" Cloe added.

"But the ER staff swore that there was no way that Harry could have hurt his own neck. They say that, because of the way he was injured, it couldn't have been self-inflicted. If he knew Dinah was there, what reason would she have had for hitting him in the head? Besides she was just a little old woman."

"She is now, Nelson, but she wasn't always. She wasn't then."

"I'm overlooking something. And I'm jumping the gun. There are still interviews to conduct and evidence to review. I was merely speculating, and a good PI doesn't speculate." Nelson pulled the truck up next to the doors at the high school to let Cleo out.

"Let me come with you today," she suggested, trying to play it cool with her relaxed expression and offhand manner.

Nelson looked at her, really looked at her, sitting next to him with one leg drawn up under her. He wanted nothing more than to say yes. He wanted nothing more than to put the truck in drive and leave this parking lot with its mass of students flocking toward the door.

"You need to go in," he said in a weak groan.

"Why?"

"Because I promised your mom I would take care of you. I don't think a prison visit would be on her list of approved activities."

She seemed annoyed as she clutched her bag to her chest and got out. She leaned in before closing the door and grumpily declared, "Suit yourself." Then she disappeared with the others who were squeezing themselves through the oversized double doors.

Nelson had never really cared that he was different, didn't desire to be in high school with other kids his age. He had always felt that he was where he belonged in the grand scheme of things, apart from them. If anything, he had felt that he didn't fit in with his peers when he was a child and able to do much more complex and advanced things than they were. He couldn't wrap his brain around how they couldn't understand what he grasped easily.

They thought he was strange; they found him peculiar. He understood that it was not his place to mingle with them and listen to the teacher recite things that were baby talk to him. But as he watched Cleo's retreating form, he felt a sense of loss that he could not describe, even to himself. As he tried to put a name to the struggle that burned the inside of his chest, it seemed pointless to try to untangle the emotions that were overwhelming him. All that he knew was for once in his life he desired to be normal. He actually wanted to fit in as he never had before, to sit with her at a lunch table, listening to her prattle, to lean against her locker while she was in between classes, and offer to carry her books for her. He wanted to be with her, to be like her. It was with reluctance that he took his foot off of the brake and put it on the gas, leaving Cleo where she belonged.

He pulled his truck on to the freeway and labored through rush hour traffic to get to the state penitentiary. After passing through the required hoops, he was sitting in front of a pane of glass, waiting for answers to his questions.

CHAPTER 13

Dennis Harvey could have been any man, with a cocky self confidence that was hard to overlook, even on the first glance. He was graying at his temples, had character in the lines of his face, and was tall and thin. He looked remarkably well for his age and his environmental surroundings. Nelson wondered if he would have had the same opinion of him if he had first seen him in a suit and tie instead of the jail attire he was now wearing, until he opened his mouth and spoke. It was clear that he was a charmer, a con artist, from the moment he sat down. He leaned back in his chair, his shoulders slumped, his head bowed slightly, and flashed a smile at Nelson.

Nelson was unfazed by the stranger's obvious charisma, and tried to brush aside his preconceived notions of what he had read of the man. He needed to remain unbiased by the premise that this man was quite possibly guilty of the murder of Caroline Fletcher. He didn't want to be easily swayed by Harvey's persuasions or by his own aversions that had been formed from the information he had gleaned in *The Darkest Night*. He would try to start with a blank slate, he told himself. But Harvey's eyes seemed hard, menacing, as he stared at Nelson through the thick glass. Nelson's eyes focused momentarily on a spider web crack in the pane, and he tried to figure out what might have caused such a crack. It spooked him a little. He leaned in toward the intercom, a round metal disc that was centered about chest height for someone sitting down.

"Thank you for agreeing to meet with me, Mr. Harvey," Nelson said, resolving to keep his face carefully unemotional.

"Sure, kid. Sure," Dennis Harvey replied with a wave of his hand, his voice sounding like a bank tellers through the intercom system. "So, you want an interview for your college paper, huh?"

"That's right, Mr. Harvey," he agreed, feeling that the deception was warranted.

"Well, it itn't the first interview that somebody's wanted. Strangest thing, how that lady just won't rest in peace," Harvey observed with a grin as he turned his attention toward picking under his nails. "Why you so interested?"

"It's a mystery, unsolved; it draws a lot of people in. There are so many twists and turns and bizarre aspects to it that it's hard to resist. It's probably one of the most famous unsolved cases of this century," he said, repeating what Cleo had told him.

"I suppose," he said. "But it has been solved. The husband did it. He was tried and convicted."

Nelson silently observed the way in which he had delivered this declaration.

"So, what'd you want to know?" Dennis Harvey finished.

"Did you kill Caroline Fletcher?" Nelson asked without taking a breath.

Dennis Harvey leaned his chair onto its two back legs and hooted. "Boy, you don't know much about the fine art of an interview. You save that question for the last," he said with a chuckle.

"I could save it for the last, but that's actually all I want to know," Nelson explained.

"Is that really what you want to know? 'Cause it's been my experience that nobody cares what the answer to that question is."

"Yes or no?" Nelson pushed.

"Sure. I killed her," he confessed with a broad grin.

Nelson felt a shot of adrenaline course through his body. "You admit to murdering Caroline Fletcher?" he asked, his thoughts incredulous yet eager.

"Why not?" Harvey countered, cocking his head and looking at Nelson indirectly with a crooked grin playing at his lips.

"Why now?"

"Hey, I got nothing to lose, do I? I'm in here for life, rotting away in this hell hole day after day. I'll never see the outside of this place again, now, will I?" Dennis Harvey reasoned. "Why not finally take the credit for it? I snuck back to their place to steal their loot, got caught, and attacked that lady in her kitchen with a knife. She was screaming something awful as I was guttin' her. Something awful." As he told his story, he seemed strangely unaffected by any of it, possibly more amused with himself than he should have been.

Nelson furrowed his brow and studied Harvey through the transparent barrier between them, trying to discern the convict's thoughts. "Mr. Harvey, I'm sincerely looking for the truth," he stressed. "I'm not looking for you to tell me what you think I want to hear."

"It don't matter if I really did it or not. They're looking for some dumb pinhead to lay it on. May as well be me," he rationalized.

"It does matter," Nelson insisted. "I *need* to know."

"Can't you just see the headline of your fine college paper? 'Harvey Finally Confesses to the Murder of Caroline Fletcher,'" he said, holding up his hands as if he were blocking off the headline that floated invisibly in front of him.

Nelson grew angry at the prospect of being played for the fool. He felt like a mouse being pounced on by a big fat feline. He grunted in disgust. "Thanks for nothing," he growled. "This has been one big waste of my time." He kicked the chair back and got up, ready to leave.

Dennis Harvey lost the spiteful smile, leaning forward in his chair, his hands pressed hard against the short ledge before him. He said low and forcefully, "Sit down, kid."

Nelson stopped and looked at him, trying to gauge Harvey's reaction, speculating whether it would be worth his while or not. After a moment's uncomfortable pause, Harvey pointed to the chair and nodded his head in a violent jerk. "I said sit down!"

Nelson obeyed, keeping his eyes carefully on Harvey, unsure of how to proceed. He cleared his throat and began again. "How did you get that brooch, Mr. Harvey? You told everyone that she gave it to you as payment. Was that true?"

"Hell no," Dennis Harvey disclosed as he folded his arms tightly across his chest. "Nobody would have believed the truth." He chortled. "Nobody believed the lie either. Let me tell you, I always got the shaft. That's been my whole life. Why would I guess it'd be any different then or now? But I'm tellin' you she didn't give it to me as payment for painting her house."

"So, in reality you stole the brooch?" Nelson hypothesized.

"I didn't steal nothin'," Harvey growled, his gestures and words becoming defensive.

Nelson could tell the man was agitated by his presumption.

"I never took that damn brooch. She *did* give it to me."

"Why would she give you her grandmother's brooch, Mr. Harvey?"

Harvey nervously ran his fingers across his chin in a firm rub. "How should I know?" Nelson's steady gaze unnerved him for some reason. It was just some stupid kid, after all, but he found himself growing agitated. "She gave it to me to hawk for her," he said reluctantly.

"She needed money?" Nelson inquired.

"Look, she was one messed up lady. Real pretty but messed up all the same. She gave me the brooch, asked me to take it and sell it. She said I could keep part of the money if I helped her out, so I took it. I said I would get the money for her, and I thought I could make something off it too. All them houses I was doin' work on and getting paid hardly nothin', and she offered me a couple hundred, just for taking that brooch off her hands. You bet your life I wasn't going to turn that down."

"Why would Caroline Fletcher need money? She and her husband were fairly well off, weren't they?"

"I don't know. It seemed like it. They sure had a nice house and all, but she gave me some crazy story about California. She needed money to get to California. Asked me not to tell anybody about any of it. She had a way of being convincing, if you know what I mean. She was real friendly," he said with a wink, "and…Well, the whore could turn heads."

"Why didn't you pawn the brooch for her like she asked, then?" Nelson asked. "Why did you keep it?"

"I never got the chance to get the money for it. Didn't have time to." He shoved his hands deep into his pockets and leaned back in his chair again.

"How's that?"

"She gave me the brooch on a Friday. I worked that day at the house. And then she showed up dead Sunday morning," Harvey said, shifting his eyes suspiciously from the guard standing watch over the room to Nelson and then back again to the guard. He came across as not just a little paranoid. "I was screwed."

"Why didn't you tell anyone about the brooch?"

"You kiddin' me? Why would I do something as stupid as that for?" he questioned, leaning toward Nelson with his elbows hanging forward, his hands still in his pockets.

"To clear your name," Nelson replied.

"Why did I need to clear my name? I wasn't a suspect then. Nobody even looked at me. I was only seventeen. So, I kept that brooch all them years so nobody would look at me, so nobody'd say I done it. Believe you me, I wanted to hawk it. Boy, it was burning a hole in my pocket, but I knew they'd nab me right up if I did. Wasn't till they busted me for stealing that guy's wallet fifteen years later that they pointed any fingers at me."

"You said that you cut yourself and may have gotten blood in the Fletcher home while working for them. Why did you tell the police that?"

"'Cause they said they found my blood there. I didn't know. That whole thing had happened fifteen years before. I couldn't remember the specifics. I mean, what was I supposed to say? For all I knew they could have. What if I said it wasn't true and it ended up being true? It very well could have been, too. I worked on that place for two weeks. I could have cut myself at some point. For all I knew they did find blood, so I just went along with what they said, 'cause I didn't know what else to do. Damn cops."

"You made up your story to explain their made up story?"

"That's about the sum of it. I knew they would try and pin it on me. They was out to get me, just like dangling a carrot in front of a rabbit. They've always been out to get me."

"Why are you telling me this now? Why not tell someone this before now, like when they wrote that book about it?" Nelson asked suspiciously.

Dennis Harvey grew angry, his countenance contorting to a smug smirk. "I never got the chance," he said with disdainful amusement.

"You're telling me that you were never interviewed by anyone before they wrote that book?"

"That's exactly what I'm telling you," he spat.

"So, the last time you told your story about Caroline Fletcher was in nineteen seventy-nine, when you were questioned by police when they picked you up for stealing a wallet?"

"Yup." Harvey nodded his head vigorously in satisfaction.

"Have you ever tried, up to this point, to tell anyone else that you had no connection to that murder, Mr. Harvey? Have you ever tried to prove your innocence?"

"I never really needed to. What was the point? I'm here for life. I messed up some old bird I worked for, then I killed a man while I was doing my time. I easily could have killed that Fletcher woman too, but they never charged me with anything. Why go out of my way to prove I didn't do it? Just a waste of breath anyway; I done been condemned because of that book. I tell people I didn't do it, who they gonna believe?"

"So, let me get this all straight. You maintain that Caroline Fletcher gave you the brooch to pawn, promised you a portion of the money, but asked you not to speak to anyone about it. You say that she needed the money for a trip to California. You left that day with the brooch, and the following day she was murdered. You kept the brooch hidden, trying to keep a low profile to keep your name out of it, until they caught you fifteen years later in nineteen seventy-nine."

"Yes."

"And the police were leaning on you and saying that they had found your blood at the scene of Caroline Fletcher's murder, and you then made up a story about possibly having cut yourself while working in the Fletcher home to explain the blood evidence that the police had invented to try and corner you."

"Yes."

"You somehow got out of it because there was no substantial evidence against you, only to be put in prison for life because you brutalized, with the intent to kill, an older woman that you were working for, and then you killed a fellow inmate while serving your prison term?"

"Yes."

"And when the author of *The Darkest Night* pointed at you as a very strong contender for a suspect in the murder of Caroline Fletcher, he never came here and interviewed you himself?"

"You'd be right on that one too," Harvey said with a nod of his head.

"Those are a lot of details to remember," Nelson slyly observed.

"I got a really good memory. You ask me anything," he said. "You ask me anything, and I can tell you. 'Cause I remember it all. I remember the day my mama died, and I was three. That's how good I can remember."

"You didn't kill Caroline Fletcher?"

"I'm sorry…I'm sorry for her, but no. No. I did not. Question answered, end of story. I said I didn't, so there."

"Well, this is just getting more and more screwy," Nelson muttered. "How am I supposed to make heads or tails out of any of it?"

Dennis Harvey shrugged his shoulders, extending his hands with his open palms turned upward. "Got me," he replied. "Maybe you should write your article on something else."

"Yeah, maybe," Nelson agreed. "Well, it's been interesting, Mr. Harvey. Can't say that I believed every word of it, but it has certainly been interesting."

"Could you send me a copy of your paper when they run it?" Harvey asked eagerly.

"If they print it," Nelson lied.

"Maybe you want my picture or something," Harvey suggested.

"If I need it, I'll let you know."

"Yeah, you're right. Probably won't want my picture. Probably won't need it," he said, trying to act as if he didn't care. "But, you know, if you do…"

"Thank you for agreeing to meet with me, Mr. Harvey. It was enlightening," Nelson said, and then he left.

CHAPTER 14

Something close to revulsion ran through Nelson's body as he pulled the door open. Why was he here? But the only reason he could plausibly come up with was that he was here for Cleo. She breezed past him through the door he held open, and he reluctantly followed her into the unknown wild of the mall, his nose assaulted by a mixture of various foods from the food court. The only place to get Mexican, Italian, Chinese, and McDonalds all in the same place—appalling.

Nelson trailed behind Cleo, who seemed to know where she was going. That was fine with him, because at this point he felt very much like a lamb surrounded by ravenous wolves. She went straight for the GAP store and began riffling through the racks near the entrance. Nelson stood off to the side, watching, with his hands in his pockets, shoulders rounded.

"What color do you think?" Cleo asked over her shoulder.

"Whatever," he mumbled. "It doesn't really matter to me."

"In that case, I'm going with the yellow," she teased, holding up a canary yellow polo. She saw the look of panic on his face and laughed. "I'm just kidding. I wouldn't make you put this on."

"So, why do we have to buy new shirts again?"

"I already told you, we're supposed to wear *matching* shirts, Nelson. That's what you do at Sadie Hawkins."

"But why?" Nelson persisted.

"That's just how it is. That's how it's always been," she said, checking a price tag.

"Oh."

"I like this one." She held up a navy and red striped long sleeve tee. "Do you?"

"It's okay," he answered with little emotion.

"You really don't want to be here, do you?" She seemed amused, maybe a little surprised by his behavior.

"This just isn't really my thing," he explained. "I don't like crowds. I don't like shopping."

"Well, but you're wearing a pair of jeans and a shirt right now. Where'd those come from? You had to buy them somewhere," she reasoned.

"Target," he replied.

"So, you had to go shopping to get them." He remained silent. Cleo held the shirt up to him to see if it would fit. "This looks like it would work. Hold it," she said as she pressed it to his chest until he accepted it. He went along with her as she moved on to the next rack.

"If you like this one, why don't we just buy it and go?"

"I need to make sure that we got the best one. What if I find one that's cheaper and looks better?" She held up another shirt. "See?" she squealed triumphantly. "On sale and a nice neutral gray color. Out of these two, which do you like best?"

His eyes zig-zagged back and forth between the two, sweat breaking out on his forehead as he tried to figure out which of the two she wanted him to pick. "The gray one?"

"You wanna try it on and see how it looks?" she asked.

"It looks like it would fit."

"Okay. Fine. I get it." She checked the tags for the sizes and took the matching shirts up to the counter to pay. Once they bagged the shirts and put the receipt in along with it, Cleo took the navy bag and spun around to face Nelson. "Anything else you want to check out?"

"Like what?"

"Like we could get you some new shoes," she proposed.

"What's wrong with my shoes?"

"They're kind of worn out, Nelson," she said as diplomatically as possible. She was thinking that it looked like his tennis shoes had seen better days, that someone else not as kind might have asked if he had been Dumpster diving, but she didn't want to hurt his feelings and suppressed the bulk of her thoughts.

"They aren't worn out. No holes in the bottoms or anything. They still work just fine," he told her defensively.

"Okay, you can still use them, but they don't look so great. Maybe you could get a nice pair of leather shoes to wear to the dance," she recommended. "Something a little dressier. And you can keep the tennis shoes for more casual wear."

"Do I really need more than one pair?"

Cleo didn't answer. Instead, she dragged him to the shoe store and began stacking boxes of shoes next to him as he sat on the cushioned bench in his socks. The sales clerk joined her in her efforts, the two of them comparing shoe styles and giving their approval or nixing them as they consulted on the latest fashions. Too polite to protest, Nelson watched them with a bewildered expression as he tried on shoe after shoe. If it made Cleo happy, then he figured he could bear it. The clerk and Cleo finally settled on a pair of shoes they felt were both practical and stylish. She held up a brown suede oxford and presented it to Nelson.

"I think these are the winner," Cleo affirmed with a nod. "What do you think?"

"They're nice," he consented, not really willing to commit wholeheartedly to it. He thought they looked good, but shoes had never really done anything for him. Fashion in general didn't mean much to him.

"Just nice?" she probed.

"I like them," he replied, still avoiding a definitive commitment.

"But you don't seem very enthusiastic," she pressed.

"If you like them, then I like them. You know more of what you're talking about than I do." He took the shoe she held in her hand and put it back in the box with its mate. "Let's just settle on these and get out of here," he said with a hint of pleading in his voice.

"All right," she allowed, as they went to the cashier.

The sales clerk scanned the bar code on the end of the box and, with a wide smile, told them, "That will come to seventy-three dollars and forty-nine cents."

"Excuse me?" Nelson asked, a sick feeling radiating from his gut.

"The sale price is seventy-three dollars and forty-nine cents. Did you want to pay with cash or debit? We no longer accept personal checks," she informed them, pointing to the sign posted on the register.

"So, you really said seventy-three dollars and forty-nine cents?"

The sales clerk seemed confused. "That's right."

He turned to Cleo with a look of shock on his face. "That's like two weeks' worth of groceries," he protested.

"They're really good-quality shoes, Nelson. How much did you think they would cost?"

"I don't know," he balked as he slapped his debit card onto the counter. "I guess I didn't think I'd have to sell a kidney to buy a pair of shoes. But if this is what you want…"

Cleo was embarrassed. She smiled nervously at the clerk as she slid the magnetic strip of his debit card down the scanner. "Would you like the receipt with you or in the bag?" she asked, trying to remain polite.

"The bag's fine," he replied with a bit of a grumble in his voice.

Cleo did not push him to go to any other store. They left without further ado. On the way out, she looked contrite. "I'm sorry, Nelson."

"What for?"

"Well, you bought those shoes just to make me happy, and I can see that you didn't really care for the mall. You tried to tell me, and I didn't listen."

He shrugged. "Look, I didn't mean to be such a bear, but I still have to pay rent and my cell phone bill for the month, you know?"

"It was really selfish of me not to think of that. If you never want to come to the mall again, I won't make you," she promised, and she casually swept her hand into his. He seemed stunned but looked straight ahead in an attempt to appear indifferent.

Cleo tried not to smile at his very red face. She noticed with delight that even his ears were a bright scarlet all the way to the tips.

"How's our case coming?" she asked, trying to make him feel at ease by bringing up a topic that was safer for him. She had noticed that when he was discussing work, he was relaxed and conversation seemed to flow easily for him.

"I don't know. It's like every time you think you might have narrowed it down, some new thing pops into the equation."

"Well, have you definitely ruled anybody out?"

"I still haven't interviewed everyone," he admitted.

"You know, I'm confident that you'll figure it out," she told him.

"I'm glad somebody is," he grumbled. "My next interview is going to be a really interesting one, but a really difficult one."

"Who is it?"

"The patrolman who was first on the scene the night of Caroline Fletcher's murder, the one who helped put Harry Fletcher behind bars."

"Can I come with you?"

"I don't know…"

"I know I messed up last time. I probably don't deserve another chance, but I would really, really love to come." She saw him hesitate. "Please! I want to help."

"I don't know. I'll think about it."

"While you are thinking about it, remember I did get you the pictures you wanted the last time—the pictures that proved that guy was faking it."

"We'll see. I'm not making any promises."

The house smelled of dogs, more precisely dog pee. With a reluctant grimace, Nelson eyed the couch with a Great Dane stretched across the length of it. When he approached, the dog growled at him. He took a step back.

"Duke, move it," Walt yelled, leaning over and taking the dog by the collar to pull him off the couch. "That's a good boy," he said, indicating for Nelson and Cleo to take the vacated spot. Nelson did not want to sit there, but he didn't see any way out of it. He tried unsuccessfully to brush some of the animal hair away before he perched himself on the edge of the cushion, trying to make as little surface contact as possible. He cleared his throat several times, unable to get the feel of choking on dog hair to dissipate.

"Nice horse you have there," Nelson muttered.

The older man ignored him and asked, "Who's this pretty little lady?" With a twinkle in his eyes, he looked Cleo over. He may have been getting up there in years, but he could still appreciate beauty.

Nelson again tried to clear his throat of pet dander. "This is my friend Cleo, sir," he said. He had encouraged Cleo not to come, but she said that she didn't want to sit around and wait to find out what happened. She told him that he was too difficult to extract information from and that she would rather hear it firsthand because then she would know all the details.

Cleo smiled energetically. "Hello, Mr. Kane," she said in her usual bubbly way. "Thanks for having us." Walt reacted with a snicker and a shake of his head.

"What can I do you for, son?" Walt Kane asked. Reaching for his glasses that lay on the end table, he slipped them on so that he might inspect Nelson closer.

"As I said on the phone, I wanted an interview with you for my Forensic Science class," Nelson said. "I'm writing a paper on the Fletcher murder case."

"You're going above and beyond, wouldn't you say?" Walt asked.

"I plan on acing my paper, sir."

"I like a man with ambition," Walt said with a laugh. "Kids these days, they suffer from a severe case of underachievement. No backbones. Lazy, sloppy SOBs."

Nelson shifted uneasily with a forced smile. Walt hiked the belt of his pants up as he burrowed deeper into his chair. Nelson thought that his pants couldn't reach any higher, but he had been wrong. The waistband was now up to his breast bone. He loosely resembled Humpty Dumpty, with his dome-shaped bald head and round middle, his pants pulled up that high. Nelson suppressed a chuckle at the thought.

"Well, what d' ya wanna know?" Walt asked, squinting through his glasses at the two of them. At this point, the Great Dane, "Duke," ambled back over to the couch, unceremoniously sticking his nose into Nelson's groin. Nelson tried to shoo the dog away.

"You were the first one on the scene, weren't you, sir?" Nelson inquired.

"Sure was," Walt affirmed. The dog continued to plague Nelson. Again he tried to divert Duke's nose. Walt leaned over and gave Duke a good, firm swat on the bottom. "Get out of here, Duke, you worthless piece of…" he said with a snarl. The dog whined and trotted out of the room.

"Could you tell me what it was like, I mean, when you got there?"

"Sure enough I can. That was the first time I saw a dead body," Walt reminisced.

"Caroline Fletcher?" Nelson said.

"Caroline Fletcher," he said.

"And she was in the kitchen?"

"Who's tellin' this story, you or me?" Walt asked in irritation.

"Sorry, sir," Nelson apologized.

"I didn't know her before. I seen him around town, but never her. When I got there, she was laying on her back in the kitchen. It wasn't pretty. A downright mess."

"Can you tell us what condition the body and the room were in?" Nelson said, trying not to seem too eager.

"She was carved up. It smelled funny. A stink that's hard to describe if you never smelled death before. She was in her nightgown, like somebody had caught her getting ready for bed. There was blood all over. Looked like someone had stood in the middle of the room with a ketchup bottle and squirted it everywhere. Looking through the rest of the house, things was tossed here and there, like somebody was looking for something. By the time everybody else got there, I had already figured that nothing would be found missing."

"How's that?" Cleo piped up.

"Well, it was like whoever went through that house was trying to make it look like they were there to rip something off, but it didn't look like the way a real thief woulda done it."

"So, how many years did you work on the force?" Cleo asked, as if she were trying to make small talk. Nelson looked over at her with a quizzical expression.

Walt pursed his lips as if he were thinking very hard. "Well, I retired twenty years ago this spring. Served forty-two years. Not too shabby in my estimation," he replied. "Had to give it up when I got sick."

"You must have seen a lot of really interesting things in your time," she told him, a hint of awe in her voice.

"Yes, I suppose I have," he conceded.

Cleo caught Nelson's slightly annoyed look but ignored it. "You should write a book or something," she teased. Walt chuckled with a modest shrug.

"A book, huh?" he mused.

"I bet you could fill a couple of books with the things you've witnessed, things that would really interest people," Cleo went on.

"I should show you two my scrap book," Walter said, shaking his finger at the two of them with a broad grin. He grunted as he wiggled himself to the edge of his chair, then hefted himself onto his feet, grabbing his walker before he shuffled out of the room. They could hear him berating Duke as he disappeared down the hall.

The second he was out of hearing range, Nelson turned on Cleo. "What are you trying to do?" he hissed.

"You're not very good at this, Nelson. I'm trying to help you."

"What do you mean, I'm not very good at this?" he fumed.

"Haven't you ever heard the expression 'You attract more flies with honey'?" she asked him.

"So?"

"So, stroke the man's ego and he'll tell you whatever you want," Cleo advised. "Don't just sit there with that straight face of yours, throwing question after question at him. You're making him defensive."

"You don't know anything about it!" he charged.

By this time, Walt had returned with a lidded box perched on the top of his walker, aiming to balance it as he walked. Cleo jumped up and took the box for him. "Let me help you with that, Mr. Kane," she offered.

"Thank you much," he said with a wink. He fell heavily into his chair, a little out of breath. Cleo put the box in front of him on the floor. Walt laboriously bent over to take the lid off and rummaged through it until he found an old photo album. "This here is my scrapbook." He leafed through it and then tapped his finger to a newspaper clipping from 1976. "See this? That's the mayor shaking my hand."

Cleo took the album from him, scanning the article before looking up at him in amazement. "You saved a woman and her child from a house fire?"

"Sure did," he confirmed. "I was one of the first there on the scene. Got there even before the fire truck. The whole place was up in flames, but I went in anyway. That poor woman was there with her girl in the bedroom, completely hysterical, trying to hide in a corner."

"And what did you do then?" Cleo asked.

"I busted out the window!" he declared. "Busted it out and passed 'em out to safety."

"That's incredible," she said.

"They put me in the paper. But I was just doing my job," he told her modestly.

"About the Fletcher case—" Nelson began.

"I bet you have some really great stories about that case, one of the most infamous of our time, and you were there," Cleo broke in.

"Like I said, I was the first on the scene. Harry Fletcher was sitting on the front steps when I pulled up. He was acting funny, the back of his head was bleeding, and he seemed shook up. He was a mess. He was crying and carrying on."

"How did he look? I mean his physical appearance?" Nelson butted in.

"Like I say, his head was bleeding, so he had blood on the back of his collar, some on his hands, and here on his shirt." Walt indicated where the smear had been on the sleeve of Harry's shirt. "When he got checked out at the hospital, he had a concussion, otherwise he was okay."

"That blood could have been from him feeling the back of his head," Nelson replied. "He wakes up, feels the pain in his head and reaches up to see what's wrong, gets blood on his hand, and rubs his sleeve in it. Don't you think it's strange that he didn't have more blood on him? I mean, he had just allegedly murdered his wife."

"He had plenty of time between her death and the call to the police to clean himself up. Plenty of time. Why he could have taken a bath by the time I showed!"

"What did you do then?" Cleo asked, overly interested.

Walt's attention was redirected to her. He seemed as though he were trying to shake his defensiveness away when he answered Cleo. "I told him to wait in the patrol car, and I went into the house. The lights were on," he continued. "I went into the kitchen, and there she was. She had slash marks on her arms, like she had been fighting, her teeth was messed up, broken out, I mean, and things in the kitchen was knocked around. There were chairs turned over, the table was pushed out of the way, and stuff that was on the counter was thrown all over. A canister of flour was spilled. I knew right away she really was a fighter."

"That must have been awful," she said sympathetically.

"I never seen anything worse," he agreed. "I mean, I saw some bad stuff, but nothing like this. It's a smaller town and not a lot of murders here. But back then, back then it was unheard of. Apart from the drunks we rounded up and the occasional domestic disturbance, it was just a real quiet place to live."

"What happened then?" Nelson interjected.

"I'm coming to it," Walt snapped. Nelson was beginning to believe that Walt didn't like him for some reason. "Anyway, I looked through the rest of the house. The bedroom, some of the drawers had been gone through. Same thing in the living room. Other than that, the place looked perfectly normal, so I went out in the back, and that's when I saw the cigarette and the shoe print next to it. Looked like somebody'd stepped in the flour in the kitchen and then left their print on the deck."

"The shoe print that mysteriously disappeared," Nelson complained.

"Well, now, things weren't like they are now. People was traipsing through there, in and out, for weeks. They were giving tours of the place. Likely somebody just didn't notice it and walked right through it. You're up at the college taking that fancy class; we didn't have none of that back then. The police were the ones that collected evidence, didn't use gloves, didn't have all this flashy equipment, and they sometimes got the locals to help 'em out. They had the little neighbor boys searching the fields round about for the missing knife, the one the Fletcher woman was done in with."

"Are you serious?" Nelson said, outraged by the prospect.

"Dead serious. There wasn't that *CSI* crap like you see on TV now a days. That stuff itn't real. It was the police that took care of that stuff, the police and the coroner. I ought to know. With everyone coming in and going out of that place, it isn't surprising that the shoe print disappeared. Write that in your paper."

"Can you describe what the shoe print was like?" Nelson wanted to know.

"Oh, it was bigger 'n my foot, by at least one or two sizes," he said, lifting his foot off the floor for them to inspect.

"What size do you wear, Mr. Kane?" Cleo inquired.

"I wear a ten. Average size. This print was bigger 'n average."

"Do you think that Harry Fletcher killed his wife?" Cleo asked.

"Sure as shootin', he did. He was there. He behaved suspiciously, what with not calling the police right away and all. Practically had a guilty stamp on his forehead. Besides, who else would have done it? I suppose there was speculation 'bout a few others, but nothin' that amounted to anything."

"What kind of speculation?" Cleo probed.

"There was some that said she was carrying on with another man. Find the man and find the killer," he explained. "But we never knew for sure if she was or not. At any rate, all roads led to Harry Fletcher, the husband."

"Well, I suppose that we've taken enough of your time," Nelson said, getting up from his seat and waiting for Cleo to follow. "I really do appreciate you meeting with us like this."

"Don't you wanna see the rest of my scrapbook here?" Walt Kane gestured toward the album.

"I think we should probably be going," Nelson replied, but Cleo held back. She felt sorry for Walt. He was obviously a lonely man.

"I'd really like to see it, Mr. Kane," she offered.

Walt perked up a little, stretching across to hand her the old album. She accepted it and started to leaf through it, asking questions here and there as she looked over his forty-two-year career all stuffed neatly in this one volume. Nelson was agitated, shifting from one leg to the other as he waited for her to finish. He had better things to do than stand around here, looking over some second-rate cop's crappy pictures. He was sick of interviewing all of these geriatrics that seemed to want to hold on to their pasts with the single determination of a child clinging to its favorite toy. Would he be the same? Would he want to tell anyone and everyone that would listen about what he was like when he was young? What he didn't understand was the terrible nature of aging, how you gradually lost your looks, your respect, your ability to even care for your basic needs. It was natural to want others to know that at some point you were something, you were somebody.

"This is very nice," Cleo praised as she turned another page.

"My late wife put it together," he told her.

"What are these?" Cleo questioned.

Walt craned his neck to see what she was looking at. "Those are my own snapshots of the Fletcher case," he explained.

Nelson came to attention. He lunged to the couch, sitting next to Cleo as he quickly scanned the page of photos, momentarily forgetting about his earlier hesitation to make contact with the dog hair laden upholstery. "When did you take these?" Nelson blurted in an urgent tone.

"Some when I got there, some just after the coroner removed the body," Walt informed him. Nelson took the photo album from Cleo and inspected the photos closely. They were nothing more than candid snapshots, obviously taken by an amateur, but it was the closest Nelson had come to seeing anything new related to the case. "Those were my little souvenir," he told them with a proud look on his face. He sensed that the two of them were impressed.

"Is there any way that you would allow me to take these and get copies made of them, sir?" Nelson requested.

"I let you look at 'em, but you can't take them."

Nelson's heart sank.

"May I take photographs of them, Mr. Kane?" Cleo asked.

"That I don't mind," he allowed.

Nelson was full of excited energy on the drive home. Cleo knew that he was onto something. She waited until they pulled out of the driveway before she asked, "What? What are you thinking?"

"Walt Kane just proved that Harry couldn't have killed Caroline."

"How's that?"

"Well, for one thing," Nelson began, "Harry's shoe size is ten too."

"And for another?"

"It's so simple, it's ridiculous. Just look at those pictures. It's all right there."

CHAPTER 15

Beautiful Caroline, her hair in a ponytail, was tearing crisp leaves of lettuce from the round green ball she cradled in her arm. Even in her most candid moments such as these, she bore a beauty that was hard to see past. Marnie, a young Marnie with auburn hair and freckles across the bridge of her nose, tall, a good head taller than Caroline, was chopping carrots on the cutting board. Only twenty-nine and in her prime, thin and birdlike, graceful in her motions and mannerisms, soft spoken and kind-faced, Marnie was the picture of a proper woman.

"You really wouldn't mind coming over on Sunday afternoon to help me with those pies for Sunday evening social, would you?" Caroline asked as she labored at her task of salad making.

"No, I don't mind. I already told you I would, didn't I?" Marnie said good-naturedly.

"Pastor Peterson wants them there by six o'clock," she went on, enveloped in her own mental to-do list. "I need to stop by the grocery store Saturday and pick up some sugar. I've run out."

"If you'd like, I can pick some up and bring it over when I come," Marnie offered.

"Would you?"

"I don't mind. It would be easier for me to do it anyhow," she replied. "After all, I live closer to town."

"Did you see Pastor Peterson the last time I brought my pies? He wouldn't touch anyone else's," she bragged. "He told me it would be a sin to let his lips touch anything less worthy." She sniggered.

Marnie rolled her eyes. "I suppose we can't all be good at everything, Caroline. Not like you anyway," she replied with a light laugh.

Caroline gave a coy, sidelong look toward Marnie and lowered her voice. "Have you thought it over? Are you coming with me?"

Marnie automatically seemed uncomfortable. She did not like telling Caroline no. Caroline was a woman prone to adult fits, pouting, and the silent treatment if she didn't get what she wanted, and Marnie did not want to be on the receiving end of that. She avoided Caroline's burning eyes by focusing her attention entirely upon the vegetables she was so diligently chopping. "I just can't, Caroline. Steven has school, and Chuck has to work. It's a bad time. You must understand; I would go if I could…"

"Would you?" she asked scathingly. Then her mood quickly changed. "Oh, never mind. You'll be green with envy when I come back from California, tan and wearing the latest styles, anyway. You can't get good fashion like that around here," she asserted. "Woolworth's would never make *Vogue*, if you know what I mean."

"Why do you need me to come along, anyhow? Won't Harry take you?" Marnie said, shifting the focus from herself. She brushed the hair from her forehead with her arm, avoiding any contact with her soggy hands.

"I don't want him to take me. He'd only get in the way, the killjoy. Can you imagine him in California? He'd ruin everything."

"You seem very upset with him. What has he done this time?" Marnie didn't want to seem too nosy, but she also wanted to know what Caroline was getting at. She waited patiently, glimpsing through the bold, daisy curtains at the window to see the children chasing one another across the lawn, squealing and screeching as they tried to elude one another's reaching fingertips.

Caroline laughed scornfully. "If you're talking about Opal Armstrong, that's over. It has been for a while. The coward broke it off with her."

Marnie finished cutting the carrots and scraped them into the salad bowl with the blade of her knife, then she busied herself with chopping tomatoes. "You act as if that were a bad thing. If I thought

Chuck was having an affair, I wouldn't stand for it. Aren't you relieved he isn't seeing her anymore?"

"What do I care? I hate him. He's just like my father. I don't care what he does or who he does it with." Caroline tore the lettuce a little more forcefully than the situation warranted. "I was going to tell him I wanted a divorce," she confided vehemently. "But I guess that's not going to happen now. He's discovered a way to keep me from leaving."

Marnie stopped chopping and turned around to face Caroline, sensing a bombshell about to be dropped. "What are you talking about?"

Caroline placed her pile of lettuce into the bowl and went over to the sink to wash her hands, prolonging the moment. She could see Marnie was dying to know what she was about to divulge. Caroline was basking in the attention it was affording her. If there was anything that could bring joy to Caroline Fletcher, it was pure, undiluted attention being poured out upon her. She went to dry her hands on the towel hanging from the oven door.

"Spit it out, Caroline!" Marnie cried, flustered by the torture she was being subjected to.

Caroline lowered her voice and drew closer. "I'm pregnant." She was pleased with Marnie's wide eyes.

"Does Harry know?"

"I haven't told anyone but you," she admitted.

Marnie turned back to her tomatoes to avoid Caroline's scrutiny, cleaning the seeds and juice from the avocado-colored countertop with a wet dish cloth. "How long have you known?"

"For certain? A few weeks. I expect I'm around three months along."

"I wish it was me." Marnie sighed. "I've been trying for another ever since Steven was a year old."

"Well, you're better off, Marnie. I swore I'd never do it again. But I suppose a woman doesn't always have control over these things," she said peevishly.

"But when will you tell Harry?"

Chuck came through the hallway and into the kitchen. "Is dinner ready yet? Harry and me are starving in here," he complained.

Caroline's mood switched completely. Marnie had seen it many times before, how she could change as quickly and as thoroughly as trying on a new coat. She became jovial as she teased. "We aren't ready yet, Chuck. You be a good boy and run along and wait until I come tell you it's time." She was being patronizing, and it was just the thing that made Chuck dislike her so. Marnie had grown very use to this slightly hostile banter between the two of them.

Chuck successfully squashed her fun by ignoring her completely. Caroline was not a woman to be put aside; it made her down right angry when someone overlooked her.

"How much longer, Marnie?"

"Go ahead and call the children in, Chuck. It's nearly done," Marnie said as she twisted partially to his view in a sidelong glance over her shoulder.

"Fine, then," he replied, leaving the two women alone again.

"Why do you have fun with him like that?" Marnie wanted to know. "It only makes him dislike you more."

"Don't be silly, Marnie. Chuck doesn't dislike me. Chuck adores me, doesn't he?" She laughed at her own joke. Marnie rolled her eyes. "Listen, don't tell anybody about what we talked about," Caroline ordered in a low voice as she brushed past Marnie and into the dining room. "Keep it under your hat."

"Don't you think Harry has a right to know?"

"What do you care, anyway? It's really none of your business. When I decide he ought to know, I'll tell him, and only then," Caroline said with a huff. "End of story."

CHAPTER 16

Nelson burst through the door of his apartment, Cleo on his heels. She followed him to his computer, watched him upload the pictures onto his screen and then intensely scrutinize each one. Her patience didn't last long. "What did you see?" she asked in exasperation.

"A picture is worth a thousand words," he mused. "It's all right there."

"What!" She was looking at the exact same pictures but seeing nothing, nothing that would clear Harry in her mind, anyway.

"I'll show you," he said, pointing to the kitchen floor in the photos.

"Nelson, there is nothing there!"

"Exactly."

"Stop jerking me around and tell me what I'm supposes to be seeing," she griped. Nelson went over to the refrigerator and pulled out a water bottle. "What are you doing?" she asked.

"I'm showing you," he told her.

Nelson grabbed her by the elbow and positioned her on the sliver of linoleum in his kitchenette and then unceremoniously squirted her with the water bottle. Cleo hadn't seen it coming. She gasped and sputtered, holding her hands up defensively.

"Are you *crazy!* What are you trying to pull?"

"Look," he ordered, spinning her around to face the opposite direction.

"Look?"

"Look at the floor."

"It's wet, you idiot. You sprayed me with water," she fumed.

"Cleo, the floor isn't wet where you were standing. You blocked this part of the floor with your body," Nelson explained, pointing to the floor directly behind where she was positioned.

"I don't get it," she said as she wiped her face with her hands.

"Whoever killed Caroline that night was standing here," Nelson said, directing her back to the computer screen and pointing to the only patch of floor that was miraculously free of blood spatters in the photo. Indeed the room was covered in Caroline's blood, but for that one spot in the picture.

"So, you know where the killer was standing. That doesn't mean that Harry couldn't have done it."

"The killer would have been covered in Caroline Fletcher's blood. You see how your body blocked this part of the floor, kind of like a shield? The blood that would have been on this part of the floor was on the murderer. His body shielded the floor from the blood spatter. See? The only blood on Harry was the blood from his head. You heard Walt Kane yourself."

Cleo rolled her eyes. "Nelson, he had time to clean himself up. Walt said so."

"He was still wearing the shirt and pants that he wore to work that day," Nelson informed her. "If Harry had killed his wife, he would have been dripping with her blood because whoever was standing here —" and again he indicated the patch of clean floor "— they would have been doused, just like you were."

"Thanks for that by the way," she said. "Think maybe you could have just explained it to me?"

"Sorry," he replied.

"Do you have a towel I can clean myself up with?"

"Yeah." As he walked into the kitchen, he continued talking with an excited chatter, as though he could hardly contain his delight. "That's not all, either. I'm looking at the blood spatter, and I'll have to inspect it more closely to make sure, but the blood arc makes me think that it was done by a lefty!"

"And Harry is right handed?" Cleo guessed.

Nelson grabbed a towel from the drawer as he shook his head with a grin. "That's right!" He came around the bar and approached Cleo with a triumphant smile. "Right handed," he said as he dabbed her face and arms.

When he looked at her again, she was staring at him intently. There was something about her expression that made him uneasy. He thought that she wanted him to kiss her, but he wasn't sure. Reading facial expressions did not come naturally to him. He had often times been wrong about his assumptions. He stood watching her for a moment, puzzling over it, feeling the rush of energy between them. Nelson began to lean in, seeing Cleo's lips part ever so slightly. He suddenly lost the nerve and pulled back.

"What are you doing?" she murmured.

Nelson was still just inches away from her face. He felt shamefully inadequate at that moment, his mind fighting his body's urge to touch her. Racing through his thoughts was the knowledge that he was eighteen and had never kissed a girl before. What if he were woefully poor at it? What if he were so completely inadequate that Cleo laughed at him? What would he do then?

"I…" he began. But he suddenly realized that he just did not care anymore if it was the right thing to do or not, or even if he would screw it up. "Ah, forget it!" He tossed the towel over his shoulder and moved in for the kiss, thrusting his lips to hers. Cleo wrapped her arms around his neck and pressed against him eagerly. If he had thought it was not a good idea to kiss her before, that notion had flown right out the window, along with his self-control. It was beyond anything that he had ever imagined it would be to kiss her.

Nelson felt an immediate rush, like warm liquid flooding through his insides. While he was perfectly aware of Cleo and sincerely hoping that she was enjoying it as much as he was, for a moment he forgot himself and was overcome by his desire. He pictured all of his neurons firing at once, his brain racing as everything around him dissolved away, and he was conscious only of how soft her lips were, how warm her mouth was. It was a marvelous, euphoric sensory overload. He drew her closer, pressing his body to hers.

"Wow," he whispered against her ear. After a brief respite, he said, "Cleo, I really like you."

"I like you too," Cleo said with her eyes half hooded and a slight smile on her blushing lips.

"You do?"

She gave a breathless little laugh, which Nelson found very pleasant. "You couldn't tell?"

"I don't know. I guess I thought you felt sorry for me," he admitted.

"Nelson, why do you think I came around? Why do you think I asked you to the dance?" She had pulled back slightly so that she could look into his eyes, but their faces remained only inches apart.

"You were trying to be nice?" Nelson replied.

"I'm not that nice," she said. And she kissed him again. He cradled the back of her head within the cup of his fingers, pulling her closer instinctively. And he thought he would never let her go, it was too good to be true, that she was here with him, that she wanted him. He wondered happily what he had done to deserve it. Perhaps he didn't deserve it. He didn't care. As long as he had this moment, he didn't care.

Nelson scrutinized Harry, the old man with the lifeless eyes who was contentedly whittling away at a small wooden figurine. He sat quietly in a chair that had been offered him in the front room of Harry's double-wide trailer. They were humble surroundings compared to the fine home Harry had once owned, but immaculate nonetheless. Nelson figured that Harry had to keep everything in its proper place in order to find his way around. A blind man could not afford to leave things lying about; it would make it difficult to navigate through rooms without injury.

"How do you do that without seeing it?"

Harry shrugged as he swiped the blade across the wood. "I get a picture of it in my mind's eye, of what I want it to turn out like."

Nelson observed with some reverence the perfect detail of the collie, with its full puff of a mane surrounding its intelligent-looking eyes and perky triangular ears. The dog figurine was standing at attention with its paws drawn up close together, its bushy tail resting along the back of its hind legs. "Very impressive collie," Nelson complimented.

Harry chuckled. "That just goes to show you that things don't always turn out the way we pictured them."

"I don't understand," Nelson replied.

"I was certain I was working on a lion," Harry jested, laying the wooden figure and the knife on a TV tray stand next to his chair.

Nelson drew his eyebrows together, puzzled over Harry Fletcher the man. It was quiet for a moment before Nelson spoke. "Mr. Fletcher, you haven't been totally honest with me," he accused, pulling no punches.

Harry shifted ever so slightly, inclining his head to one side, admitting nothing. "How's that?" he asked quietly.

"You knew that Christy wasn't your daughter, didn't you?"

An uncomfortable silence filled the room as Nelson gauged the reaction on Harry's face. The man shuddered and cringed, his brow wrinkling as if he were deeply pained. He opened his mouth as if he might speak, but could not. Nelson felt a genuine sense of compassion spread through him, watching the broken old man before him. He imagined Harry as young, successful, with a nice home and the respect of his community. In one decisive blow, that had all been stripped from him. Now that Nelson had come to the conclusion that Harry was innocent of the crime for which he had been imprisoned, he couldn't help but feel sorry for the man.

Through his quest for the truth, he had come to realize that Harry had a deep affection and devotion for his only daughter. It had become abundantly clear that all of Harry's reasons for not defending his own innocence up to this point had been out of concern for Christy. The question that had plagued Nelson from the beginning—why Harry had silently suffered—had finally been answered. Now the dark secret had surfaced, and Harry was facing it full on after all the deteriorating years had seemingly rotted his secret away. But no matter how deeply a secret might be buried, there are always traces left behind for the diligent who hunt them, much like the bones of a mammoth dinosaur, hidden for hundreds of thousands of years, unearthed by the earnest seeker armed with shovel and brush.

Harry finally found his voice. "How did you know?"

"Your sister," Nelson informed him quietly.

"Dinah?" Harry was legitimately perplexed. "She didn't know."

"She said that you had a severe case of the mumps when you were young. In some cases, mumps can cause sterility," Nelson explained.

"That's right. Not many people know that," he confirmed with a frown and a nod of his head. "I didn't even know it myself for a long time."

"Something else, something you probably didn't realize yourself until Christy was diagnosed with Huntington's disease."

"Yes, there was that, too."

"A genetically inherited disease that didn't run in your family line. The carrier, someone who ends up suffering from the disease themselves, has a fifty percent chance of passing it on, and I did a little looking around and found out Caroline's family line had no traces of it either. One of Christy's parents had to have passed it along to her, and it wasn't you, and it wasn't Caroline. It was her father, her real father."

"No one else has put that together." Harry shrugged. "Maybe they just didn't want to."

"The thing is, I couldn't figure out why you did what you did. Why you rotted in prison for all those years when you knew you hadn't done it. I figured that you were protecting someone, but why? That's when it came to me. You were protecting Christy."

"Sweet Christy," Harry said. "She was such a good girl. She was always so eager to please others, to make everyone happy. I wanted to protect her, but it ended up hurting her more than anything."

"It doesn't make sense, Mr. Fletcher. It seems like she lost her father anyway. I mean, you weren't exactly there to raise her if you were in prison."

"If they had discovered the truth, they would have taken her away. I had no legal right to her. At least going to prison meant that I knew where she would be, who would be caring for her. I knew she would be loved and that she would still believe I was her father, that she would feel some sense of belonging. That meant more to me than my freedom, knowing where she was and how she was being treated." He looked utterly defeated in that moment. "It didn't start out as me being the martyr."

"What do you mean, Mr. Fletcher?"

"I knew I was innocent. I had no doubt that I could prove it. In the beginning, I kept silent because I thought it would never be relevant, that it would never need to come out. But when it came down to it, when they said that terrible word—guilty—that's when

I had to make some tough decisions. I didn't want to be accountable for a murder I didn't commit. Although I loved Caroline, in some terrible way it was a relief that she was gone. I suppose I shouldn't admit that, but we had a difficult relationship, she and I. The only problem is, Christy was the one who suffered. She was too young to understand most of what was going on. All she knew was that she had lost her mother. I'm sure Caroline loved her in her own way, but she never showed it. Poor Christy spent the rest of her life wondering, 'Why was my mother taken from me? Why didn't she love me?' When someone is dead, it's awfully hard to make your peace with them. She had such a sad and difficult life. The only solace I have these days is knowing that she is at peace now."

"They put you in prison. You could have continued to fight for your freedom, but you didn't."

"She had lost her mother. Would it have been better if I had told the truth and she had lost a father too? The only thing I had to look forward to at that point was her monthly visits with my sister. That's all I had. I had kept my mouth shut up to that point, and I figured it was worth paying for a crime I hadn't committed to keep her safe, to keep her mine."

"But you missed out on so much. You missed out on seeing her grow up, on being there for her. I mean, do you think it was worth all of that?"

"I paid the price. We all did. Should I have told the truth? I don't know. I don't know that it would have made a difference. Just the fact alone that Caroline had an affair was no proof that I was not the man that murdered her. I could have ended up still in prison and without my daughter. Christy wouldn't have had a father, and what fate would have awaited her then? I really felt that they wouldn't have let her stay with me. What if I had cleared my name, exonerated and let out of prison? Even if I had told the truth, what would have happened to her? I just didn't feel that the gamble was worth it."

"Whose was she?"

"I don't know." He waited a long while before he continued. "I never knew. As far as I knew, she was mine because I loved her. Just an innocent baby that needed a father, a baby that never did a thing to deserve *not* to be loved. Why should she be responsible for the mistakes we had made? For the fools we became? When you're young, you don't understand that the things you do, all of them, have consequences, sometimes more serious than we have the ability to understand in our limited experiences, in our impetuous stupidity."

"Is that why you waited to clear your name? You waited until Christy wouldn't find out the truth, couldn't find out the truth? She wouldn't find out you weren't really her father?"

Harry's voice broke as he said, "But I *was* her father."

"You didn't want her to find out she wasn't really your daughter. You didn't want her to believe that she wasn't yours biologically."

"She was my daughter. I raised her. I cared for her. I was there for her, and I loved her."

"Caroline was pregnant with another child when she was murdered. Did you know about that as well?"

"Not until after she was dead. She never told me," Harry insisted. "It came out with the autopsy."

"Do you know who the father of that child was?" Nelson pressed.

Harry dropped his head and shook it dejectedly back and forth to indicate he did not. Nelson knew that he was telling the truth, he could sense it. For the first time it all made sense, he understood why Harry had waited for so long to be cleared. He waited for a moment before he proceeded, worrying about how he was affecting Harry Fletcher, wondering if he should let it go at that. He didn't want to appear disrespectful or impolite, but he had to know. This might be the break he had been looking for.

"Did Caroline know that Christy was not yours?"

"I'll never know," Harry murmured dejectedly. "So many mistakes, so many senseless mistakes. 'Pride cometh before the downfall,'" he quoted. "I should have cherished her. I should have told her every day that I loved her. I should never have taken her for granted. But then Christy came from all of this idiocy. That's the only good thing that came from the two of us messing up so badly." A tear coursed down the deep wrinkles that furrowed his face. Nelson thought he looked a hundred years old, worn out, marked by the cares of the world. "Look at me and learn, son. Look at me and decide that this will never be you. Learn from my thoughtless mistakes and be better for it."

Nelson ignored his solemn words of warning and pressed on. "Mr. Fletcher, did anyone else know about Christy? Did anyone else discover that she was not your daughter?"

"Only one person I ever discussed it with. Only one person I ever trusted it with."

"Who was it?" Nelson pushed.

"Chuck Donner. I wouldn't have told him, either, only Christy, she didn't exactly look like me. Didn't look like Caroline either. Chuck was messing around one day and said that he knew Christy wasn't mine. I didn't think he was kidding. He seemed serious enough. I asked him how he knew, how he had discovered the truth. He was shocked, couldn't believe it. Well, the cat was out of the bag so I admitted to him that I couldn't have children. He was a true friend and kept that secret till the day he died. No one else ever knew that Christy was not my child."

"Chuck Donner?" Nelson repeated, somewhat surprised.

"That's right," he said.

"Look, Mr. Fletcher, I'm doing my best to figure this out," he told Harry. "But you've gotta help me out."

"I didn't think that it had any relevance to what you were doing," Harry said defensively. "I'm sure you can appreciate how sensitive the information you possess is. It is something I was willing to go to prison for, to protect it."

"Yes, sir. I keep all of my clients' information completely confidential," he assured, with a twinge of guilt because he knew that he would be sharing all of this conversation with Cleo.

"I certainly would appreciate that."

"Now tell me, Mr. Fletcher, is there anything else you're keeping from me?"

"Nothing."

"Mr. Fletcher?" Nelson began.

"Yes?"

"I know this probably isn't exactly relevant…But out of sheer curiosity, do you mind me asking you a personal question?"

"What is it?"

"How did you become blind?"

"We are all blind, son. One way or another, we are all blind," he said with a small smile. "But me, I met my fate in prison. Ironically, the very thing that kept me going all those years was the thing that took away my sight. It was working in the wood shop."

"The wood shop?" Nelson was stumped.

"I became a very competent carpenter. It passed the time. It was something I was very passionate about. Just four years left on my prison term and there was an accident. One of the chemicals we used in our woodworking—formaldehyde, to be specific. I was exposed to it. Blinded me. As you said, no relevance to the murder, though."

"There might be more than you think," Nelson confided.

"How's that?"

"To be honest, Mr. Fletcher, I don't think you would have ever hired me in the first place if you hadn't been blind."

"I don't understand."

"If you had seen me, sir, more than likely you wouldn't have thought me competent enough to take your case."

"How old are you, Nelson?" Harry asked. "It seems to me that my sister Dinah was somewhat concerned by your apparent inexperience."

"Is that what she said?"

"Well, no, she said something more to the effect that you were some kid that didn't know his rear end from a hole in the ground, wet behind the ears, something like that. But then, Dinah's always been a bit on the dramatic side."

"I'm eighteen, sir," Nelson told him.

"Maybe you were right after all," Harry replied with a hint of a grin.

"About what?"

"If I had seen how young you were, I may not have hired you. But you haven't given me a reason to fire you yet, so I think I'll just take my chances and stick with you."

"I appreciate that, Mr. Fletcher," Nelson said. "Your confidence means a great deal."

"Has nothing to do with confidence," Harry joked. "You're still the cheapest PI in the yellow pages."

Nelson smiled. "There's that too," he agreed.

CHAPTER 17

"You again?" Marnie plaintively remarked when she saw Nelson come through the door.

"I brought a friend this time," Nelson said, motioning to Cleo. Since their kiss the other night, they had been joined at the hip. When she wasn't at school, she was with him. "This is Cleo."

"Hello, Mrs. Donner," Cleo said, extending her hand. Marnie was sizing Cleo up as they shook hands. Her eyes seemed large and a bit menacing behind her bifocals as they wandered over Cleo from top to bottom.

"Well, this is more traffic in here than I've had in the six years I've been here." She chuckled sarcastically.

"How have you been, Mrs. Donner?" Nelson asked politely.

"Cut the bull, kid. You didn't come to visit me, I'm sure," she said. "I'm not so senile as to believe that."

"I came because I have a few more questions for you," Nelson admitted. He caught Cleo looking at him in wide-eyed astonishment. She obviously wasn't expecting Marnie Donner to be such a feisty old bat.

"You bring your tape recorder so I can give you an earful?"

"I sure did," he replied, ignoring her obviously condescending tone. He pulled it from his pocket and placed it on the arm of his chair.

"So, what's the burning question this time?" Marnie asked, trying to appear as if she didn't care.

"Here's the thing, Marnie," Nelson began. "The last time I spoke with you, you said that Caroline told you about a baby. She told you not to tell anyone, especially Harry."

"That what I told you?"

"Yes, ma'am, that's what you told me," Nelson affirmed.

"So, what's your point?"

"Did you tell anybody else?" Nelson asked.

"Didn't have to. It all came out after she died. It wasn't exactly a secret anymore," she said. "It was on the news, it was in the papers, it was the thing everyone was talking about. So much for secrets, huh?"

"Yes, I understand that, but did you tell anyone *before* she died?" Nelson stressed.

"No," Marnie said simply. "She told me the day before she died."

"Mrs. Donner, you didn't tell your husband, Chuck?" Cleo interrupted. Marnie again looked Cleo over with a hard squint, but she didn't reply. "It's just that some women aren't very good at keeping secrets," Cleo went on. "They have a hard time not telling *someone*. And I would think, you being married, that it would likely be your husband you would have confided in. I mean, you couldn't tell Caroline, your best friend, because she was the one that told you in the first place, so the only other person you would have turned to would have been Chuck. Am I right?"

Marnie half smiled. "Smart girl. I wish I had been so savvy at your age, could have saved myself a lot of grief," she mused.

"Mrs. Donner, did you tell your husband about Caroline?" Nelson coaxed.

She pursed her lips, as if she might not speak, and then she said, "What are you trying to get at?"

Nelson drew his eye brows together. "I just want to know if you told your husband about Caroline's pregnancy," Nelson clarified. "Did you tell Chuck?" he asked again, emphasizing each word.

Marnie seemed torn. She answered quietly, "Yes, I did."

"What was Chuck's reaction? Did he tell you something in return?" Nelson continued.

Her expression did not change. She said stoically, "Yes, he did."

"Was it about Caroline's baby? Did he tell you something about Caroline's baby?"

"Yes," she said simply.

He could see that he was going to have to drag it out of her. "What did he tell you?"

"That Caroline's baby was his baby."

The room grew silent but for the sound of people in the courtyard just beyond the window. Cleo and Nelson looked at one another in shock. It wasn't exactly what they had thought might come out of their meeting with Marnie Donner. Nelson had supposed that Chuck had told Marnie the truth about Harry being unable to have children and that Marnie may have passed that information on to someone else. He had never expected to find out that Chuck had a deep, dark secret of his own.

"I'm sorry, what did you say?" Nelson questioned.

She looked him square in the eye. "You heard me," she replied, and there was something like relief that passed over her.

"Could you expound?" he requested. She did not readily react.

Cleo saw the elderly woman's weakness, saw that she had carried this heavy burden for many years. She exploited it. "Mrs. Donner, please. This has been a lie you've had to live with for so long. Please, just tell us what really happened...the truth. Think of Harry Fletcher and what he's had to endure for the past forty-five years."

"I don't give a flying fig about Harry Fletcher. He was too stupid to get out while he could. He looked the other way, knowing full well what she was. If he had been home taking care of business like he should have been, none of this would have happened!" she cried.

Cleo thought for a moment and then said gently, "Do it for yourself, then. Tell the truth for you."

Nelson thought that it hadn't worked, that Cleo hadn't been convincing enough. The old woman sat positively rigid in her chair, her lips pressed together in a hard line. Surely she had given them more information than she had intended, and now she was going to ask them to leave. But he was wrong; Marnie opened her mouth to speak.

"We went home that night," she began. "And it was hard for me not to say anything, but I didn't. Not right away. But she just wouldn't grow up. And it bothered me. It bothered me how she was playing Harry for the fool. I can't say that I was close to him, but just the thought of her keeping her pregnancy from him. Well…I thought it was a sin!

"You're right, young lady. I couldn't keep it to myself. I shouldn't have, I know that now, but I told Chuck what Caroline had said, that she wanted to go to California, that she wanted a divorce, that she was pregnant and hadn't told Harry. I told him I didn't know what she had in her head, but I thought she was certifiable." She laughed, but it was more of a grunt. "Chuck looked like he might throw up. He was shaken, deathly white, very upset."

"And then…" Cleo prompted.

"He wanted to know how far along she was, so I told him. Three months, I said."

"And he said…" Nelson added.

"He said he had something he needed to tell me," she went on. "I could see that it was bad. I said, 'Chuck, what is it?'" She looked as if she were speaking to him and not to Nelson and Cleo. "Funny thing is I told him it couldn't be that bad, nothing could be that bad. That's when he said that it wasn't Harry's baby. Now, that wasn't so unbelievable because I knew she could be a real vamp. I didn't like to admit it, but it was true. I was different back then. I tried to overlook a lot of things that you didn't talk about in polite society. So, I said to him, 'That isn't exactly the bombshell you made it out to be.' But then he said that it was his." She spoke with a total lack of feeling as she sat there rather dejectedly.

"Did you know or suspect anything up to that point?" Nelson asked.

"No," she confessed. "I thought he hated Caroline. And she was my best friend. Why would she betray me like that?" Marnie said, most likely asking the question of herself. "I didn't blame him as much as I blamed her. Out of the two of them, I knew who the pursuer was. I have no doubt she instigated it. And who was Chuck to resist her charms?"

"What happened after he told you?" Nelson persisted.

"We fought." She got a little emotional. "I told him that I hated him, that I wanted him out, that I never wanted to see him again." She dropped her gaze to the speckled teal and tan flooring. "My heart was completely broken. I've never felt so betrayed…so…I don't know. At that point, I left. I just stormed out. I left him there."

"Where did you go? Did you go back to the Fletcher home?"

"You're a stupid boy!" she cried. "Do you think I wanted to see her? Do you think I wanted anything to do with her? There I was in her home, a guest, supposed to be her friend, and she knew all the while that she was carrying on with my husband. *My* husband! I'll tell you right now I was the only one in town that stuck up for her, that treated her good, that…that stood by her, *and she would do that to me?*" Marnie hissed between clenched teeth.

"Where did you go then, Mrs. Donner?" Nelson asked.

"I drove around. I tried to calm myself," she told them. "I tried to think things through, to put my head right, to figure out what I should do."

"What about Chuck?" Cleo questioned.

"What about him?" Marnie said, growing instantly defensive.

"Do you know where Chuck was while you were out driving around?" Cleo asked, a hint of an accusation in her voice.

"I don't like what you're implying," Marnie said. She drew herself up a little taller in her chair and gave Cleo a side long glare.

"Mrs. Donner, if you weren't there that night, if you can't vouch for the whereabouts of your husband, then you can't say definitively that he did not go back to the Fletcher home and kill Caroline," Nelson explained.

"Chuck didn't kill anybody," Marnie said firmly.

"How do you know for certain?" Nelson inquired.

"He didn't kill anybody!" She was shaking now, raging at the two who sat across from her. "You didn't know him! I knew him. And I know he didn't kill her! I know! Do you have any idea how he fretted, how he worried over why Harry killed Caroline? He was afraid that Harry had discovered Caroline's pregnancy and that that's why he killed her. Nearly ate him alive that he thought he might be the cause of it."

"Mrs. Donner, did Chuck smoke?" Nelson asked.

"I don't see what that has to do with anything."

"I'd like to know if Chuck was a smoker," Nelson continued. "I already know that Chuck died from emphysema. Was it because he smoked?"

"I want you to leave," Marnie spat. "I want you to leave now!" She picked up her pager and pushed the button forcefully with her thumb. "I don't like what you're saying, what you're thinking. Chuck *didn't* do it. He couldn't have!"

"Mrs. Donner, Harry Fletcher served thirty years in prison for a crime he did not commit. He wants answers. Frankly, he deserves answers," Nelson said in a firm tone. "You may be the only one who can give that to him."

"I said I want you out!" she growled, her thumb continuing to press down on the button in a death grip.

"Chuck is dead and gone. Harry is still alive. Don't you think he should be able to finally know the truth?" Nelson continued. Cleo was tugging at his arm, trying to get him to go, but he resisted.

"Nelson, we should leave. She wants us to leave…"

"An innocent man wasted half his life rotting in prison for something he didn't do. Don't you feel the least bit sorry for him?" Nelson was raising his voice frantically.

A nurse appeared in the doorway, alarmed and on the defense. "Mrs. Donner?"

"No, I don't feel sorry for him. I don't feel sorry for her. They both got what they deserved!" Marnie was yelling. "What they deserved!"

"What seems to be the trouble here?" the nurse asked authoritatively. "Mrs. Donner, are they bothering you?"

"I want them out!" Marnie shouted.

The nurse took a step toward Nelson and Cleo with an angry look on her face. She was a large woman with an imposing presence, a woman who could take care of business if need be. Cleo shrank toward Nelson, her adrenaline pumping. "What's going on here?" she bellowed at them.

"Nothing," Nelson lied. "We were just leaving." He leaned over to grab his recorder, but Marnie made a lunge for it as well. She got a hold on it and pulled it to her chest, gripping it fiercely.

"I need my recorder," Nelson demanded as he tried to pry it from her grasp.

"No!" Marnie screamed. "You can't have it!" She tried to elude him as they struggled over it.

The nurse shot forward and tried to pull Nelson away, wrapping her arms around his waist. She planted her feet, and the tug of war ensued. The nurse was shrieking, "Security! Security! Somebody call security!" as she wrenched at Nelson's lean waistline.

Marnie bent over and sunk her teeth into Nelson's hand. Although he cried out, he would not lose his grip on his digital recorder in a bizarre sort of stalemate. Cleo watched the chaos from just behind the nurse. She was confused as to what she should do, but then the thought of being arrested propelled her to action. She dodged past the grappling bodies and pried the recorder from Marnie's hand. Then she took off at a sprint out the door and down the hall, shrieking over her shoulder, "Nelson, run!" as she made her escape.

The nurse let go of Nelson, confused as to whether she should detain him or pursue Cleo. Nelson took the opportunity to make his exit as well. He dashed past the nurse, hot on the heels of Cleo. They jumped into his truck in tandem, with all speed, and peeled out of the parking lot before anyone could stop them.

"Do you think Chuck did it?" Cleo burst out in between her heavy panting.

"He would have had motive. But so would Marnie. She didn't have an alibi," Nelson pointed out. "She said she drove around all night. And for either of them, it would absolutely have been a crime of passion."

"Nelson, two people could have easily done it. Think about it for a minute. What if they both went back to the Fletcher house together? Or what if Marnie left in a rage, went to confront Caroline, and Chuck came after her? Chuck walks in, sees what Marnie has done, and helps her cover it up. Chuck could have easily left the foot print, and he could have hit Harry over the head. It all fits."

"It doesn't matter. We've got no proof, only speculation," Nelson pointed out. "We have to find something solid, something that would leave no doubt. Right now all we've got is a woman who could have but maybe didn't do it."

"She was sure acting guilty," Cleo complained. "I mean, she completely flipped out, Nelson. Why else would she have behaved that way?"

"I don't know. Maybe she thought Chuck had done it and was covering for him. Or, like you said, she did it. It doesn't matter. We're still in the same boat. I need to review the evidence again."

When they had made it back to Nelson's apartment, Cleo carefully bandaged Nelson's hand and gave it a sentimental peck with her lips. "She got you pretty good, you poor thing," Cleo remarked as she snuggled in close to him.

"To be honest, I'm completely surprised that her dentures aren't still buried in there somewhere," Nelson replied, inspecting his hand as if he were looking for them still.

Cleo giggled. "You're so full of it, Nelson."

"I'm serious," he insisted. "Why do women always seem to resort to biting?"

"I don't bite," Cleo taunted. "Not hard, anyway." She gave him a challenging glance with her eyebrow raised. Nelson laughed, using his arm around her shoulder to draw her near so that he could give her a kiss.

"It's a good thing you were there with me," he said as he gave her another kiss. "You saved the day."

"Oh, Nelson, that's so sweet. Are you saying you need me?" she continued to jest.

"I wouldn't say *need*."

Cleo gave him a little slap on the back of the head. "Watch it," she warned.

"Cleo?" Nelson grew serious.

"Huh?"

He waited until he had her full attention and she was meeting his gaze and not staring fixedly at his lips. "Why are you hanging around with a guy like me?"

"I don't know…You're different, you know." She turned her concentration back to his hand and her bandaging job. "It's like you can't be anybody but you. Like you can't deceive people about the kind of person you really are. You're true, no crap." She met his eyes again. "You're a good person, Nelson. But it goes beyond that…You're smart, and crazy serious, but then you can say some really funny thing out of nowhere, and well…I don't know how exactly to put it into words, but I just feel good when I'm around you."

"You really think that?"

"Yeah, I do." She put a hand on each of his cheeks and kissed him with a broad grin. "So, why do you like me?" she challenged.

"I…I don't know. I just do," he said with a shrug.

A hint of a troubled expression played on Cleo's face, but he seemed oblivious to it. "But why?"

"You kick butt with old women and hefty nurses," he teased.

This was not the answer she had wanted. She pulled away from him and went to grab her purse on the chair close to the door. Cleo slipped the strap over her head so that it crossed over her torso, pulling her hair out from under the strap and letting it fall free. She looked like she might cry or scream, one or the other.

"I gotta go. I have a paper due tomorrow that I need to finish," she said.

"Why don't you work on it here?" Nelson offered. "You could use my computer if you wanted."

"No, I don't think that's such a good idea. My mom'll be home soon, and I should be there when she comes."

"Okay, I'll see you tomorrow, then."

"Yeah, maybe," Cleo said as she opened the door and headed down the hall.

"Bye," he blurted after her.

She didn't turn around when she told him, "Bye," over her shoulder. Nelson felt completely confused by the turn of events. One moment, they had been playfully messing around, and the next, she was abruptly out the door. He wondered if Cleo was upset about something, but he couldn't figure what it might be. Eventually, he let it go. After all, she had told him she needed to do her homework, and there was no reason to believe otherwise.

CHAPTER 18

Caroline pulled at the cuff of her short white glove, nervous at the prospect of someone overhearing her conversation with the bank teller. What she was doing here was no one else's business, she thought defiantly. But it was taking every bit of her effort to appear unaffected by his words.

"I can certainly get you the money, Mrs. Fletcher. Only it will take some time. We'll have to move some things around."

"How's that?" she asked, an edge to her voice.

"Well, Mr. Fletcher has wisely put the bulk of your savings into investments, stocks and bonds, life insurance…and then there's the retirement fund, a savings account for young Christy. By the time she heads off for college, it will all be paid for." The man was smiling generously, unnerving Caroline. She grew agitated at his polite veneer.

"We've been banking here for years. You're trying to tell me we don't have any money?"

"That's not what I'm saying at all, ma'am. You have plenty of money, but at your husband's discretion, much of your savings has been put elsewhere. It's simply not readily available for withdrawal, you see?"

"Then, where is it?"

"Well, it's invested, you see."

She smiled sweetly. "There must be some way to access it…" She batted her lashes for that extra touch.

The man grew uncomfortable. "Yes, of course. It would need to be arranged, but absolutely, it is, after all, your money."

"Yes, my money. All right, let's do that. Let's arrange for it."

"I would be glad to help with that. We just need Mr. Fletcher to sign a few items so it can be made available."

"But I am his wife. Why can't I do it?" Her mood quickly changed when she didn't get her way. She was nearly pouting.

The teller was downright flustered, possibly afraid of upsetting Caroline with his refusal, but unsure of what else to do under the circumstances. "You can. But we also need Mr. Fletcher. He is the one who signed the paperwork in order to open the various accounts."

"How long would it take to become 'available'? How long would I have to wait?" Caroline barked.

"I couldn't say. It all depends on what Mr. Fletcher decides to do. If you would like to have Mr. Fletcher come in and make arrangements, we would be more than willing to accommodate you."

Caroline shifted gears. "How much?" she asked with a toss of her head and a reserved lift of her eyebrow, physically demonstrating her superiority over him.

"Pardon, ma'am?" he asked, confused.

"How much is available?" she clarified.

"You have roughly five hundred and twenty-seven dollars and thirty-nine cents available for withdrawal," he informed her.

"Fine. I'll take that," she said with a look that dared him to defy her. She waited for him to dole the fresh bills, stacking them in bundles of hundred dollar increments, his monotone voice counting it out as he went. When he was finished, she gathered it all up and slipped it into her patent leather purse.

"Can I help you with anything else, Mrs. Fletcher?" he asked politely.

"You've done quite enough, thank you," she told him, unable to keep a hint of sarcasm from her voice. She snapped her purse shut and walked away, keeping her back as straight as was humanly possible.

Five hundred and twenty-seven dollars and thirty-nine cents was not going to stretch far enough. She knew that. She felt like seeking Harry out and giving him a piece of her mind. But then he would know what she was up to if she did that. She pushed her way out the double doors and headed down the sidewalk, seething inside. "You've managed to spoil everything again, Harry," she said under her breath.

Chuck saw her from the window of the deli. She was wearing a cream colored suit and black pumps, moving her lips ever so slightly as she talked to herself. He hastily dropped his sandwich, wiping his hands on the front of his coveralls as he headed for the door. He burst out just as she had passed.

"Caroline!" he hissed, trying to keep his voice low enough for only her to hear as he trotted after her.

She absent-mindedly slowed to a stop and turned around to see who was calling after her. She saw it was Chuck and attempted to push her ill mood aside with a beguiling smile. "Chuck, how nice to run into you like this," she purred.

He glanced around casually, taking note of who was about. "You got a second?"

"I don't know. I was on my way over to Woolworth's to pick up a few things," she said, making him squirm a little. If Caroline Fletcher had a gift, it was for playing hard to get, teasing, tormenting.

"Fine, then, I'm not gonna beg," he said indifferently.

"But for you, I'll put off Woolworth's," she said, giving in without being persuaded. "My car is parked just over there." She pointed her gloved finger to the black Cadillac waiting next to the curb. He followed her in a slight jog across the street, climbing into the passenger side of the car, watching as she turned the keys in the ignition and pulled into traffic. The two of them did not realize, as they left together, that Dinah Gert was watching from the post office parking lot, wondering what they might be up to.

"Where did you want to go?" she questioned.

"I don't care. Any place quiet," he said, keeping his eyes carefully watching out the passenger side window.

She pulled onto the two-lane highway, driving for a few miles outside of town before making a turn off onto a dusty lane that lead to the reservoir. It being fall in the middle of a weekday, no one was there. Caroline parked the car just beneath an ancient oak tree, letting the engine idle. She sat there, her gloved hands clasped tightly on the steering wheel, watching the sun reflecting and playing across the water.

"Won't they miss you at work?" she asked, her words void of any kind of emotion.

"I'm on lunch break," he said, turning his body toward her. "You got a cigarette?"

"You know I don't smoke." Her voice was reproachful, critical.

"Yeah, I guess I did know that."

"So, what is it you wanted, Chuck?" She knew very well how to play this game, and she didn't have the time for it today.

"What is it I want? Do I have to want anything? Isn't it enough to be in your fine company?" he taunted.

"Someone isn't in a good mood," she replied, chortling.

"Do you want her to find out? Is that why you behave the way you do?" The accusation had been dripping with hostility, but Caroline didn't let it affect her.

"It's been going on and off for nearly a year now, Chuck. She hasn't suspected anything yet, has she? And she won't."

"How do you know that?"

"Oh, Chuck, are you so blind?" Caroline challenged. "She thinks the sun rises and the moon sets by you. She doesn't think you're capable of betraying her, stupid girl. If you weren't such a bonehead, you'd understand that."

"Don't talk about Marnie that way," he defended.

"What's gotten in to you, Chuck?"

It amazed him that she could be so cool, so emotionless, especially since she had riled him so thoroughly. He could hardly keep his temper in check. There was something about her control over him that made her all the more attractive. She was an exciting, intoxicating creature. He had identified that as the reason he had always been drawn to her, jealous when she turned her flirting to other men.

"I'm tired," he admitted. "I can't keep it up anymore. I just want out." He was suddenly weary, his expression haggard.

"Is that really what you want?"

"That's what I said."

"I don't believe it, though."

"I can't keep lying to her." He was fervent, almost sad as he continued. "She's a good, loyal, kind woman. I never should have turned my eye from her."

"A good, loyal, kind woman that just so happens to be simple, gullible, and just plain boring," Caroline observed.

"That's not true!"

"Why do you think you turned your eye from her in the first place? It was all just a little too predictable, wasn't it, Chuck? She wasn't interesting anymore, was she? Too tame for your blood."

"Not true..." He shook his head adamantly, rage in his voice.

"She doesn't have what it takes, Chuck. She doesn't have what you need. You'll never be happy with her because she doesn't understand what you want. That's the truth."

"Don't talk about her that way! Don't!"

Inside, she was frightened. Inside, she could see she was pushing her limits. But she didn't want him to see that she was affected by his temper flair. He was so easy to control, despite his manly act, but when he grew too hot, she feared what it might be like if he boiled over. Caroline kept her demeanor calm.

"You need me. I'm something you can never give up, a compulsion you just can't seem to put aside."

"I love my wife! I love my son! You want to take that away from me!" he declared. "You won't be happy until you destroy me! Isn't that what you want, to destroy me?"

She winced a little as he barked at her, his voice rising to a fevered pitch. "What do you want, then? You want to end it, finish it here and now? Is that what you wanted to talk about?"

"Yes, that's what I want. I want to tell her what I've done."

"You would if you were man enough." It was barely audible, but it was enough to send him through the roof. He raised his hand as if he would strike her. Struggling to gain control of himself, he drew in a sharp breath and let his hand fall without incident to his side. Chuck had many faults, but he had never struck a woman, and it was something he didn't want to add to his list. He turned away from her, as if the sight of her would induce him to change his mind.

"If that's what you want, Chuck. I don't need you like you need me. If you want to come clean to Marnie, you go right ahead. Only don't come begging to have me back again, like the last time, when she puts you away."

"Caroline, I..."

"You what?" she challenged. "I'll try to forget everything you've just said, because I know that when you think it over, you'll change your mind. You'll realize what a mistake you've made, and you'll change your mind."

"One of these days you'll go too far, Caroline," he grunted back.

She pulled the gear shift to drive as she replied tritely, "Yes, one of these days. But today is not that day." The car kicked up dust as she followed the dirt road back to the main highway, headed toward town again.

CHAPTER 19

Nelson knew without having to be told that there was something amiss. It was easier to pretend that he didn't know, that by ignoring the obvious it might fade away, and he wouldn't be confronted with it. Cleo had always quite openly told him what she had on her mind before. Why should now be any different? But she was quiet and aloof when he came to pick her up for school the next morning.

"My mom can take me," she told him through the door. "You don't have to."

"I don't mind," he told her with a silly grin spread across his face.

"That's nice of you, but my mom's leaving for work, and I told her I'd drive with her today."

"Well, okay, but I can pick you up if you want," he offered.

She hesitated. "I guess."

He spent the remainder of the day burning time. He felt the clock had never moved so slowly. He attempted to fill it with mundane tasks — laundry, buying groceries, cleaning out what little there was in the fridge. He had it in his mind to make a nice dinner for Cleo, something he rarely did. There was really no point in cooking if you were just cooking for yourself. It struck him, in a moment of clarity, just how lonely his life had truly been since his grandpa had died. And yet, Nelson had never been one to need human companionship.

He had always been a loner, even from his early childhood, until Cleo had come along and filled that void.

He had attributed his lack of socialization to his mother, recalling how she had moved him around from one town to the next, making no ties, leaving no friends behind when they had moved on. For some reason he remembered her in a drunken stupor, lecturing him on trust. "Don't count on anyone, Conroy," she'd instructed with her slurred speech. "Nobody to trust but you. Nobody to count on like you can count on yourself." And then she had begun to cry. She didn't cry very often, but when she did it was loud sobbing that wracked her whole body, shook her frame as tears streamed down her face.

His grandpa had told him, when Nelson had come to live with him, that his mother was sick. This was not something that he understood, even with his accelerated intellect, at his young age. He had taken his grandpa's words for their literal meaning, not for the kind way his grandpa had devised for saying that his mother was mentally unstable. Nelson thought it must have hurt his grandpa a great deal to have his daughter, his only child, lose it like that.

When his grandpa had passed on, it was up to Nelson to clean out the house before it sold. He kept a few things, some photos, and some pieces of furniture. Of course he had kept the old truck and his grandpa's hunting rifles. The thing that really left an impression on him had been the box he had found in his grandpa's closet. He still was left to wonder if it had been his grandfather who had compiled the collection, or his grandma before she had died and left his grandpa alone.

Buried in the depths of that box was a mystery all its own. Yearbooks from high school; awards for swimming; photo albums of a smiling baby girl, a precocious toddler, a shy adolescent, a confident and beautiful teenager; a pair of roller skates; a high school and college diploma; a scrapbook with newspaper clippings from a variety of different places—Boston, New York, Los Angeles, Miami, Houston. He had been somewhat surprised that the articles were written by his mother; he'd had no idea that she had been a newspaper reporter, and a somewhat decent one, by the looks of it.

These manifestations had only confused him even more. The thought of his mother, a train wreck of a woman, living a normal life, being a contributing member of society, was too farfetched to believe. It frightened him. He wondered if the mental break down had been genetic, if he would, at some future date, suffer the same fate, crack like she did under the pressure. He felt all right. He felt stable. But looking at the photos, reading the articles penned by her hand, she had seemed just as sane. Eggs, even seemingly flawless ones, when held up to a light source, often revealed fine lines, a vein of fissures spread through the shell. Perhaps he was just as defective.

Now that his grandpa was gone, he couldn't discuss his concerns with anyone else. No one that would understand, anyway. Nelson thought that perhaps it had been giving birth to him that had put her over the edge. Maybe it had been he that had ruined his mother's life. She had waited to marry, older than some. She wasn't exactly a young girl when she'd had Nelson. But there were things he did not understand, chunks of the past that were still lingering in a gray area that had been off limits to him. His grandpa knew very little about his father, knew very little about the circumstances involving his parents' divorce, and subsequently his father's whereabouts once the divorce was through.

Nelson pondered these things as he set the coffee table for a dinner for two. He was salivating a little over the smell of roasting chicken and vegetables, slowly cooking in the oven. It would be easier to eat at the coffee table than to clear his computer and file folders, with a collection of loose papers, from the small table off of the kitchenette. That would take all day to do, he reasoned. He checked his wrist watch, calculating that he would have just enough time to run and pick up Cleo before the dinner in the oven would be ready to take out.

When he pulled into the parking lot and up to the curb, she was waiting there, her bag in her hand, watching as he came to a stop. She climbed in, her face purposefully blank. "Hey," she greeted him.

"Hey, how was your day?"

"Okay," she said.

"I hope you don't have plans for dinner," he told her.

"Why?"

"Because I was going to make dinner for you," he divulged.

"That's thoughtful, but I don't know if it would be a good idea."

"Don't worry," he teased. "I won't give you food poisoning or anything."

"That's not what I meant, Nelson."

"What did you mean?"

"I meant that I think we should take a break from one another," she said.

There was an awkward pause, and then he replied, "Oh, I see." How was it that last night she seemed totally in to him, and today she was telling him she needed space? Women made no sense, no sense at all.

She avoided his gaze, remorseful for what she was doing. "I don't know that we're really right for each other," she went on.

"Why not?"

She seemed to be searching for the right words. "Nelson, we are complete opposites, and, well, I just don't think it's going to work out. You know?"

"Did I do something?" he probed. "I mean, last night everything seemed fine. You were telling me why you liked me and now you're telling me you don't. I just don't get it."

"I don't think you care about me the way that I want to be cared for. You…you just don't need anybody, Nelson. You're kind of a loner, and I'm not made that way. I don't want to be the only one who really cares."

"I care," he said defensively.

"Look, I just don't want to get my heart broken. I don't want to fall in love with you and be the one all wrapped up in it, and then have you decide you don't feel the same." She paused. "Besides my mom thinks I need to concentrate on my final year in high school and my SATs and stuff. She's afraid I'm spending too much time with you. Maybe we should just take a break from one another for a while. See how it goes."

Nelson was a little stunned. He didn't know what to say or what to do. He tried to figure out a way to talk her out of it, but his brain felt empty. It was like a giant blank. She had apparently made up her mind, and he had no idea how to change it. "Okay, Cleo, if that's what you want," he murmured. "I guess I can't say anything that'll make you feel any differently."

Like most men, Nelson didn't realize that he could say something that *would* make her feel differently. He dropped her off at her door and then went back to his own apartment alone. When he walked in, the smell of roasting chicken invaded his nose, making his mouth water. He pulled the roasting pan from the oven and helped himself to a portion, using only one of the place settings at the coffee table he had set for two. He eyed the other place setting and then pushed it off of the edge, where it clattered on the floor. For the first time in weeks, he was utterly alone again. He reasoned that he had been used to it. Solitude had been his way of living for many years. So, why did it bother him so much? It was then that he realized that before Cleo, he had never known what he was missing. He never knew how good it was to be with someone, to carry on a conversation, to touch and be touched. He figured that it must be what a recovering alcoholic feels when they know the taste of booze. How they must crave it, but can't have it. How the memory of it must torment and canker.

Now that he was alone, he began to think of things he should have said to her. It seemed funny that, just a short while before, he couldn't think of a single thing to say, and now his head was full of all of the reasons she was making a mistake. He entertained the thought of going to her door and knocking and telling her that he was sorry for whatever he had done. He would explain that he was not very good at reading people. If he had only known what she was feeling, he would try to make it right. He would try to fix it.

He picked up his cell and began to write a lengthy text message.

I thought your eyes would be that one thing about you, then I remembered your lips. Not what you would think…I mean you're a good kisser, but you always know what to say too. Then there's your hands. Or maybe it's your skin. It's like ivory. Certainly it has to be part of your beauty. But then I thought of your patience—the one thing I should love more than anything because, for a brief moment, you put up with me when no one else ever has.

His finger hovered over the send button for a moment, and then he realized how stupid and desperate he must sound, and he quickly deleted it. One thing was certain: Cleo deserved something much better than him, not some loser who clung desperately to her after she had dumped him.

CHAPTER 20

Dennis was cleaning his paint brushes in the kitchen sink when Caroline Fletcher breezed in, wearing a pale yellow sun dress and red high heels. Her large, loose curls were pinned up in a bun, creating a soft halo of hair atop her head. Dennis thought her smile was nice, her teeth white and even.

"You're finished?" she asked him.

"Yeah, I got the bedrooms done," he told her.

"You'll be back Monday to start on the living room?"

"Yes, ma'am," he affirmed, bending down to put his brushes in the bucket he had the rest of his work gear in.

"Would you like a lemonade, Dennis?" she offered.

He stood up to his full height, rubbing his hands nervously on his pants. "That would be real nice, Mrs. Fletcher."

"Why don't you sit down and let me get that for you," she said.

"All right," he agreed, ambling over to the kitchen table and taking a seat. He watched her as she pulled a pitcher from the refrigerator. The lemonade was nearly the shade of her dress. She poured it slowly into a tall glass, then turned to him with a smile, brushing her hand against his as she handed it to him.

"How's that?" she asked as she watched him drink.

"That sure hits the spot, ma'am," he said, wiping his mouth with the back of his hand.

"You know, Dennis, you and I are a lot alike," she said.

"How's that, ma'am?"

"What's all this 'ma'am' business? Just call me Caroline, will you?" With a satisfaction that was hard to conceal, she noticed Dennis look away. "Let me hear you say it."

"Yes...Caroline," he obliged.

"That's better," she said with a provocative smile. "What I was trying to say is that I know what you're going through."

"You do?" Dennis asked, completely lost.

"My daddy left too, you know."

"I didn't know that," he replied hesitantly.

"I was only seven when he left. Not so much as a goodbye. Not even a note," she confided and she looked on the verge of a pout.

Dennis was suddenly acutely aware of the emotions she was drawing from him, feeling a bit guarded by her admission. He wondered if she wanted him to tell her about his own father. But that was something he didn't like to talk about. He looked at her dumbly, wishing vaguely that he could get out of this house, not have to listen to her prattle. He felt ill at ease, worried that he was being set up or something.

"Dennis, how much money do you make doing these odd jobs you do?"

"I don't know, it depends on what folks will pay me," he answered cautiously.

"Maybe a few dollars an hour here and there?"

"I suppose." He finished with his lemonade and stood up, walking past her to put it in the sink. "That's what most figure is fair."

"How'd you like to make some extra money besides that?" she coyly put to him, moving in closer with a somewhat provocative expression on her face.

He tried to dodge the question. "I got plenty of work around here. I'm doing all right, ma'am," he said. "You always pay me what's right."

"Caroline, remember?" She laughed a little as she reached her hand out and swept her fingertips across his face. He was a bit skittish and drew back. "You have paint on your face," she told him.

"Oh," he replied.

"Tell me something, Dennis. You got a girlfriend?"

"No."

"A good looking boy like you? That's a shame," she lamented. "But then, you never seemed like the type that fit in around here. You'll move on to bigger and better things. Mark my words."

Dennis slipped his hands into his pockets. "I plan on getting out, as soon as I graduate."

"I knew it!" she cried.

"What?"

"You ever been to California, Dennis?"

"No," he said.

"I plan on going," she whispered.

"When?"

"As soon as I get all my ducks in a row," she said with a giggle.

"You and Mr. Fletcher are moving?" he asked, confused by her banter.

She looked around suspiciously, as if someone might be listening to their conversation. "You mustn't tell anyone else what I'm about to tell you, Dennis. I'm not going with Mr. Fletcher. As a matter of fact, I don't want him to know about it at all," she said. "Can you keep a secret?"

"I guess so."

"I'm leaving town," she informed him.

He looked surprised. "But—"

She put a finger to his lips. "I'm trusting you," she said, "not to tell a soul." Her finger on his lips did something to him; he felt a little weak in the knees. When she stepped closer to him, so that she could speak more intimately, he liked it. "I'm going to California, and no one else must know. You understand?"

"Yes, ma'am."

"Yes, Caroline," she corrected.

"Yes, Caroline," he said, her name like honey in his mouth.

"I have something," she said, putting her hand in her pocket and pulling out a brooch. It was old, he could tell, with a large, oval onyx the size of an egg in the center, surrounded by smaller, but still generously sized, diamonds. He studied it in her petite hand, curious.

"What's this?" he asked.

"Our ticket out of here," she said softly with a lift of her eyebrow.

"I don't understand."

"You know where I can trade this in for cash?"

He was silent for a moment, running his tongue over his bottom lip anxiously. "They got a pawn shop in Guthrie, twenty or so miles from here."

Caroline reached out and took his hand gently from his side, pressing the brooch lightly into his palm. "I need you to take this to Guthrie and get money for it."

"I don't know…" He hesitated.

"I figure it should be worth six or seven hundred dollars. But they won't give us that much for it. We'll probably see four or so out of it," she went on. She was still holding his hand in hers.

"I don't want no trouble," he said, feeling the perspiration trickle from his armpits.

"There won't be any. All I'm asking is that you take it and pawn it. That's not asking much, is it, Dennis?" She moved in even closer still, an imploring pout on her plump lips. "It's just a small little favor. And you get something out of it, too. I'll share a hundred of it with you," she promised.

"What about Mr. Fletcher?" Dennis asked.

"What about Mr. Fletcher?" she huffed. "He's got nothing to do with this. Nothing to do with us. There's no need to tell him. No need to tell anyone. Don't you see? This would be our chance to get out." And she closed his fingers tightly over the brooch.

Dennis wrapped the brooch in some old rags and shoved it deep into his pocket once he was gone. He could feel the slight weight of it with every step he took, with every move he made, the way it might feel with a stone in his pocket. When he got home, he tucked it in the coffee can he kept his wages in, pushing it to the back of the cupboard in the kitchen.

When his brother Carl got home, he said nothing of it to him. Carl worked at the factory just on the edge of town, fixing steering wheels to brand new automobiles coming off the assembly line. Only two years older than Dennis, he had dropped out of school to secure a job and had been working there ever since, for nearly three years now. It was monotonous work, predictable and loathsome to Carl. But he kept at it, realizing that without the steady paycheck, he and Dennis would be out of luck.

Dennis knew that Carl was as miserable as he was. It would have been hard not to know this about his brother. Carl was not shy about verbalizing it. "If I wasn't here, bringing home the bacon, where would you be when Pop left?" he would berate his brother. "I work that rotten job so you'll have food to put in your mouth."

It was something that Dennis had never grown used to. The rebuking left him feeling like he was inches tall instead of his impressive six foot five. Carl reminded him very much of the father that had abandoned them, the man that had hurled insults and blows as easily as he could toss beer cans across the room into the trashcan. Looking back, Dennis had never really been sorry that the man had gone. There was a relief that was hard to describe. At times, he wished Carl would leave too, but then, as his older brother was quick to point out, Dennis would have nowhere to go, no way of taking care of himself.

"You got dinner ready?" Carl barked as he slouched heavily onto the couch.

"I picked up some chicken from the deli," Dennis said. "It's in the refrigerator."

"Whatcha standing there for? Go get me some."

Dennis disappeared into the kitchen and returned shortly with a plate of cold chicken. Carl grabbed it from his hand and began shoving the food into his mouth, licking his fingers every now and then.

"Carl, I need the truck tomorrow," Dennis said, trying to appear nonchalant.

"No way. I'm taking Nan to the dog track tomorrow." He continued to wolf down the chicken, oblivious to the pieces of food that spewed out of his mouth as he spoke. "Besides, you got the front porch to paint. You ain't goin' nowhere tomorrow."

"I'd be gone for an hour or so. I'd have it back before you got to go to the track, and I can paint the porch in the afternoon."

"I said no," Carl said, unrelenting.

Dennis knew better than to push his luck at this point. He decided he would figure a way to take the bus to Guthrie. He would have to do it without the truck. He wondered how long it would take to catch the bus, take care of his business in Guthrie, and get back home. The last thing he wanted was for anyone to see him, but then, he didn't have much of a choice. Without the truck, the bus was his only option, and if he rode the bus, he was sure to be seen by someone. The memory of Caroline Fletcher exposing the brooch to him burned fiercely within his mind, and he figured that it was worth the risk if it made her happy.

He consoled himself with the fact that his miserable life would be vastly improved in a short time. He could stand to put up with his brother, with this pit of a house, because he would be in California in a week, maybe two. All of this would be behind him, a distant memory.

CHAPTER 21

With nothing else to keep him occupied, Nelson threw himself back into his work. He reviewed everything he had pertaining to Harry Fletcher's case and had come to the conclusion that there was nothing that he hadn't overlooked in his own trove of records and evidence. He determined that he would have to figure out a way to actually look at the evidence from that night. He would try to talk his way into being allowed to see it; that's what he would do. But how?

When he inquired into the matter, he was told that no one was allowed access to evidence, even to a case as old as the Fletcher case. It was an irritation, much worse than a burr under a saddle. To come so close to wrapping it up, to nearly having all of the loose ends neatly tied, and then be rebuffed was more than he could bear.

And then it dawned on him. As he struggled with sleep one night, the answer came to him in a soft sibilant murmur to his brain, as if someone else had given him the solution to his problem. If he wanted to see the evidence, he was going to have to steal it. He couldn't sleep for the thought of it. It churned around inside his head, sparking new thoughts, leading off into tangents that took him to dead ends, and then quickly jumped onto a different track with a new train of thought that led him down still another route.

By morning, Nelson was showered, shaved, dressed, and ready to go. He drove downtown, parking in the street just in front of the police station, his heart fluttering as he deposited his quarters into the meter before entering the building through the front door. With deception in his heart, he requested an application for employment, filling it out completely, carefully leaving out some details. His college diploma, for instance, wouldn't evoke the effect he was trying for. His GED did. His age was something else that he was sure would paint them the right picture when they reviewed his qualifications, because the desired effect was to make it appear as if he were a high school dropout, seeking employment as a janitor. Nelson turned the sheet of paper in at the human resource desk with a smile and a polite nod of his head. The woman who took it from him smiled back. It was as easy as that to beguile, he thought as he climbed back into his old truck.

He was on pins and needles for the next two days, waiting in agitation for some word about his request for employment. The case of Caroline Fletcher's murder consumed him. He sat for hours, with photos, records, and handwritten notes laid out before him, trying to gather from them the key to the mind-bending mystery. He half expected Caroline Fletcher to raise herself up from the soiled kitchen floor, open her dead eyes, and share her secret with him, exonerating her poor wretch of a husband for good. But she continued to lie there in her pool of blood, limbs sprawled, face slackened and lifeless. There was not even a hint of who had assailed her that night on the slain woman's lips.

It wasn't until Thursday that he got a call about the job. An energetic voice on the other end inquired, "May I speak with Nelson Rune?"

"This is he," Nelson replied, feeling the excited rush when he realized who it must be.

"I was calling about the janitorial position you applied for," she said.

She made arrangements to interview him on Monday. That seemed as close to eternity to Nelson as anything had. He would have three days to sweat it out. And there was nothing to do but wait, wait and try to be patient. The only thing that broke up the monotony of it was a visit from Cleo.

She knocked on his door on Saturday morning, sheepishly fidgeting with the buttons on her blouse when he opened it to her. She smiled nervously, and for the first time he could remember, she seemed unsure of herself. "Hey, Nelson," she said, a little too overzealously. Then she waited for a response from him, eyes wide and expectant.

"Hi," Nelson replied, slightly dazed by her presence, or perhaps from his lack of sleep. He was beyond glad to see her. It had been a whole week since they had last spoken to one another, but he kept his excitement in check. There was really no point in making a fool of himself, even for the barefoot goddess with a strawberry-blond ponytail standing before him now. Without her makeup and in her glasses, she was still a vision of beauty to him. His exhaustion took the edge off of his adrenaline rush just a little.

"How are things?" she inquired.

"Okay, I guess."

"May I come in and talk to you for a second?"

He scratched his head absent-mindedly, ruffling his hair in the process. "Yeah, come on in," he allowed, stepping aside for her.

She noted right away the dishes piled in the sink, the disorder of his apartment, a pizza box stained with grease marks lying on the floor next to the futon, the scattered photos, papers, and trash littered about. Nelson made no attempt at tidying for her benefit; he went and sat heavily on his easy chair, leaving the futon for Cleo.

"Jeez, Nelson, you're a wreck," she told him, sitting on the futon with care, trying not to disturb the police reports stacked on the other end. Her mind was racing. She had never seen him this way before, and from the looks of the apartment, he was in a bad place. She wondered at his state of mind and worried that it was her fault.

"Was there a point to your little visit?" he asked, slightly perturbed. He thought maybe she was just there to torture him.

"What's going on? Are you all right?"

"Fine," he lied. "Just a little preoccupied."

"I can see that," Cleo responded, pointedly allowing her gaze to roam the disheveled place. "Working on the Fletcher murder?"

"Yep."

"Anything new?"

"I don't know, not really," he said.

"You're acting funny. You've got something you aren't telling me," she urged. "I know you."

"I told you, not really. I'm just trying to work out a way to see the actual evidence from the case."

"Will they let you do that?" she inquired doubtfully.

"Probably not. What did you want to talk about?" he asked, trying to take the focus off himself.

She watched him warily. He yawned and rubbed his bloodshot eyes. "I wanted to talk to you about the dance," she admitted. "I know you didn't want to go. I mean, I know it was my idea and all… but I would really be grateful if you would still go with me."

He gave her a cautious glance, trying to detect her thoughts from her expression. "Why?" he asked simply.

"I thought we could go as friends," she explained. "It's only a week away, and I thought that since we had already planned on going that you wouldn't mind." He didn't say anything. "It's okay if you don't want to," she added. "I'll let you off the hook."

"No, Cleo, I would very much like to take you," he said with a look in his eyes that made her twitch a little. He leaned forward and took her hand in his. "I'm sorry," he said, his gaze sincere.

"For what?" she asked, feeling that she should bolt for the door. She questioned her motives for even coming. But there had been some small hope that she would end up in his arms, that maybe he would profess the feelings she wished he had for her. Now she wasn't sure what to think. He was behaving so strangely, and the state of his place seemed to be in direct correlation to the state of his mind. She fleetingly thought that she should have just left him alone. Really, that probably would have been the kind thing to do.

"You deserved someone better. I let you down," he said.

"Nelson, there is no one better," she confessed. "I know it sounds lame, but I really would like to still be friends."

He let her hand go. "Yeah, that'd be good."

She noted the change in his demeanor. "Are you mad at me?"

"No."

"You aren't acting like yourself. I'm a little worried."

"I'm just tired."

"I can see that. Have you been sleeping?"

Nelson shrugged. "Not really."

"Why not?"

"Just a lot of things on my mind," he said.

"Anything I can help you with?"

"No."

In the end, she left with a sense of apprehension, unsure as to whether she should leave him or not. Something was not quite right with Nelson, and it bothered her that he wouldn't confide in her. But then, she reasoned, *she* had broken things off with *him*. It was her own fault. Why would he share anything with her after what she had done?

Monday brought an end to the torture of waiting. They offered him the position, and he would start just two days later. The first night on his new job as a custodian, he had little time to think about how he might obtain the evidence he so desperately wanted to possess. Instead, he followed the head custodian around, making mental notes of the layout of the place and memorizing the schedule and the particulars of his assigned tasks.

The station was a nondescript brick building with several floors. On the first level, a large room housed cubicles for patrolmen coming in or leaving from their shifts. The walls were a putty color, with berber carpet in varying shades of gray. This was also the floor where the evidence room was located, down a hall, and tucked away near the back of the building. The upper floors were offices for the chief of police and another large room for the detectives and their desks.

Nelson did his best to listen to his boss as he passed through the rooms and surveyed the building, tagging along behind him as he spouted the ins and outs of the job. Guy Larsen, the head custodian, was a goofy man but kind-hearted nonetheless. He joked a lot, but he also offered words of encouragement to his new charge. While Nelson felt he should appreciate Guy's praise, he felt a little patronized by it and resented it. Guy never noticed, because Nelson simply smiled and nodded and tried to seem pleased by it. It wouldn't do to be insubordinate to his superior or to foster any kind of doubt in his abilities to perform the job. After all, he was in no position at this point to be proud.

"I know it's all a lot to remember, but you'll have it down in no time," he told Nelson with a broad grin at the vote of confidence he had bestowed upon the teenager. "I'll go around with you for the first couple of days, so you won't have to do it on your own right away."

Nelson wanted to roll his eyes at the man who was talking down to him, but he smiled and nodded. "Thank you, Mr. Larsen," he replied.

"Just call me Guy. There's no formalities around here," he said with a laugh.

"Yes, sir."

Emptying the trash cans next to the maze of desks, vacuuming the carpets, cleaning the restrooms, wiping fingerprints and dirt form the glass windows, mopping the vinyl floors in the entryway and hallways were all part of his duties as a janitor. Nelson found it strangely satisfying, almost therapeutic. While his mind still worked over how he would pull off his heist, his hands were busy, and it took some of the anxiety away from his overly stimulated mental state. He asked questions, very carefully worded, paid close attention to anything Guy might divulge without being prompted, and observed closely all things pertaining to security and protocol.

"Is it always this quiet?"

"Shift change. It settles down a little around shift change," Guy answered.

Later, they passed a door that was clearly marked *Evidence Room.* Guy didn't even slow down. "Are we supposed to clean that room?" Nelson asked, feigning ignorance.

"No. No, we don't clean that room. Only two people have got the key to that room, and I ain't one of 'em."

"Why not?" Nelson asked. As they passed, he kept his eyes on the sign until he was craning his head, and then he forced himself to look back at the hallway in front of him.

"That room is off limits. Not just to us, to everyone. The chief has the key and the guy who's over evidence has a key. If any of the other fellows want something from there, they gotta get permission from one of them two."

"I guess I can see how they wouldn't want a lot of people going in and out of there."

"Yeah, well, it gives us one less thing to have to worry about."

"No kidding," Nelson agreed.

By the time his shift was over, he was exhausted. For the first time in over a week, he fell onto his futon and settled into a deep, dreamless sleep. He woke up late afternoon with a burning hunger. Over a peanut butter and jelly sandwich, Nelson took notes of the layout and specifics he had gleaned from Guy Larsen the night before on a legal pad. The trick would be in getting one of the two keys that was required to unlock the door to the evidence room.

He was speculating as to how he could filch one of the keys, make a copy, and return it before anyone noticed it was missing. In his opinion, the chief would be the least likely to note the missing key right away. He would be the one that wouldn't regularly have a use for it. After all, the primary reason for his key was just as a back-up, used in the event of an emergency.

Nelson realized with some amount of frustration that it would be a nearly impossible task. The chief and the detective in charge of evidence were never around for the night shift, when Nelson worked. He would report to work, observing things in a laid-back but sincerely interested way. Guy would make comments on how clever he was, and Nelson would laugh it off as if it were a joke. He wondered what Guy would say if he knew that the teenage boy he had taken under his wing was technically a genius. By the end of the week, Nelson realized that he would have to find another way in to get into the evidence room. As disheartening as it was to come to this conclusion, his job became easier without Guy tagging along beside him. Without the supervisor scrutinizing his every move when his training had come to an end, Nelson was free to roam where he might, cleaning meticulously as he listened and watched.

It was difficult for Nelson to observe these men coming and going, discussing a case, talking about the game on Sunday, relating a story about their wives or their children. He envied them more than he wanted to admit to himself. They were living the life he had wanted. They wore their badges and their guns with a casual confidence, comrades in their profession. Some of them talked to him and were friendly and polite. But he felt very much like an outsider, not really one of them, lingering beyond their sphere in his gray work coveralls, pushing his cleaning cart in obscurity, a silent observer to their informal exchanges.

After his first week of working on his own, a curious thing happened. Nelson's epiphany of exactly how he would pull off his crime struck him like lightening. Mulling it over, he had considered picking the lock of the evidence room, letting himself in, helping himself to what he was looking for, and then slipping out. But how to lock the dead bolt back once he had left the room—the unlocked door would certainly not go unnoticed. And then providence smiled on him, and he knew that it was as close to divine intervention as he was going to get. He would let himself into the evidence room, review the Fletcher case evidence box, and let himself out again, without anyone being the wiser. It was so simple it was brilliant. And no one would ever know.

CHAPTER 22

Nelson sat stiffly, uneasy on the sofa next to Cleo in her apartment. He was out of his element, as usual, when it came to Cleo, but more so tonight because of their recent relationship that had freshly ended. If he didn't have feelings for Cleo, he never would have agreed to such an arrangement. No point in wooing a woman who had made it clear she was not interested. He was a fool for going along with this. He knew it, but he was unwilling to disappoint her anyhow.

Cleo was dressed casually and looked very nice. Her hair was curled, her makeup done in a way that was natural but noticeable, her lips a blushing pink. It depressed Nelson that she looked so good. They both wore the matching gray polos they had picked out at the GAP just three weeks ago. The twin pair of them smiled for photos as Sandi snapped a few off before they left.

"Okay, Mom, that's enough." Cleo groaned as her mother took a few more.

"All right, all right," Sandi reluctantly assented, putting the camera on the bookshelf.

"We're going now," Cleo playfully grumbled.

"Take care," Sandi warned, giving Cleo a quick hug as she and Nelson walked out the door. She threw in, "Be back by curfew. And no drinking!"

Nelson and Cleo sat in a quiet booth at the back of the restaurant, an upper-scale Chinese place. The waitress wore a bright red geisha-style kimono peppered with golden colored oriental flowers, a gold comb in her hair. She brought them drinks, took their orders, and then disappeared, leaving them to their privacy.

"This is a cool place," Nelson remarked.

"One of my favorites," Cleo divulged, sipping her drink.

"You look very nice, Cleo."

She grinned at him. "Thanks. You clean up well yourself." She turned the ice around in her glass with her straw. "What have you been up to lately, Nelson? I see you coming and going at all hours."

Nelson cleared his throat. "I sort of have a job."

"A new job, besides the Fletcher case?" Her interest was piqued.

"Not quite like that," he said.

"What, then?"

"I got a custodial job."

"Are things not going well with your private investigation business?"

"No, that's going pretty much the same as usual," he told her, his eyes roaming over the silk fans, paper lanterns, and Chinese characters, bold and black, that adorned the walls. Daring colors in golds, blacks, reds were emblazoned everywhere in the quaint place, adorned with white orchids, simple but elegant.

"Is there something you don't want to tell me?"

"I guess so," he said.

"Oh."

She seemed to have a way of getting things out of him without forcing it. All it took was her melancholy "Oh" to get him to spill his guts. He felt instantly guilty. "I'm doing custodial work at the police station," he admitted, the words tumbling out of his mouth before he scarcely knew what he was saying.

Nelson realized how pathetic he must seem, dumping it all on her with so little provocation, but he was so relieved to be talking to her again that he didn't care. It struck him as odd that he had never needed anyone before Cleo, but once he had gotten used to having her around, it was painful now that she was gone. Once his best friend, his comfort and constant companion, the silence was now a distasteful trespasser that he politely endured.

Cleo gave him a shrewd glance. "Why?"

"The steady paycheck is nice," Nelson commented. "My savings account is growing quite rapidly. I'm toying with the idea of buying a house in a year or so. Nothing fancy, of course. I don't know, with the housing market such as it is, maybe I should wait a little longer."

Her eyebrows curved dangerously. She obviously wasn't put off the trail by his decoy. "Are you going to tell me the truth?"

"That is the truth. It's nice to have some money I can count on."

"And the other reason you took that job…"

At this point, the server returned with a small rectangular serving tray of egg rolls, two small dishes, and a bottle of soy sauce. She rearranged the place settings, giving them each a dish and putting the eggrolls within easy reach of both of them. "Your pork egg rolls," she informed them, as if they weren't able to see for themselves. "Your dinners will be out shortly." They watched her float to another table to greet a new batch of customers.

"Why do you think?" Nelson answered with a question.

"I don't think it's for the steady paycheck," she leveled.

"That wasn't the initial reason I took the job, but it is a nice added bonus. Plus I get benefits."

"Are you doing something that's going to get you into trouble?" she continued, watching him pluck up an eggroll and crunch into it.

"Possibly."

"Are you going to tell me or not?"

"I'm going to break into the evidence room," Nelson said in a low deliberate tone as he gazed from side to side, making sure that no one else but Cleo was listening.

"What? You can't do that!"

"Keep your voice down," he cautioned when he noticed a few patrons looking their way curiously.

"Nelson, you can't do that," she whispered fiercely. "If they catch you you'll be serving time. Tampering with evidence is a federal offense." His unruffled demeanor irritated her. "It's serious!"

"I know all of that better than you do," he said with a frown. "Much better. But I'm not going to get caught. And I'm not going to tamper with evidence, just look over it, that's all."

"If they catch you, I doubt they would differentiate between the two."

"The key word being *if,*" Nelson pointed out.

"I don't understand. Why can't you just tell Harry Fletcher that it was either Chuck or Marnie that murdered Caroline? Let him listen to the interview. You got it all on your recorder. That should be enough."

"But it's not enough," he said. He noted her crestfallen expression and smiled reassuringly. "What do you care?" he teased. "Afraid you'll have to admit your ex is a con?"

Cleo cringed when he used the word "ex" as though she found it physically painful. "It's not funny," she asserted. He could joke all he wanted, but it was not humorous to her. She had always taken people's feelings very seriously. And the fact that he was making fun of their situation hurt because she knew he was doing it defensively.

"I didn't mean to upset you," he said, his brow furrowed. "That's really the last thing I wanted to do."

"How did you think this wouldn't be upsetting to me?"

"You're making a big deal out of nothing, Cleo. I'm not going to get caught. I have a plan."

"Well, that makes me feel so much better."

"It should. Don't you trust me?" he asked, not really wanting a response from her.

"Nelson, I care about you. I don't want anything to happen to you."

"Then why did you break it off with me?" He hadn't meant to say it out loud. It had been in his brain, rattling around, and he had thought it so many times that it just came out, unbidden. Cleo looked as if she had been slapped in the face. She sat morosely across from him, unwilling to meet his gaze. He waited, toying with the idea of apologizing. "You said you were the one that was more invested in the relationship, but you don't seem to mind being apart. I'm the one that's still messed up over it. You don't seem to care one way or the other. While I…I miss you, Cleo. That's all. I miss you."

"Why?"

"Excuse me?" Nelson said, confused.

"Why do you miss me?"

"I miss having someone to talk to that listens and someone that talks to me back. I miss your company, you know. And you're funny and smart. I'm comfortable with you. I feel like you understand me. No one else does. Nobody. But you do. And as if that isn't enough, as if all those things weren't deal makers, you happen to be completely beautiful…totally irresistible."

"Don't worry, Nelson. You'll get over it," she finally said, obviously upset by his admission. She was suddenly very torn and confused by all of it. Just a little over two short weeks ago, he couldn't think of a single thing to say about why he liked her, and now here he was, in a Chinese restaurant of all places, making a public declaration like this one. Why not sooner? Why had he let her walk away without the slightest attempt at trying to talk her out of breaking up with him? She was finding it difficult to remain peeved with him, his penitent expression shadowing his lean features as he watched her across the table.

"I don't want to get over it," he said, reaching over to take her hand in his.

The server took this most inopportune moment to return with their dinner plates on a bamboo-style tray. "The cashew chicken?" she inquired with a pleasant smile.

"That's me," Cleo acknowledged, accepting the plate from her.

"And the sweet and sour pork," the server said, giving the plate to Nelson. "Everything else all right?"

"Yes, thank you," they chimed in together, a little too eagerly.

"Just let me know if you need anything else," she offered.

Cleo waited until the server was out of hearing range, taking her fork in hand and picking at her plate, somewhat preoccupied by her thoughts.

"That's maybe the nicest thing you've ever said to me," she replied.

Nelson could see he was gaining some ground. He looked at her earnestly. "I meant it."

"I just don't want to get hurt, Nelson."

"I don't ever want to hurt you," he reiterated, pushing her hair gingerly back from her face with his fingers.

"But you will. Eventually you will…" She took a generous bite of her meal. "It's good," she said. "You should eat before it gets cold."

Nelson picked up his chopsticks, plucking up a piece of meat and popping it into his mouth. She watched him with interest. "You're right, it is good," he agreed as he chewed.

"You can eat with chopsticks?"

"Yeah."

"Show me how," she said.

"Start with your thumb," he advised, taking one of her chopsticks and laying it across the length of her thumb. "Use your middle finger to brace it. Then lay the second one against your pointer finger, like this." He placed the remaining chopstick between her pointer finger and the tip of her thumb. "Now you just pinch it together by moving only the top one. See?" He took up his own chopsticks and demonstrated for her, picking up a clump of sticky rice and placing it on his tongue.

"Like this?" Cleo asked, attempting to pick up a piece of chicken. The chopsticks slipped, launching the chicken against Nelson's chest, leaving a saucy stain behind.

He laughed. "Exactly like that," he said.

Cleo was laughing too as she dabbed at his shirt with her napkin. "Sorry."

"You might just want to stick to the fork," he joked.

"I think you're probably right." She set the chopsticks down in favor of the fork.

"And after all the trouble of picking these stupid shirts out," he noted ironically.

"Don't feel bad, looks like I got something on mine too," she said, taking her napkin to blot at a spot on her chest.

"Need help with that?"

She gave him an amused smirk. "No thanks."

"Just offering," he said.

"What a gentleman."

They arrived at the school gymnasium with the dance already underway. The basketball hoops had been retracted, folded up toward the ceiling, and every square inch of the place had been transformed into a fall harvest theme with bales of hay, bundled corn husks, pumpkins, and gourds. The music was playing loudly, the bass vibrating with an infectious pulsation, enough so that they had to bend close to one another and raise their voices to converse.

"Do you want some punch?" His lips brushed just slightly against her ear. She smiled and nodded her head yes. They moved together to the punch bowl, and he ladled a cup for each of them. Cleo and

Nelson stood just on the edge of the dance floor watching a throng of people gyrating to the fast-paced beat.

Nelson crushed his cup when he was finished and pitched it into the trashcan. Cleo followed suit. "You wanna dance?"

"What?" Nelson cupped his hand to his ear.

"You wanna dance?" Cleo said, raising her voice to be heard.

Nelson was reluctant. "I don't know how to dance," he revealed with a grimace.

"It's not that hard," she yelled back.

"The only thing I know about dancing is the 'Macarena' from gym class in the third grade," he announced with a grin.

"This I've gotta see." She chuckled. She held up her finger as she left his side. "I'll be right back."

He watched her weave her way through the crowd to the DJ, making her request before finding her way back to him.

"What'd you do?"

"It's all set," she assured him. "No worries."

As the fast-paced music ended, the thrum of the "Macarena" took its place to the boos and hisses of everyone around them. Cleo took his hand and led him out onto the dance floor, standing next to him as she went through the motions of the dance. She messed up and began to laugh at herself. "Come on," she commanded. Nelson gave up and started to dance too, surprisingly proficient at it. By the end of the song, everyone else was trying to join in too.

"Let's switch tracks here," the DJ said into his microphone. "Here's a slow one."

Cleo took Nelson's hands tenderly between hers and set them on her waist. It was so innocent, yet so intimate, and Nelson felt his heart knocking loudly against his ribs. She wrapped her own hands around the back of his neck and began to sway back and forth with the music. He followed her lead, not taking his eyes from hers. Her lips curled into a half-smile, and she leaned into him, resting her cheek against his shoulder. He knew then that he had won her over again, and that for that small moment she was all his.

CHAPTER 23

Dennis pulled his T-shirt on in the gloom of his bedroom, intentionally not turning on the lights so that his brother wouldn't be bothered. His plan was simple. He would walk two miles to town, grab a bus to Guthrie, hawk the brooch, and be back by noon. He didn't know anyone to speak of in Guthrie, no one that might spot him and tell Carl. It would be easy, he thought as he tied his boots with quick, angry strokes.

When he opened his bedroom door, it creaked slightly. He paused, holding his breath, and then pushed it the rest of the way open. All was still. Dennis noted with relief that Carl's door was closed. It would muffle much of the stealthy sounds he was making. Tiptoeing down the hall, he was making plans in his head, imagining what Caroline Fletcher's reaction would be when he presented her with the money. Maybe he could finagle more money out of the pawn shop owner. That would sure surprise her.

Once in the kitchen, Dennis went straight for the coffee can, peeling the plastic lid back and reaching his hand in to rummage through the bills, searching for the brooch. His fingers did not brush against it right away, so he began dumping its contents onto the kitchen table. Dread did not take long to set in when he saw the brooch was not there.

"Looking for this?" Carl asked from behind him.

Dennis jerked violently, recoiling from Carl with conditioned reflex. He was used to Carl knocking him around some, taking his frustration out on him in a savage pummeling. His usual gut reaction was to cower. Carl was not in the mood to brawl just then, however. He was tossing the brooch casually into the air and catching it again, as if it were a toy.

"Carl...I was just—" Dennis stammered.

"Just what, Dennis? What is my little brother up to?"

Dennis fell silent with a look of pure dread clouding his expression. "Nothing," he said simply, not taking his eyes from his work boots.

"Something," Carl countered. He strode across the room and shoved the brooch under Dennis's nose. "What's this?"

"A brooch."

"I know it's a brooch, you freak," Carl bellowed. "Where'd it come from?" When Dennis didn't answer, Carl took him by the front of his shirt and pushed him back against the wall. "Spit it out!"

"I was gonna tell you, Carl. I swear—"

"Cut the bull. Where'd you swipe it from?" Carl interrupted.

"I didn't steal it," Dennis protested.

"You didn't steal it?"

"Carl, I swear...I swear I didn't steal it," he said with a pleading in his voice.

"Where'd you get it from if you didn't steal it?" he demanded, pressing him more firmly into the wall.

"Look, it's not what you think. Somebody gave it to me," he said, his heart pounding violently in his chest.

"Who? Who the hell'd give you something like this? Who's gonna give some snot-nosed loser like you something expensive like this?"

"Carl, I'm telling you, she gave it to me."

"She who?"

"Mrs. Fletcher. She gave it to me," he insisted.

"Mrs. Fletcher?"

"Yeah, she gave it to me and asked me to pawn it for her," he explained. "Yesterday."

"What's a classy broad like her want to pawn her jewelry for, Dennis?" he asked in disbelief. "And why's she asking you to do it for her?" Carl began to relax his grip.

"I don't know. But that's honestly what happened."

"You're lying to me," Carl said, getting into Dennis's face.

"I'm not…"

"Why did she want to pawn it? They got plenty of money," Carl pointed out with a scowl on his face.

"I don't know. I don't know. She didn't want Mr. Fletcher to find out. She said she was going to California, Carl. That's all I know."

Carl inspected the brooch closely. "How much she say it was worth?"

"She didn't."

"How much, Dennis?"

"I don't know."

"Do you know who you're talking to, bonehead? You may as well spill it cause I'll get it out of you one way or the other," Carl threatened.

Dennis weighed his options in silent misery. "Three hundred," he mumbled, hoping his lie was convincing.

"Three hundred? Woohoo!" he hooted.

"I told her I was gonna bring her that money, Carl. If I don't, she'll call the cops or something."

"She ain't calling nobody," Carl said with a laugh. "You think she wants people to know what she's up to?"

"She could lie. She could say I took it or something," Dennis complained. "It isn't your ass on the line."

"Shut up, Dennis!" Carl's eyes were menacing. "You better damn well do what I say, when I say it."

"Just think it through, Carl. Don't be stupid," Dennis pleaded.

Carl lurched toward Dennis, belting him in the face. Dennis shrunk away from him, his lip busted and bleeding. He fell silent, realizing that no matter what he had to say to his older brother, Carl was past listening. He pondered what he would say to Caroline, how he would explain his failure to her. She had trusted him. He had let her down.

"I already thought it through. You'll do what I say, Dennis. You'll shut your big mouth, and you'll paint the front porch today, and it'll be done by the time I get back from the dog tracks, you hear? Just like nothing out of the ordinary, just like any other day," Carl snarled contemptuously.

CHAPTER 24

Nelson felt that after having worked as the janitor at the police station for four weeks, becoming a familiar face and a credited employee, he had gotten to the point of no return. It was time to focus on his main objective: getting to the evidence on the Caroline Fletcher murder case. And so he went to work one night, determined to make it happen. After this night, there would be no turning back. Either he would meet his objective, or he would be spending the night in jail. One way or the other, this night was when it would happen.

There was no vocal agreement between Cleo and Nelson, but after the dance they were an item again, falling into a comfortable routine of spending time together during their spare moments. As Nelson's girlfriend, Cleo felt that she had a right to voice her misgivings about his plan to steal evidence. She endeavored to talk him out of his mad scheme with no luck. She reminded him that if he were caught, the consequences would be severe. Not only was he plotting a felony and could possibly serve prison time, but he would forever lose his eligibility to attend police academy, which was his lifelong dream. The more she worked on him, the more resolved he became. He would not argue with her. He would simply nod his head, as though he were listening to every word she said, but he would not respond.

It was infuriating to Cleo, but she also knew that he was his own person and, regardless of anything she had to say, he would choose for himself what he would do. Still, she had some hope that something she might be saying was sinking in. Cleo was with him one evening before he left for his night shift. She could sense something was different. When he left for work that night, he had tried to act as if nothing were out of the ordinary. He didn't want to upset her. There was no point in it, he told himself, because everything would go off without a hitch. He had to believe this to get up the courage to actually follow through with it. But she knew instinctively that something was up.

"You should call in sick hang out with me," she suggested, cuddling close to him, wrapping her arms around his waist and draping her leg over his.

"I can't do that. I'm not sick," he reasoned. "Besides, you'll be home in bed soon anyway. Your mom's not going to let you skip curfew."

Shortly after, Nelson got ready for work and dropped Cleo off at her apartment before heading out. She was irritated, messing with the buttons on the front of his shirt with the hint of a pout on her mouth. "I'll miss you," she said. Leaning toward him on her tiptoes, she gave him an extra-long kiss. "Try to be good, won't you?"

Nelson's body was full of adrenaline, knowing what he knew about his plans for the night. Having her kiss him that way was almost too much. He responded to her, moving his mouth over hers with an intensity that left them both a little surprised. He moved in to her, pushing her back against the door jamb as his thumbs held her jaw and his fingers curled around her neck.

When he finally pulled away, he hesitated. "I've got to go. I'll be late if I don't go."

"Stay."

"I'll be late." He gave her one last, much more chaste kiss and then turned to leave.

"You better be here in the morning to pick me up for school!" she called out after him.

He turned around, continuing to walk backward. He smiled and nodded. "Bright and early."

He would wait until shift change, when there were fewer people about and he wasn't as conspicuous. It had been his good fortune to be breaking into an evidence room of a smaller police station. A larger one, in a busy metropolis, would have surveillance equipment monitoring the hallway, keeping careful track of everyone and everything. As it so happened, there was very little that Nelson had to be concerned of in his police station. A few cameras were set up around the perimeter of the building itself, around the parking lots and sidewalks, at the main doors, and in the lobby on the main level.

As long as no one suspected him of any wrongdoing, there should be no snag in his plan. He rushed through many of his duties to begin with, dumping trashcans in the janitor's cart with haste. Then he vacuumed, not taking the usual care with getting every last crumb in his customarily meticulous fashion. Lastly, Nelson took out the mop, slathering the hallway in a nice wet coat as he went, until he reached the hallway where the evidence room was. He set a *Wet Floor* sign where it could clearly be seen and ducked down looking both ways to make sure the coast was clear. No one was around.

He remembered the day the idea had come to him. A detective with evidence he'd used in court that afternoon had been his inspiration. The detective had stopped in this hallway, lined with lockers of varying sizes, chosen a locker, opened it, deposited his evidence, and then locked the locker door with a small key, round and orange on top. When he was finished, he poked the key through a hole which had been drilled near the top of the locker door and was just big enough for the key to fit through. These lockers were very much reminiscent of the lockers you might find at an airport, a pool, a gym, only some here were rectangular, long and thin, some small, and some large and square-shaped. Nelson saw all of this and marveled.

"What are you doing?" he had asked the detective, a thirty-something in a short-sleeved polo.

"It's evidence. I don't want to get stuck with it over the weekend," the detective had replied. "They put these lockers here so you can put the evidence in and lock it up, and then the guy who's in charge, he opens the locker on the other side and puts it away for me. See? They're two sided." He showed Nelson by opening one of the empty lockers and rapping his knuckles against the door on the back side.

All kinds of evidence, all different sizes. It was so simple, Nelson couldn't believe it. He doubted that anyone else would have even thought of it. It was like looking into the face of a man with crooked teeth and not noticing it because you were distracted by his large, obtrusive ears. Obvious but completely taken for granted. Why not? Why couldn't it be that easy?

The next evening, he had come back to the lockers, discreetly testing out his theory by opening each locker and testing the back to see if the door would give. This is how he had discovered that a whole section of lockers would give him admission to the evidence room. Apparently the lockers could be accessed from the other side from a panel of larger doors; you open one door and you could get the items from a whole set of lockers on the other side. One of these doors had a broken latch, thereby giving him a literal portal into the room that was the object of his quest.

The coast was clear. If he wanted to back out, the time would be now. But he couldn't. It was something he had to do. He knew that he wouldn't ever be able to let it go if he didn't find out for himself once and for all who killed Caroline. He ducked down, checking the locker that was large enough for a man to squeeze through, roughly three feet by three feet. He pulled the door open and pressed against the back door that led inside the evidence room. It gave. His heart gave a little flutter as he bent down and crawled through. Much like a doggy door, he thought to himself.

His window of opportunity was short. He had to find the box, sift through it, and get out before someone noticed that he was missing. He took a small flashlight from his pocket, turning it on as he scanned the room to get his bearings. It was large in size, with a cement floor, exposed ductwork and rectangular fluorescent lights suspended from the ceiling, and rows of metal shelves lined neatly like appendages from the walls. These shelves were littered with brown paper bags or boxes, descriptions of their contents labeled and stapled to each.

Nelson quickly ran the flashlight over the shelves, surveying them in a hurried but thorough hunt for the old evidence. He knew that in a homicide case, evidence was never destroyed, it was kept indefinitely, and it had to be here somewhere. Near the back corner of the room, he found a group of boxes, the old evidence, the prize in his conquest, stacked neatly with their case numbers facing toward the isle. He could recite by heart the number of the particular box he sought. It was, however, a very different thing to find that number on one of the many boxes he was checking through now.

With speed and precision, he began at the bottom of the shelf and worked his way up. And there it was, like the golden ticket peeking out of the candy bar wrapper. He put the flashlight in his mouth, holding it steady with his teeth as he tugged the box off of the ledge it was nestled on. Laying it carefully upon the floor, he lifted the lid and let the beam of his flashlight sweep across the inside with a tantalizing glance of what was to come.

Nelson removed the contents of the white cardboard box carefully as he inspected each item and laid them neatly on the floor before him, his insides quivering with anticipation. The photos were ones that he had already seen, but he leafed through them before placing them in a stack off to the side. It was the evidence that he was here to see, the thing that had drawn him here with unrelenting persuasions.

He was missing a puzzle piece, something crucial that held the rest of the pieces together. What looked random very often was not. If he were to prove that Marnie or her husband, Chuck, had killed Caroline, he was going to have to dig up something more concrete than the rantings of an older woman confined to a retirement home. The problem with today's society was that they relied wholly on DNA evidence to prove the innocence or guilt of a person. Not everything was as substantial as DNA. How many guilty men had been let off on a technicality because there was not *enough* proof they had committed the crime?

As he went through the box, he knew each item backward and forward. There was nothing new to the random collection of objects. It was all as it should be, as it had been for over forty-five years, collecting dust in a cardboard box.

"What are you looking for?" he asked himself in a desperate whisper.

He didn't really know what he was looking for. He had just been hoping that something would manifest itself, or perhaps that he would stumble upon something new that hadn't been there before.

He pulled Caroline's silk nightgown from an ancient-looking paper bag, spreading it out before him. It wasn't the same milky color it had been when she'd worn it that night. The fabric had sallowed with age, as fabric often does. He saw the angry slashes where she had been stabbed and the darkened blood stains, almost black after lying entombed in the box for so long, dominating the front portion of the bodice. It gave him chills to witness it first hand, to actually have only the thin latex gloves as a barrier between his fingers and the gown.

Nelson inspected the fabric more closely, noticing something he hadn't seen in the old photos of the nightgown. He bent over the night gown and squinted. There was something on it, he realized, and he ran his gloved fingers over the trace marks of the mysterious smudges that were smeared in random patterns across the silk. They were a pure ivory, probably the same as the original color the fabric once was, before it had grown old and discolored.

It was like the fabric hadn't aged in those spots, as if the something that had soiled the silk had somehow preserved it. It was vaguely stiff to the touch, much like the blood that had soaked it, crusty and somewhat inflexible. He marveled over it for a moment longer, wanting more than anything to collect a sample from it, to have it tested. Knowing that wasn't a possibility, knowing that his even being here, if he were discovered, would ruin any chance of him being able to use this new discovery at all. He folded the gown and slipped it back into the wrinkled, brown paper bag.

He heard voices in the corridor, two men talking as they passed the evidence room. Evidently the *Wet Floor* sign had not deterred them. One of them cursed and the sound of rubber squeaking on the wet vinyl made Nelson freeze in the middle of his inspection. Whoever it was that had slipped was not happy. To make matters worse, his buddy was laughing at him. "You're gonna break your freakin' neck if you aren't careful. Didn't you see the wet floor sign, moron?"

This was a wake-up call. He had to get out and fast. Nelson scrambled to put everything back in the box as neatly as possible, tossing the lid back on as he jammed it back into its empty socket. If he got caught, all would be lost; the hard work would have been for nothing. He found his way back to his doggie door, extinguishing his flashlight and stowing it in his pocket again, listening intently as the footsteps disappeared down the hallway.

His next step was to push the outside door just slightly, enough to peek out and see if anyone was about, and then he crawled through it again, getting his hands and knees wet as he came out onto the damp floor. Nelson jumped up, grabbed his mop, making a beeline for the bucket, and quickly wheeled it off, headed for the bathrooms to finish up his work for the night. He had done it. He had broken into the evidence room and gotten out without being discovered.

CHAPTER 25

Twenty-nine-year-old Harry sat at the kitchen table, cutting his pot roast deliberately with his fork and knife. He was a quiet man, decisive in his thoughts and movements and words, a man who made lists, who kept a detailed itinerary of every aspect of his daily life. To distract his mind, he was thinking that he should take the car in to get it serviced down at the Kwick Stop. He was trying to tally in his brain exactly how long it had been since the last time he'd had the oil changed.

Christy, displeased with her peas, began to push them around her plate with her fork, watching them roll about in bored fascination, attempting to delay having to eating them. She looked over at Harry, who grinned and winked good-naturedly. He didn't want to eat his peas, either. "How was school today, Bug," he asked her.

"I get to compete in the spelling bee," she told him, brightening up a little.

"That's fabulous," he said. Whenever he spoke to her, he grew animated, not generally how he reacted to others. "Perhaps we should celebrate. What do you think, Caroline? You think we should go out and get a milkshake to mark the occasion?" Christy seemed thrilled with the prospect, her eyes growing big with excitement.

"I'm not sure that I feel up to it tonight," Caroline replied, slightly aloof, as if she had other things on her mind. "I just haven't felt well lately."

Harry saw the little girl's face fall and felt a twinge of guilt for getting her hopes up. "Another time, Christy. Tomorrow is Saturday; maybe we can do it then," he suggested. He hated that she was always in the middle of Caroline's power plays. It made it worse in his mind that she was too young to understand what was going on here. He knew that she must think it was somehow her fault. That she was somehow the cause of it.

"I've got Marnie coming over tomorrow to help me with the pies for the church dinner, Harry. I told you that days ago," Caroline complained. "I can't change my plans now." He could feel the patronization in her tone, and it set him even more on edge than he already was. In all the years he had known Caroline, the last few had been the most difficult. Where once she looked at him with longing eyes and adoration, now she showed him nothing but contempt, disdain, an all too familiar loathing that lingered just below the surface of all of their conversations. Harry had learned to avoid any serious talk with her. He had grown more aloof in attempts at dodging the inevitable fights. When confronted head on, he simply sidestepped the situation and headed for a safe place until it all blew over. It was like living with a ticking time bomb. You knew it was bound to go off, but the when always loomed overhead, destroying any semblance of normality that you hoped for, dashing any confidence you might feel.

"I'm sorry, I must have forgotten." Frankly, Harry was relieved. He paused for a moment as if he were thinking it through and then said, "Tell you what; I'll take Christy with me tomorrow. Then we'll be out of your hair so you and Marnie can work on those pies."

She was pouting and chose not to reply. Where Harry masked his feelings behind a sober face, Caroline was an emotional creature that wore her sentiments quite openly on her sleeve. He almost laughed now to think that that had been something that had made her so appealing to him in the beginning. Christy dared not say anything for fear that her mother would protest the ice cream date. She looked slyly over at Harry, who was trying not to smile at her. The two of them were always conspiring with their unspoken language, which didn't escape Caroline's watchful eyes, even if she chose to ignore it. Christy decided that she didn't want to give her mother a reason to nix tomorrow's plans, so she grudgingly ate the peas until every last one had disappeared from her plate.

Harry observed Caroline across the table as she ate, taking in the delicate way she held her fork, her lips as they closed over her food, the way she gingerly chewed. She had always held a fascination for him that he couldn't shake. It made him angry at himself. What's more is she knew it, she knew what she did to him, and she used it, always to her advantage. He had known her for so long, and yet a stranger may as well have been sitting across from him now. The woman may have looked like Caroline, wore her clothes, smelled of her perfume, but he did not know her.

This realization gave him the startling sensation of being voyeuristic, of prying into some private moment he was not meant to observe. It only added to his discomfort when Caroline's eyes suddenly met his, and for a brief moment they exchanged glances. She lifted an eyebrow to him, as if she were trying to figure something out, ponder an enigma, and she continued to stare at him until he dropped his gaze back to his plate.

A small smile played at the corner of her lips. It was something like a victory that she could get him to look away. She savored her next bite with unusual relish. "The Channings have invited us over for barbeque next week. You haven't got any plans, have you?" she asked.

"No, I haven't got any plans."

"Good, because I told them that we would love to come."

"I'll make a note of it on my itinerary," Harry said dryly.

"Apparently, Ted has gotten himself a new barbeque grill, and he's just dying to show it off."

"Yes, well, Ted's always got something he's dying to show off. He's a big phony, if you ask me," Harry grumbled.

Caroline gave a little laugh. "Are you jealous, Harry?"

"What would I have to be jealous of?"

"I don't know, his grill, maybe."

"I've got a perfectly good grill myself. I don't really give a hoot about his." Harry abruptly scooted his chair out, grabbing his plate and cleaning it off before he set it next to the sink.

"What's the matter? Don't you want any dessert?" she asked.

"No, I don't want any dessert. I don't feel like it," Harry retorted, trying to keep the annoyance from his voice. He didn't want Christy to pick up on their very subtle arguing. Harry chose to remove himself from the situation by retreating to the living room where he relaxed in his lounger, stretching himself out and extending his toes out as far as he could reach them.

Christy trotted in shortly and curled up on his lap while he watched the news. The anchorman announced, "While the president and first lady were attending a dinner for the Women's National Democratic Club at the Sheraton Park Hotel, a bomb threat was telephoned in. President Johnson remained in the hotel for no more than five minutes, and then he and Mrs. Johnson were driven back to the White House. Insiders say that if the president was aware of the bomb threat, he appeared unconcerned. In other news, Barry Goldwater has won the presidential primary in California…"

"What is the world coming to?" Harry asked himself out loud.

"What's wrong, Daddy?" Christy asked, craning her neck so that she was looking up at his face. The news droned on in the background, but Harry now focused his attention on the little girl and didn't hear anything more.

"Oh, nothing important, Bug," he said. She took her small hand and stroked his cheek as if she were petting a kitten.

"Are you sad, Daddy?" Her eyes were so serious, so intense. It melted his heart. What could he say to that? He certainly couldn't admit that he was indeed very sad. That he was so terribly alone. That at times the melancholy he felt came very close to swallowing him whole. No, that would not do.

"How could I be? I have the most beautiful and the smartest girl ever. I'll never be sad as long as you're my girl."

She beamed. "Oh, Daddy, you're so silly."

"I mean it," he insisted. Caroline floated into the room at that point, finished with the dishes. She stood in the archway with her hand on her hip, watching the two of them with something close to envy.

"It's time for you to get ready for bed, Christy," Caroline announced with a no-nonsense tone.

"Can't I stay up for just a little longer?"

"Not tonight. You need to go to bed tonight," Caroline maintained. "It's getting late, and you need to get your rest."

Christy left her father's lap and retreated to her bedroom to slip into her nightgown, leaving Harry and Caroline alone. Harry turned his attention back to the news, hoping that no words would have to be exchanged.

"Are you going to mope all night?" Caroline asked with that irritating condescension in her voice.

"I'm not moping, Caroline. I'm just trying to catch the news."

"It's really a shame, Harry, how pathetic you've become. You were a man once. I remember it well. In high school, when you played football and I was proud to stand beside you, the guy that socked Donald Stump in the nose when he asked me out on a date…" As she made her admission, she dropped her voice to a whisper so that Christy wouldn't hear in the other room. "I thought something of you then, when you were strong enough to fight for what you wanted."

"That was high school, Caroline. You're not the prom queen anymore. Clinging to something that happened eleven years ago is borderline delusional. We all have to grow up at some point." He kept his demeanor distant and aloof.

"You may go gently, but I refuse. I'm sick of this little town, with all of these little people. You promised me once we would move to New York, we would live in an apartment, and go to all the parties and plays on Broadway. Here I am, still stuck in this dull little town, Harry." She didn't even attempt to hide the sarcasm in her tone. "But not for long, if I have anything to do with it."

Harry put the footrest of his chair down and got up. "There are some things that I forgot to clear up at the office," Harry said, slipping past her into the hallway.

"That's right, Harry, run away! Turn tail and run away like you always do. You don't care about me. You don't care what I want or need. Go ahead and go." Harry continued toward the front door. "Don't even bother coming back, for all I care," she cried to the slamming door.

Harry's face was burning, his scalp tingling, as he grabbed his briefcase and keys and left. He climbed into his car and peeled out of the driveway, glimpsing the house with a few lights twinkling behind the window panes in his rearview mirror. He berated himself for allowing Caroline to get to him. At least for Christy's sake, he should have waited until she was asleep. As he drove down the dusty lane, hit the main road, and drove to his office, his conscience pricked him. Poor Christy. He only wanted to make her life as normal as possible. A child shouldn't have to worry over such things. He wanted nothing more than to seal her away in a bubble, to give her the security that she deserved, that she craved.

CHAPTER 26

Dennis Harvey looked pleased to see Nelson again, and his smile was that of a serpent's lying in wait in a patch of tall grass as a mouse was happening along. He resumed his same slouching position in the chair, appearing a little more comfortable with Nelson this time around.

"Back, huh?" he sniggered.

"Good to see you again," Nelson lied, pulling out his trusted digital recorder.

"If you say so." He acted as if he were doubtful of it, though. "You figure out who done it?"

"I was hoping you could help me with that. I thought that, since you had such a good memory, you'd agree to answer a few more questions, if you don't mind. Shed some light on what happened. It would make writing this article a whole lot easier for me."

"Fire away," Harvey said with an excitement that was apparent. He seemed to like the prospect of aiding Nelson in his task.

"Who do you think was responsible for Caroline's death?" Nelson probed.

"I think it was him," the man said without blinking an eye.

"Him who?"

"Her husband."

"Harry Fletcher?" Nelson clarified.

"You bet, Harry Fletcher."

"Did you know him well?"

"No, not well. He was never around when I was there painting. At work, I suppose."

"What makes you think he did it?"

"Everybody went on about how smart he was, how much money he had. But nobody's perfect. Between you and me—" he leaned forward as if he were confiding in Nelson "—I don't think she liked him much. Never said anything; she was too much of a lady for that, but I could just tell. He put on all these airs, but really he was just a, well, inside he was just an arrogant jackass. He didn't deserve her."

"What was she like, Mr. Harvey? How was she?"

"Caroline?"

"Yes, Caroline."

"She was a looker. Everybody thought so. She had these eyes…" He used his pointer finger to draw an imaginary circle around his own eyes as he spoke. "They just went right through you. If I had been Harry Fletcher, well, I would have done her right. She wouldn't have had a reason to want to go to California, if you know what I mean." He smirked.

"Do you remember the last time you saw her?"

"Oh yeah," he said.

"What was she wearing?" Nelson asked.

"You mean—you mean, what she was wearing that afternoon? The day before she died?"

"Yes, that is the last time you saw her, right?"

"That's what I told you, wasn't it?" Harvey snapped, agitated by Nelson's question. "Yeah, I saw her the day before she died. She was wearing a yellow sundress, fitted up top and then it kind of flowed out at the waist. I thought it looked like the same color as the lemonade she gave me."

"Do you remember where you were the night she was murdered?" Nelson continued.

"Hell, I don't know. I guess I was home." Dennis Harvey shifted with a graceless jerk in his seat, scratching his forehead with his thumb.

"I can't imagine how full of rage Harry Fletcher must have been to have done that to his wife," Nelson said as though he were marveling over it to himself but out loud. "To do that to that poor woman."

"I thought over that before. For him to have gone at her that a way, to just keep stabbing her and stabbing her like that, she didn't stand a chance. It was probably some sight, all that blood. Some really awful sight when he finished with her. He must have just snapped," Harvey speculated, then he pursed his lips and shook his head as if it were a real shame.

"Could you tell me, Mr. Harvey, where you got that scar from?" Nelson asked, indicating the sizable white scar that made a jagged line on the inside of his right arm.

Harvey instinctively covered it with his hand, rubbing it with fierce, agitated strokes. "That little old thing?" he scoffed. "Damn, I don't know. That was too long ago to remember how I got it. Why do you wanna know about that?" But his eyes became sly, shrewd. He took a more defensive posture, crossing his leg and turning his body sideways so that he was no longer directly facing Nelson.

"Did you know that Caroline Fletcher bit her attacker?" Nelson enjoyed watching him squirm, enjoyed watching him trying to remain cool, unaffected.

"I guess I heard that…from somewhere."

"I thought you told me you had a *really* good memory. Uncommonly and exceptionally good. You remembered the day your mother died, and you were three? Isn't that what you told me that last time we spoke?"

"What are you getting at?"

"Mr. Harvey, did you go over to the Fletcher home that night?" Nelson interrogated. "I mean, the night she died?"

"No. I already told you I didn't," Dennis Harvey growled.

"Did you stab Caroline Fletcher—"

"No!" he said before Nelson had finished.

" —with a knife from her home? Did you murder Caroline Fletcher in her kitchen?" Nelson remained level-headed while Harvey raged.

"No! I did not!" His composure gone, his hands balled to fists and his knuckles bearing down upon the ledge on his side of the glass, Harvey's face had turned a deep scarlet.

"I think you did. I think I have proof that you did," Nelson asserted. "And if you'll sit down, I'll tell you what I've got."

Dennis Harvey summed Nelson up, weighing his options carefully in his head. He slowly lowered himself back into the chair, squinting his eyes warily at Nelson. Nelson, still stoic, didn't seem bothered by the smoldering glance. "You ain't got nothing," he said with a laugh. "You're all bluff. You're a damn liar."

"What color did you use to paint the porch that day, Mr. Harvey?" Nelson asked. "Did it take you all day, into the night, to finish?"

Harvey folded his arms tightly across his chest, slouching further down into his seat. "Beats me." He shrugged with both of his shoulders.

"For a man with such an accurate memory, you're certainly having a difficult time remembering some of the simplest of details."

"That was forty-some years ago!" he defended.

"I suppose it would be hard to remember that far back. I'll help you out. It was a shade of white."

Harvey wouldn't look at Nelson. He focused his attention on a hole that had begun to wear through his pant leg close to the seam.

"Am I right? Was it a shade of white?" Nelson continued.

Harvey was done answering questions; he just sat there and glared.

"I think you killed Caroline Fletcher that night, Mr. Harvey. I think you butchered her in her own home, in a most barbaric manner, with her daughter sleeping down the hall. She was screaming, she was fighting for her life, she bit you, and you just kept stabbing her and stabbing her."

"You can't prove that! You can't prove it," he said just under his breath. "I never killed nobody, and you can't prove it."

"You're in here for life for murder, aren't you, Mr. Harvey?"

"That's—that's not what I meant. I meant, you—you can't prove that I killed *that* woman. I never…You got the wrong man. I never did it," Harvey said, and he got up and walked away.

CHAPTER 27

Caroline sat before her vanity in her white silk nightgown, stroking her hair firmly with a brush. It was uncomfortably still elsewhere, in the shadows of the house, only the katydids' chirp from the clipped grass just outside her window to keep her company. Caroline hated the hush that enveloped her at moments like this. She preferred not to ponder anything too deep, to reflect upon her life, her circumstances. Noise, and activities, and people were her diversions. Funny thing about Caroline, despite trying to subdue her conscience, endeavoring to dash the memories of her sinful existence, she could not disremember the harmful and loathsome decisions she had integrated into her life with her power of choice. Like a child, she feared the dark for the monsters it brought with it.

Like a child, she also stubbornly refused to admit that she was wrong, that she was accountable for her own actions. The blame game was so much easier than bearing the weight of her indiscretions on her own weak shoulders. It was too frightening to face her reflection in the mirror with the knowledge that she had destroyed her life and the lives of others, too terrifying to confess in any way, shape, or form that she was liable for the irreparable ruin she had left in her wake.

Caroline was so proficient at employing guilt upon others that she gave herself little opportunity to dwell on her share of responsibility in the problems that revolved around her. So, when she chanced to have a moment of introspection, she ran from it with all haste and speed. Caroline set the brush down, restlessly walking down the hallway to Christy's room. She hovered over the sleeping child, feeling an emotion that was perplexing.

Since Christy's birth, she had struggled with resentment, inadequacy, and confusion, yo-yoing between uncertainty and outright anger, over this child that had been born to her. But sleeping there upon her pillow, she looked like an angel, soft skin aglow from the moonlight filtering through the window, her face soft and vulnerable. Caroline nearly cried because, despite all of the mixed and varied emotions that were a product of her little daughter, she loved the girl. She loved her. Why did life have to be so complicated? Leaving a tender kiss on Christy's brow, she left her room, shutting the door softly behind her.

Standing in the hallway, Caroline thought she heard something. She stood still and strained to listen. Yes, it was a hushed tapping at the front door. Moving soundlessly to the door, she peeked through the peep hole, her eyebrows drawing together. Caroline opened the door and whispered, "What are you doing here so late?"

Shifting uneasily from one foot to the other in the inky shadows of front porch, his gaze darted from her back to the welcome mat. He looked around apprehensively before asking, "Could I come in?"

Caroline craned her neck out the door, taking her turn at looking around, making sure that no one else had seen her late night visitor. She stepped aside and let Dennis Harvey, the young house painter, inside. "You're lucky Mr. Fletcher isn't home tonight."

"I knew he wasn't. The light's on at his office," Dennis told her. "I saw him there before I come over."

"Keep your voice down. Christy is asleep," she warned.

"I had to talk to you," he said in a hushed tone.

"Come into the kitchen so that no one sees the lights from the front road." Caroline showed him into the kitchen. When she turned around, he was close, close enough to make her uncomfortable. Instinctively, she crossed her arms over her chest. She was used to being the one that initiated contact with a man, the one in control. In her home, in her nightgown, she felt uneasy. She felt exposed, but she refused to show it. Caroline was not about to relinquish her power to him. She took a step back, realizing with a small sense of amusement that he was nervous. "What's so urgent you couldn't wait until

Monday?" she asked. She noticed his disheveled appearance in the light of the kitchen. "You're a mess."

"Sorry. I been painting all day. I just finished before I came over here," he said as he looked himself over for the first time. His cheeks pinked, and he dropped his eyes to his work boots. She thought it was a habit of his, to look at his boots when he didn't know what else to do.

"So, why are you here?" she demanded, raising her eyebrow ever so slightly.

"I-I…" he stammered, shutting his eyes and screwing his face up in anguish.

"You what?"

"My brother…He found the brooch," Dennis continued on in what appeared to be pure torture.

"So?" she pressed.

"So, he says he's going to keep it."

Caroline allowed this new revelation to sink in. "What do you mean he says he's going to keep it?" she fumed. Then she jerked her head, paranoid by a sound. "Did you hear that?" she whispered fiercely.

"What?" Dennis asked, trying to listen too.

Caroline cocked her head, straining to hear any further disturbance. "Sh!" She glided toward the kitchen entryway. "Harry is that you?" No answer. "Harry?" She waited, expecting her irate husband to fly through the entry way, raging that he had caught her with someone. No one materialized. She cautiously crept to the front door. No sign of Harry. Caroline went back to where Dennis waited in the kitchen. "It was nothing," she told him. "You want to tell me how your brother got his hands on my brooch?"

"He found it. He found it, and he says that he won't give it back to me," Dennis explained.

"Well, you just tell him it's mine."

"I did. He still won't give it back."

"That was my grandmother's brooch," she said, growing upset. "If you don't return it to me, I'll call the police."

"I told 'im that too." Dennis reached in his shirt pocket and pulled out a cigarette, twisting it agitatedly between his fingers, putting it between his lips without lighting it.

"And what did he say then?"

Dennis removed the cigarette from between his lips, inspecting it pressed between his thumb and pointer finger. "He said you wouldn't call the police because you'd gotta admit that you gave the brooch to me in the first place."

"Dennis, that's my brooch. I need that money," she cried.

"I know, I know," he said, holding his hand out to quiet her.

"You go tell him that if he doesn't return it to me, I will call the police and I'll tell them he stole it or something," she threatened.

"Won't do no good. He'll tell 'em the truth."

"Who'll they believe, him or me?" She grew all the more angry.

Dennis drew closer to her. He slipped his fingers to the base of her neck, cradling the back of her skull in the palm of his hand. "Caroline, I know you need the money. But listen, I been putting some money aside, without my brother knowing, and I think I got enough for the two of us to make it to California," he murmured softly. "I can get us to California, and then I'll get me a job there and I'll take care of you."

In her agitated state, Caroline did not pick up on the tenderness his voice carried. She looked at him with distress joined with annoyance. She pulled away from him, turning her back to him as she leaned against the table top. "You've got enough money to take me to California?" she asked incredulously. Dennis didn't seem to notice her sudden mood change.

"Yes. I've saved up a couple hundred," he admitted.

"A couple hundred, huh?"

"Yeah."

"And you think that's going to pay for gas and food and hotels?" she questioned doubtfully.

"You could pack some sandwiches. We could sleep in the car if we needed to," he reasoned.

"You want me to sleep in the car…with you?"

"Now, you said you wanted to go to California," he replied defensively.

"I'm not packing sandwiches, and I'm not sleeping in a car with you!" she hissed. "And I'm certainly not going with you, either." Her words were vicious, meant to be hurtful, meant to be final.

Dennis reacted as if he had been slapped in the face. His mouth fell open, and his eyes grew wide. "I know you're upset about the brooch," he began, "but—"

"Upset? That's an understatement."

"Look, I'll make it right. You might have to wait a little longer, but I'll get you to California. I'll do it in style, like you deserve. I promise."

"You won't get me anywhere!"

"You said you wanted to get out of this place. You told me you and I could leave together."

"I never said together, Dennis. I said I would give you part of the money, but I never agreed to go anywhere with you. You can just get that out of your head right now." She turned on him, fire burning in her eyes. "Did you honestly think I would run off with some kid and live the life of a handyman's kept woman? I think I could do better than that." She laughed scornfully.

Dennis was hurt to the core. He looked at her, bewildered and humiliated, stung so badly by her comments that he didn't know what to say. He realized then that she had only been using him, using him to get what she wanted, making a fool of him. He saw Caroline Fletcher now with fresh eyes, someone of the same make and build as his brother, as his father. His chest burned, his fingers trembled.

"Get out of here, Dennis, before Harry comes home," she commanded. "And don't show your face here again until you can bring me back that brooch. You understand?"

"I told you, I don't got the brooch."

"You'll find a way to get it back, or I'll phone the police station and tell them it's been stolen, and then I'll point them to you."

"That's a lie," he seethed.

"I don't care if it's a lie or not. I want that brooch, and I'll do what I have to to get it back."

No sooner had she gotten the words out of her mouth when he lunged at her, knocking her back into the table, shoving it into the wall, his body on top of hers, his fingers curled around her delicately small neck. Caroline was completely taken off guard and tried to push him off of her, grunting from the effort. She was choking, gasping for breath, coughing from asphyxiation. Struggling against him yielded no results. He was stronger than she was, too strong to fight against.

Instinct kicked in, and she closed her teeth down on his arm, biting as deep and as hard as she could.

Dennis let out a yelp and pulled his arm away, the force of it breaking off a few of Caroline's teeth, her mouth bloodied, but it gave her a split second to wiggle out from beneath him. She made a run for the back door, crazily desperate to get away from him, her brain unable to even form thoughts before he caught her wrist, reeling her back in. She tried to pull away, launching herself against the counter top, flailing her arms wildly, knocking off canisters of flour and sugar, overturning the knife set, a bowl clattering as it fell from its perch. The two struggled for control, grappling in a fevered frenzy, until Dennis's fingers brushed against the smooth wood of a knife handle. He grabbed at it, squeezing it deliberately in a hard grip in his hand.

His next lucid moment was standing just beyond the back door, breathing in the night air. He was shaking, his heart pounding. To steady his nerves, he pulled out a cigarette, lit it, and puffed deeply a few times. He realized what a mess he was when he observed his hands, bathed in blood, cast eerily in the moonlight. He turned them over and inspected them with a morbid curiosity. Spooked by what he saw, he attempted to wipe them on his pant legs, finding it futile. His jeans were wet with her blood as well. He dropped the cigarette, crushing it with the toe of his boot.

Dennis went back through the kitchen, grabbing the knife he had used, extinguishing the lights, leaving her behind. He was alarmed, yes, although his primary emotion was exoneration. She had gotten what was coming to her. It was a sense of power he had never felt in his seventeen long years of living. Each strike of the knife had unleashed in him a fury that grew in its own strength, until he was powerless to even have the will to fight it. But he discovered, as he let it out in a torrent of violence, that he didn't want to control it. He was the one in the driver's seat, his hands on the wheel; he was the one calling the shots for once in his miserable life. It was liberating beyond anything he had ever done before. After taking it for so long, he had dished it out, and he vowed to himself he would never be the one taking it again. This night was the first night of his life, the beginning of his destiny's changing.

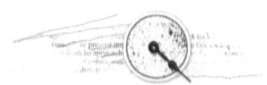

After Harry had calmed down, working methodically on the sums before him, keeping each number in its own neat and meticulous column, he could breathe again. Order was the thing that gave him back his composure. His eyes began to blur as he continued working the numbers in his head; they swam and swirled together on the paper before him. He was suddenly startled by the telephone ringing. He jumped and made a lunge to answer it as it rang again.

"Hello," he said a little breathlessly.

"Harry?"

"Yes," Harry answered, his response guarded, for he knew immediately who it was on the other end of the line.

"I saw the light on in your office," Opal said softly.

"Just finishing up on some paperwork."

"I'm sorry, I shouldn't have called. I just wanted to see how you were doing." She hesitated. "I miss you, Harry."

"I'm doing fine." He paused for a long time. "How have you been, Opal?" He could sense that she was crying softly. "Opal?"

"I'm sorry I bothered you. I'll let you go," she whispered, and then the line was dead. He put the phone back on the receiver and leaned his elbows on the desk, rubbing his face vigorously with his hands.

The next thing Harry knew, he was waking, his head lying on the top of the desk, a pool of saliva on the papers he had been working on. He ran the back of his hand across his mouth and sat up with a start. He checked his wrist watch; it was one thirty in the morning. He should have gone home hours ago. Harry collected his things, shoving them into his briefcase haphazardly as he headed for the door. His brain was fuzzy as he found his way home along the quiet concrete and then back down the dirt lane to his home. A solitary light shone through the bedroom window. All was stillness but for the sound of insects in the night, katydids and crickets searching for a mate in the vague stillness.

Harry opened the front door, not needing his keys to the unlocked entrance. He dropped his briefcase on the floor and loosened his tie as he went toward the bedroom. He had just passed the front room when he heard footsteps in the darkness.

"Caroline?" he murmured into the shadows. Just as he turned to see who it was, he was struck over the head. That was the last thing that he remembered before coming to. The pain shooting through his skull was nearly unbearable when he came to his senses and realized he was sprawled on the carpet in the hallway. He crawled onto his haunches, feeling the room spin around him. Harry collapsed onto the floor again.

The second time he attempted to get up, he used the aid of the chair next to the credenza in the entryway. He sat himself on the chair for a moment, running his finger along his neck line, where rivulets of blood had dried and crusted, and then closer to the base of his neck to the place where it still ran fresh. Harry struggled to his feet and staggered to his daughter's room, opening the door in a burst and rushing to the bedside. Christy's even breathing came in rhythmic rising and falling as she slept peacefully with her stuffed rabbit next to her.

Harry shut the door quietly behind him as he warily made his way to his bedroom. He stood in the doorway and gazed upon an empty room. He noticed the twin beds, both made; Caroline wasn't in hers. Her jewelry box was tipped on its side, the contents spilled out onto her dressing table. He backed out, spinning with confusion, his brain reeling, retracing his steps through the house, lingering in the archway of the living room. Finally, he went to investigate the kitchen.

In the murky darkness, he smelled something strange that he couldn't quite place. It was an earthy smell that he thought similar to dirt, perhaps. His senses reeling, he struggled to focus his eyes, and then he saw it, the light from down the hallway lending enough illumination to cast his shadow on the cabinets, giving an eerie feel to the once familiar and comfortable place.

He dared not move, dared not believe what his eyes were seeing. The lack of substantial light lent to the scene the feel of an old movie washed in grays, the collecting blood on the linoleum seeming black as it spread and puddled across the floor. One leg was propped up on the edge of an overturned chair, bare foot with painted red toe nails dangling in the air, her other leg stretched out before her, the ivory colored slipper that matched her silk night dress still on that foot.

Revulsion ran through him, turned his stomach, made his gut quiver. He backed away desperately, tripping over the transition from the linoleum to the carpet in his haste. Harry fell hard onto his back, flipping over and crawling with all urgency away from the horrific scene. He sat with his knees drawn up to his chest, panting hard, shaking violently.

Harry's mind focused on Christy, sleeping in the bed just down the hall. He feared that she might wake up, might happen upon Caroline, laid out on the floor in the kitchen. What should he do? With great effort, he forced himself back to his feet and retraced his steps to his bedroom, picking up the receiver to the red telephone on the table between the twin beds. He plugged his finger into the hole next to the number seven and pulled the rotary around to the silver hook under the zero. He repeated this process until he had dialed his sister's number, and then he waited, the phone ringing in his trembling fingers, an eternity passing.

"Hello," came Richard's sleepy voice.

"S-Something's h-happened…" Harry stammered.

"Harry?"

"I must speak to Dinah," he said, his voice growing frantic.

"All right, Harry, all right," Richard said. Harry could hear him waking Dinah in the background.

Dinah spoke in a confused and groggy muttering. "Harry, it's three o'clock in the morning. What's the matter?"

"I think they've killed Caroline," Harry cried. "I think they've killed her."

"What? What are you talking about, Harry? You're not making sense," Dinah said, catching the panic she felt from the other end of the line.

"Dinah, listen to me. I need you to come and get Christy. I need you to come and get her before this all hits the fan."

"I'm on my way," Dinah said. "I'll be there in half an hour, Harry. Just stay calm. I'll be there."

CHAPTER 28

"It's all there," Nelson informed Harry as he dropped the large manila envelope on the desk.

Harry's age-spotted, withered hands reached out and caressed the smoothness of it, a look of confusion passing over his features. "What is this?" he asked in his inherently gentle yet commanding voice. He waited a moment for Nelson to answer.

"My report, sir. I've finished, and that is a write-up of what I've discovered during the duration of my investigation."

"Not to be rude, but you see, it doesn't do me a lot of good with my eyes. I won't be able to read it."

"I know."

Harry cocked his head to the side, wondering at what Nelson was up to. "You know?"

"To be honest, sir, everything that I've included in that report could be very damaging to you as well as others I came across in the course of my inquiries."

"I see," Harry replied.

"If you still wish to know all of the dirty details of it…Well, I figured you'd find a way."

"Were you able to exonerate me, prove that I didn't kill my wife?" Harry asked, eager and on the edge of his seat, still with the cane in his grasp.

"Yes, sir. You'll be glad to know they're in the process of reviewing the case and will be looking over the evidence again. I am confident that it will prove you were not responsible for Caroline's murder. That you were innocent."

"Who?" he whispered. "Who was it?"

"Dennis Harvey," Nelson answered.

"He was just a boy," Harry said in horror. "I never knew him really, but he was just a boy."

"That was no indicator of what he was capable of."

Harry left Nelson's office with his shoulders rounded, his steps lighter. He could live with a small semblance of peace now. Soon the world would know that Harry Fletcher was not a murderer, he was not the vile man they had made him out to be. After forty-five years, Harry could finally let the past be the past and crawl out from under the shroud of suspicion that had loomed dark and heavy on those shoulders for so long.

Harry was not the only person privy to the report. Nelson had attempted calling the retirement home to see if Marnie Donner would allow him to come see her. She gave him an emphatic no. Nelson didn't feel that he could leave things as they were, and so he mailed her a copy of the report. Marnie ran her crooked finger along the seal when she received the fat, yellow envelope, and after opening it, she read every word as if it were life or death. And it was life and death. Not just Caroline's, but hers as well.

In the darkness of night, Marnie lay upon her pillow, her mind wandering over the sheets of paper Nelson had sent her. Caroline's face floated before her, haunting as it always was. Some might defend her by saying that she was in shock, that she didn't realize what she was doing, she thought, but Marnie had known exactly what she was doing. She had known that she had condemned Caroline to die. She had known that she had chosen to allow Caroline to suffer, in agony, alone on the kitchen floor.

Just as surely as the man who wielded the knife that had ripped through Caroline had murder tarnishing his soul, so did Marnie. Turning her back on Caroline was nothing less than a death sentence. Marnie knew this. She knew it deep down in the depths of her conscience, but she didn't care. It was a burden that she had borne upon her shoulders for all of these years.

As her mind worked over these things, she began to feel something, a strange sort of tingling in her fingers. A horrific pain seized her head, shooting tremors through her body, and her eyes quivered and slid shut. It was Caroline she saw—her angry, vengeful, contorted face—and then nothing. Eventually life catches up to you. We all come to the inevitable end when we must meet our maker and account for what we've done with these fragile lives we possess for the short time we're given. Marnie's end had finally caught up with her. Her end was quick—a flash of pain and then she was gone. What more could you ask for than to die in your bed? Marnie's stroke was quick and somewhat merciful in its nature.

"It's snowing," Cleo squealed. "I mean really snowing! Get your coat and come play with me!" It was December now, frigid with a few inches of powder on the ground.

Nelson shrugged his coat on as he followed her down the hall and out into the cold. She tromped through the snow, white flakes collecting in her hair, on her eyelashes, clinging to the wool of her coat, as she crouched, hiding around the corner of the building. Cleo stooped to grab snow from the ground in her cupped hand. Waiting for the opportune moment, she stood and launched the snowball, hitting Nelson as he exited the door.

"Hey!" he cried.

"What's the matter, Nelson? You can't handle a little snow?"

Her taunting spurred him to action. He chased her across the parking lot and tackled her as they reached the soft grass, padded with inches of white snow. She fell flat, pinned to the ground with Nelson holding her wrists in his hands. She was laughing and so was he. "The question is, can *you* handle a little snow?" He raised an eyebrow mischievously.

"You wouldn't dare!"

With a determined smile, Nelson pushed her wrists together above her head and secured them with just one of his hands so that he had the other hand free to scrape up snow. He took the snow and unceremoniously rubbed it in her face.

She wriggled beneath him, hollering in protest. "My hair!"

"Your hair?" he said sarcastically.

"I just spent a half an hour straightening it," she complained.

Nelson rolled off of her, lying flat on his back next to her as the snowflakes floated down, blanketing his hair and eyelashes, making him slightly dizzy as he watched them coming toward him. He was chuckling. "I didn't know you were so vain, Cleo."

She rotated on to her side so that she was facing him. "Vanity is only one of my many charms," she replied.

"I see." He reached out and rubbed a snowflake off of her nose with his thumb. "Well, I can see how it would be hard to not become vain if I were looking at a face like yours every morning. As a matter of fact, I might never get anything done. I would just stand there all day, watching myself in the mirror."

She smiled sweetly. "I have a secret," she said conspiratorially.

Nelson was smiling back. "You do?"

"Uh-huh."

"What is this secret?" He turned his head to get a better look at her.

She dropped her voice to a whisper, her gaze growing intense. "I think," she said, "that I've fallen in love with you, Nelson Rune." She could see the surprised expression he flashed her. For a moment, she considered that it was not the best thing for her to admit to him. After all, didn't guys have commitment issues? But it was Nelson, and she could tell him anything, couldn't she?

Cleo got up and ran away, laughter trailing over her shoulder. He chased her. He figured that's what men were put on the earth to do, chase the girl they wanted.

Before they went back in, Cleo collected the mail and the paper from her box in the front hallway and then followed Nelson back to his apartment. She flipped the paper over, catching sight of a familiar face. It was Marnie, a picture of her young and vibrant next to the picture that Cleo had initially recognized. A strange sort of before-and-after, the before image showed a girl expecting only the best from life, believing that her dreams would come true. The after image was of a woman jaded and worn from the cares of the world, her face creased and wrinkled with a look of experience, a look of knowing in her eyes.

Cleo showed it to Nelson, shaking the moisture from her hair and hands, sending droplets of water flying, like a dog shaking after a bath. "That's an odd coincidence. Mrs. Donner has passed away," she said, holding the page up for him to see. Nelson took it from her and read through it. She snuggled up next to him, trying to warm herself from the chill she felt. "Terrible, isn't it?"

"Yeah," Nelson agreed.

"I'm so cold," she said, through chattering teeth, rubbing her hands together.

Nelson pulled his favorite afghan, a hideous rusty-orange and brown throw he'd had for years, from the end of the futon, and draped it over Cleo. "Let's get you warmed up," he said as he wrapped his arms around her.

They sat gazing at the miniature tree they had picked out together just last week. Nelson had no decorations to fancy it up with, just a plain string of lights, so Cleo had spent several hours cutting snowflakes from white paper to scatter on the tiny branches. It was simple, but they both were happy with the results.

Cleo glanced over at the floor near the entryway and noticed the snow she had tracked in. "Look what I've done," she lamented, eyeing her boots on the floor in front of her. "I've made a mess."

"It's no big deal," Nelson told her. "It'll dry out eventually." He eyed the beads of melted snow Cleo had sprinkled in her haste at drying off and the tracks in the shape of her size-seven shoes, and it dawned on him. Like a smack upside the head, it hit him solid. "Oh, crap!" he yelled.

Cleo was confused. She looked at him as if he had fallen off his rocker. "What's wrong?"

"I screwed up," he bellowed, running his fingers through his hair, sitting at attention on the edge of the futon. "I wasn't thinking."

"What are you talking about, Nelson?"

"No blood."

"No *blood?*" she asked, shaking beneath the blanket.

"There was no blood, Cleo."

Cleo was just as dumbfounded as she had been before. His revelation meant nothing to her. "I don't understand what you're talking about."

"There was no blood through the rest of the house," Nelson went on. "None."

"Get to the point," Cleo urged. She was growing impatient. She could generally wait until he was able to collect his thoughts; able to work through it in his head so that he could tell her exactly what he had on his mind, but patience was not a strong point with her. She didn't like being in the dark, and the longer he prolonged it, the more agitated she grew.

"Who hit Harry Fletcher on the head? Who knocked him out when he came home that night?" Nelson posed.

"Dennis Harvey," Cleo answered. "Dennis Harvey killed Caroline. It's been all but proven. They reopened the case, and it's been all but proven, Nelson."

"He left out the back door. The only footprints they found were in the kitchen and on the back walkway. And we already figured that Harvey was covered with blood. No blood. You see?"

"No, not really."

"There was no blood found in the rest of the house. If Harvey was in the living room, there would have been blood evidence. He would have tracked it in or dripped it along the way," Nelson said.

"But there was none," she finished.

"Dennis Harvey didn't hit Harry over the head. He would have left a trail from the kitchen to the living room if it had been him," Nelson went on.

"But it doesn't make sense," Cleo said. "Dennis Harvey did it, didn't he?"

"He wasn't the only one in the house that night," Nelson told her. "He couldn't have been."

"Who, then?"

"Good question. I don't think it's as much of a coincidence as you do," Nelson said, reaching over to grab the paper, then holding the obituary up for her to see.

"Marnie?"

"Who else had the motive? Who else had no alibi?"

"Well, Chuck, for one."

Nelson shook his head. "What did Marnie say?"

"Chuck admitted he had a relationship. Marnie blew up. She stormed out," Cleo summed up. "Am I missing anything?"

"No."

"So…"

"So, Marnie drove around for hours by herself?" Nelson asked. "No one but Marnie knows that for sure. She went back there that night — to confront Caroline. She was there. Do you remember how adamant she was about Chuck's innocence? She said she *knew* he hadn't done it."

"We'll never know absolutely," Cleo pointed out. "She's dead."

"I guess not."

"Don't get all brooding on me," she said, watching his face turn to a scowl. "The important thing is that you figured out who really killed her. If Marnie was there that night, it doesn't change things. Dennis Harvey was the one responsible for Caroline Fletcher's murder."

"Maybe you're right," he agreed. "Best to let sleeping dogs lie."

"This isn't going to ruin your day, is it?"

"Don't think anything could ruin my day at this point. Am I mistaken, or did you say you loved me?"

"Hm, I get what you're doing here. Making me say it again when you have made no such declaration yourself. Well, Nelson, I am far too clever to fall for that sort of trick. I am willing to wait. And let me be perfectly candid, I can wait a very long time."

"Who says you have to wait?" Nelson asked.

"Stop!"

"Stop what?"

"Don't say it yet."

"Why not?"

"Because I have time. Because sometimes the waiting makes it better somehow. And I'm not going anywhere, Nelson. You are stuck with me."

"If you couldn't tell, I wanna be stuck with you, Cleo. Stuck is a very good place to be."

CHAPTER 29

It was more than Marnie could bear—the thought of Chuck with Caroline. She wondered how she hadn't seen the signs, hadn't realized there was something amiss. She'd always tried to keep their marriage fresh, their romance alive, even after long days of chasing their young son around. It turned her stomach, made her quake, to feel so betrayed, to be so vulnerable. She drove in the dark, and it was as if the car steered itself, turning corners, following the familiar route on autopilot. She came to a stop, parked beneath the huge oak tree just down the street from the Fletcher home. She turned off the headlights and sat in darkness for a moment, eyeing the house anxiously. Harry's car was gone. Good, that made things much less complicated, she thought.

Marnie drifted to the back of the car, unlocking the trunk and rifling through its contents. She pulled the bulky pipe wrench, the size of a man's forearm, from the assortment of tools Chuck kept there, the tools he used down at the tow yard. It fell heavy to her side, fifteen pounds of dead weight, as she approached the house. She stealthily opened the front door, carefully shutting it with as little noise as possible.

Marnie noticed right away the faint light from the kitchen and the hushed tones of two people talking. She quickly hid in the front room, pressing herself up against the wall. Caroline called out. "Harry, is that you?" she said. "Harry?" Marnie felt the hairs on her neck rise as Caroline floated through the hallway. If the wall hadn't been there, they would have stood side by side. Caroline paused there for a moment, but, seeing no one, returned to the kitchen.

Just barely able to make out the urgent murmurs from the other room, Marnie realized that Caroline was arguing with a man. It was Caroline's soft song-like voice, mixed with the deeper base of a male's. Who it might be was not immediately clear to her. As the fight progressed, Marnie got the gist of it—something about a brooch, a brooch that belonged to Caroline, a brooch that had somehow become lost to her. The fighting heated up, escalating, until the two were in a physical struggle. Marnie could make out the sound of the table scooting across the linoleum, things crashing about, objects clattering to the floor.

She could sense that Caroline was in peril, her heart thrumming violently in her breast as she realized what must be happening in the next room. She had come to kill Caroline, and someone had beaten her to it. The irony of it was incredible. The worst of it was hearing Caroline's muffled cries, her frantic gasps, her brutal struggle to preserve her life. The sound of the back door opening and closing again marked the end of the scuffle between Caroline and her assailant. It seemed unnaturally quiet in the aftermath.

Marnie stood there with weak knees, holding herself up against the wall, her cheek and hand pressed against the cool plaster. She could hear the clock on the wall ticking, the sound magnified to a loud drum in her ear. Should she creep from her hiding place? Should she chance giving up her safe spot? Before she could make a definitive decision, she heard the back door open again. He hadn't gone yet. There were a few slight noises as the mystery man walked about the kitchen. The lights went off, pitching her into darkness, and then the back door opened and shut again.

Standing there in the shadows of the living room, Marnie's eyes began to grow accustomed to the dark. Moonlight trickled through the windows, casting the rooms with an eerie light. The clock continued to tick, and then the faintest of moans wafted through the silent home. There was no mistaking who it came from.

Marnie waited a minute longer before she abandoned her hiding place. She tiptoed down the hallway, stopping on the edge of the carpet as if it were a barrier, a line she was not supposed to cross. She stood there with the wrench at her side, her knuckles white from gripping it so determinedly. The scene before her was horrifying beyond anything she had ever seen. She shut her eyes tight, opened them again, hoping it would erase what she was registering. But the view was just the same as it had been.

Caroline was sprawled on the floor, covered in her own blood. The physical beauty that had once been an aura around her was gone. Her face was contorted in fear, in pain, her teeth broken, her hair tangled. Her eyes met Marnie's with a pleading that took Marnie's breath away.

"Help…me," she said, hardly able to force the words from her throat. Marnie could hear her breathing, heavy, raspy, and seemingly difficult.

She simply stood there, indecisive, grasping the wrench in something close to terror. But what was she afraid of? What was it that frightened her so badly? Was it the thought of Caroline lying before her in the last moments of her mortal life? Was it the thought of the man who had done this to her, that he might come back?

It was none of those things. The thing that Marnie feared the most at that instant was herself. She looked at Caroline's bloody body, completely helpless and vulnerable, and she felt no pity. None. It was as if she was empty inside, as if the heart that beat in her chest was gone, a vacant cavity left in its wake. The moment stretched itself; Caroline's eyes locked with Marnie's, until the sound of a car pulling into the driveway and the accompanying headlights flashing across the wall broke the spell.

Marnie ran to the front room, back to her hiding place against the wall. She heard the footsteps on the front walkway, and then the front door opening. It was Harry, and Marnie realized, with a sinking feeling in the pit of her stomach, that she was trapped. There was no way out. She sensed Harry passing, his silhouette, an impressive size, cast against the far wall. It was now or never.

She stealthily moved in behind Harry, raising the wrench above her head. He started to turn toward her, calling out for Caroline, before she let the wrench fall, knocking him with a solid crack on the back of his skull. He fell in a crumpled heap to the floor. Marnie stood over him, wanting to make sure that he would not get up. When it was apparent that Harry was down for the count, she took a gingerly step around him and went toward the kitchen one last time.

Caroline had not moved. The scarlet pool of blood was growing, expanding. Her eye lids fluttered ever so slightly, and her mouth hardly moved as she begged, "Please…" It was no more than an exhale, something close to a weak whimper.

"I know what you did," Marnie murmured, just loud enough for Caroline to here. "I know about Chuck." And then she turned her back to the dying woman. She turned her back and walked away. In a frightened fluster, Marnie ran to the bedroom, pulling drawers open in a rush, turning the jewelry box on its side, dumping its contents. She backtracked through the hallway, sweeping everything from the credenza in the entryway to the ground. She went back into the living room, turning things over in a frenzy as she went. When her work was done, Marnie slipped quietly out the front door, securing it behind her.

The betrayed woman had come to kill her best friend, and by some strange twist of fate, had been beaten to it. It was something, she thought as she tossed the pipe wrench with a heavy clatter into the trunk of the car, that she was willing to live with.

Marnie brushed her hands together, as if dusting minute specks of dirt from them, and climbed into the driver's seat, looking back only once as she pulled away, headed home to make sure that her boy Steven was safely tucked into bed.

The End

AUTHOR'S NOTES

After extensive research and study of some high-profile unsolved mysteries, I was able to construct the story of the murder of Caroline Fletcher. This story is a work of fiction, invented through the inspiration of several collated stories that really did happen, but with my own twist on it. While some of it is based on factual evidence from cold cases, the people in my book are merely a concoction of my imagination, characters of a story.

I would like to recognize the help and support of those around me who listened to me, inspired me, and helped me come up with some plausible resolutions to the problems that I encountered while writing, including my parents Doug and Sharon Beaty for their continued and constant help and support, my husband Ben, and my close friends and family who read the manuscript and gave feedback. First off, thanks to my sister Ashley for inventing the boy genius Nelson. What a fascinating and fun character, and he wouldn't have been if it hadn't been for her. Thank you to my husband and daughter for getting me through the last few chapters. Thanks to my sister Jennifer whose suggestions led me to my surprising finale.

Also, my appreciation goes to Dean Livingston and my brother-in-law Steven Westfall for answering all of my questions about law enforcement, police procedure, and generally helping me make Nelson's evidence-room break-in and janitorial work accurate. I simply couldn't have written this book without all them.

ABOUT THE AUTHOR

 Tracy Winegar enjoys cooking and gardening in her free time. She loves all things vintage and considers several family heirlooms to be her prized possessions. She's also always on the lookout to score pieces to add to her growing Jadeite collection.

Tracy lives with her husband and four beautiful children in Northern Utah. Although she doesn't mind living in a desert, she still misses the green of the Midwest where she was born and raised.

New Adult

Three Daves by Nicki Elson
Streamline by Jennifer Lane
The Shades series: *Shades of Atlantis* & *Shades of Avalon* by Carol Oates
The Heart series: *Beside Your Heart, Disclosure of the Heart* & *Forever Your Heart*
by Mary Whitney
Romancing the Bookworm by Kate Evangelista
Fighting Fate by Linda Kage
Flirting with Chaos by Kenya Wright
The Vice, Virtue & Video series: *Revealed* & *Captured* by Bianca Giovanni

Erotic Romance

The Keyhole series: *Becoming sage* (book 1) by Kasi Alexander
The Keyhole series: *Saving sunni* (book 2) by Kasi & Reggie Alexander
The Winemaker's Dinner: *Appetizers* & *Entrée* by Dr. Ivan Rusilko & Everly Drummond
The Winemaker's Dinner: *Dessert* by Dr. Ivan Rusilko
Client N° 5 by Joy Fulcher

Paranormal Romance

The Light series: *Seers of Light, Whisper of Light* & *Circle of Light*
by Jennifer DeLucy
The Hanaford Park series: *Eve of Samhain* & *Pleasures Untold* by Lisa Sanchez
Immortal Awakening by KC Randall
The Seraphim series: *Crushed Seraphim* & *Bittersweet Seraphim*
by Debra Anastasia
The Guardian's Wild Child by Feather Stone
Grave Refrain by Sarah M. Glover
Divinity by Patricia Leever
Blood Vine series: *Blood Vine, Blood Entangled* & *Blood Reunited*
by Amber Belldene
Divine Temptation by Nicki Elson
Love in the Time of the Dead by Tera Shanley

Historical Romance

Cat O' Nine Tails by Patricia Leever
Burning Embers by Hannah Fielding
Good Ground by Tracy Winegar

←———→Romantic Suspense←———→

Whirlwind by Robin DeJarnett
The CONduct series: *With Good Behavior, Bad Behavior* &
On Best Behavior by Jennifer Lane
Indivisible by Jessica McQuinn
Between the Lies by Alison Oburia
Blind Man's Bargain by Tracy Winegar

←———→Anthologies←———→

A Valentine Anthology including short stories by
Alice Clayton ("With a Double Oven"),
Jennifer DeLucy ("Magnus of Pfelt, Conquering Viking Lord"),
Nicki Elson ("I Don't Do Valentine's Day"),
Jessica McQuinn ("Better Than One Dead Rose and a Monkey Card"),
Victoria Michaels ("Home to Jackson"), and
Alison Oburia ("The Bridge")

←———→Singles and Novellas←———→

It's Only Kinky the First Time (A Keyhole series single) by Kasi Alexander
Learning the Ropes (A Keyhole series single) by Kasi & Reggie Alexander
The Winemaker's Dinner: RSVP by Dr. Ivan Rusilko
The Winemaker's Dinner: No Reservations by Everly Drummond
Big Guns by Jessica McQuinn
Concessions by Robin DeJarnett
Starstruck by Lisa Sanchez
New Flame by BJ Thornton
Shackled by Debra Anastasia
Swim Recruit by Jennifer Lane
Sway by Nicki Elson
Full Speed Ahead by Susan Kaye Quinn
The Second Sunrise by Hannah Downing
The Summer Prince by Carol Oates
Whatever it Takes by Sarah M. Glover
Clarity (A *Divinity* prequel single) by Patricia Leever
A Christmas Wish (A *Cocktails & Dreams* single) by Autumn Markus
Late Night with Andres by Debra Anastasia
Poughkeepsie (enhanced iPad app edition) by Debra Anastasia

coming soon from
OMNIFIC PUBLISHING

Playing All the Angles by Nicole Lane
The Small Town Girl series: *Keeping the Peace* (book 3)
by Linda Cunningham
The WORDS series: *Better Deeds than Words* (book 2)
by Georgina Guthrie
Exposure by Morgan and Jennifer Locklear
The Kiss Me series: *Kiss Me by Moonlight* (book 2) by Michele Zurlo
One Smart Cookie by Kym Brunner